"Okay, Dad. I'll meet her. But I'm not going to like her."

Jay was relieved when his sons agreed to meet Faith. With his hands on the boys' shoulders, he walked them to the kitchen. The boys brightened immediately when they saw Faith, a picture of hedonistic color.

Sam stared at her. "She's not like—" he said loudly, before Andy hit him.

"Andy, Sam. This is Faith, er…" Jay realized suddenly he didn't know whether she had ever married.

"Weaver," she supplied.

"Weaver. We went to school together," Jay added, wondering why he was so pleased. No wedding ring. No new last name. Did that mean she'd never married? Did it matter?

Andy looked at her skeptically. "You're as old as my dad? How old does that make you?"

"Andy, it's not polite to ask a lady's age," Jay said reproachfully.

"She's *not* a lady!" Sam almost shouted, his gaze fixed on Faith. "She's a m⸻

Dear Reader,

When I first moved from a more urban coastal town in California to Los Banos six years ago, I didn't fully appreciate the meaning of community. However, when the El Niño storms threatened to flood all of California, I discovered a particular benefit to living in a small town.

After finding out that my new hometown wasn't designated as a "flood zone" by the National Flood Insurance program, I showed up at my very first city council meeting to bring this to their attention. I was immediately impressed by the dedication and care with which the mayor and the council members treated my concern and how quickly they acted upon my request. I went away with the distinct satisfaction that I had effected change in my community.

From that one encounter, Jay Whitfield was created—a compassionate, dedicated man whose time is tightly stretched between his commitment to the town he serves, his job and his two sons, who desperately need a parent, a *mother*. Faith Weaver, Jay's high school sweetheart and a professional drifter, is willing to step into that role only temporarily. Although she makes no promises to Jay or his sons, Faith learns quickly that even a drifter needs a family.

Please join Faith and Jay as they discover that love is the easy part—it's trust that's hard. I love hearing from my readers, so please feel free to write me at: P.O. Box 2883, Los Banos, CA 93635 or visit my author page at www.superauthors.com. If you'd like to know more about the real town of Los Banos, you can visit their Web site at www.losbanos.org. Happy reading!

Sincerely,

Susan Floyd

Books by Susan Floyd

HARLEQUIN SUPERROMANCE

890—ONE OF THE FAMILY
919—MR. ELLIOTT FINDS A FAMILY

Faith and Our Father
Susan Floyd

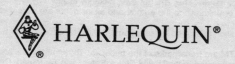

HARLEQUIN®

TORONTO • NEW YORK • LONDON
AMSTERDAM • PARIS • SYDNEY • HAMBURG
STOCKHOLM • ATHENS • TOKYO • MILAN • MADRID
PRAGUE • WARSAW • BUDAPEST • AUCKLAND

ISBN 0-373-70983-8

FAITH AND OUR FATHER

No book is written without the generosity of others.

With much gratitude to Mayor Mike Amabile and council members Nikki Smith, Gerald "Obie" O'Brien, Mike McAdams and Tommy Jones.

A very special thank-you to my CPA, Jim Valentine, who took the time to meet with me during tax season, and his wife, Sherry, who shared the experience of being married to a CPA during tax time.

Kudos to my very careful readers Nikki, Jim and Sherry. I appreciate your insight, your suggestions and your willingness to make this book as accurate as possible.

(Please note that all inconsistencies are mine.)

Finally, this book is dedicated to my father, Tad Kimoto, who gave me his sense of humor, his gift of words and his unfailing support in all my dreams. You are greatly missed.

CHAPTER ONE

THE TOPSPIN ON THE FROZEN Cornish game hen was alarming, even to Faith Weaver, and she was the one who'd thrown it. True—she had been an all-state fast-pitch softball champ for three years running, but nearly two decades later, Faith was astonished that she could still hurl one-pound objects with such velocity. She watched with distinct satisfaction when the hen sailed irreverently through a makeshift hoop and hit its intended target—a large throw pillow from her sister's designer couch—right in the middle, splattering pink frost everywhere.

Her sister's charity brainstorming committee cheered.

After two weeks of living under her sister's roof, Faith was already feeling the strain of being Patty Young's prodigal sister, recently returned after an eighteen-year hiatus to her hometown of Los Banos, a small, isolated farming community located on the westernmost edge of the California's San Joaquin Valley.

The teenage Patty Weaver had always circulated on the periphery of the ''in'' crowd, until Bruce Young, the son of one of the wealthiest, most influential families in the area and a major axis of the admired, took notice of her. The adult Patty Weaver had been able to crack the inner circle and secure a position as part of the town's elite and revered citizens by marrying Bruce. Patty took her role seriously, liberally associating their names with several charity events, committees and community activities.

As a free spirit who had spent most of her life avoiding such commitments, Faith shuddered internally at the extent of Patty's involvement and wondered how she would last until her parents' fortieth wedding anniversary party, scheduled for the second Saturday in April. Two and a half months—*long months*—away.

She was surprised that she'd even managed to get home, much less agreed to help her sister plan the party. But her father's call before the Christmas holidays had coincided with the expiration of the lease on her apartment and another more disturbing circumstance—for the first time in eighteen years, she was comfortably unemployed. During their brief conversation, she'd found herself entertaining the thought of going home, rolling it around in her mind and trying it on for size.

It might be fun to help her sister plan the party, regardless of the fact that she and Patty didn't necessarily have the most genial of relationships. It might be worthwhile to set aside old hurts, for lack of a better term, and venture back home.

Her mother had given her a follow-up call the week between Christmas and New Year's, traditionally a vulnerable time for Faith, a time when she was more reflective and slightly melancholy about the passing of the old year, intent on trying to form her resolutions for the new one.

"You'll want to stay with Patty and Bruce," Dearie Weaver had said to her, assuming her daughter would definitely return. "Bruce said the guest room was all ready for you."

"I'm not even sure I'll be coming," Faith hedged. "If I do, I'll find my own accommodations." In all her years of travel, she had slept in some unsavory places and actually enjoyed the adventure. However, she was reluctant to live under the same roof as her sister and brother-in-law for a day, much less three months. Eighteen years could only blur, not erase, some memories.

"Of course you're coming," her mother dismissed. "And it's absolutely ridiculous to think that you'd be paying rent for three months when Patty and Bruce have a perfectly nice room for you. They've fixed the old house up. You'd think you'd stepped into *House Beautiful*. Didn't you say you were between positions? Why would you stay at a motel when you can stay with your sister?"

"You know why, Mom." Faith's voice was flat.

There was a long pause, until her mother cleared her throat and said, "You two are adults, for heaven's sake. That's water under the bridge."

Faith had winced. Apparently, eighteen years hadn't improved her mother's ability to discuss sensitive topics.

"There's more to it than that." Faith's throat felt raw.

"We miss you, Faith," Dearie had said finally.

"Phone calls aren't enough. We deserve to see you more than a weekend once every five years. We'd like to be able to go to dinner with you, drop in on Saturdays. I've got seven pages in my book just for your addresses. It's like you're a missing person."

Faith had inhaled sharply, the irony of her mother's observation grazing her heart. When she'd left Los Banos that was exactly what she'd intended. More than anything, she'd wanted to be swallowed up by the world, achieving blissful anonymity. She'd found there were hundreds of places she could physically hide, but unfortunately, she could never forget who she was.

"It was a long time ago. You've been forgiven." Her mother's tone was benevolent. "Maybe it's time you came home to stay."

Home.

That word had made Faith sit down to look around her spare apartment, filled with temporary furniture, nothing lasting, nothing particularly attractive. It wasn't a home; it was the place she slept. At thirty-six, she had slept in many such places, in a lot of latitudes, both above and below the equator, searching for a way to put things right. She'd often dreamed a real home might do that, but she was also practical enough to know that while real homes with real families existed for some, for her home was merely an illusion.

Since the New Year did signify new beginnings, she'd allowed her lease to expire, sold her furniture and packed up her few belongings to begin her journey back home. She'd ended up where she'd left off—her parents' home, sold to Patty and Bruce, remodeled to pristine condition.

''Hens for Health!''

''Chickens for Charity!''

''Birds for Words—literacy, that is.''

''Come on, Faith. Try to make it two for two,'' a friendly voice egged her on. ''I think we're on to something. Hit the pillow and you get the chicken. A dollar a throw. It'll be a great fund-raiser.''

''There's got to be a way to rig it up to the dunking machine.''

Applause broke out around her when she hefted another bird from the row of one-pound hens. Trust Patty not to serve hot dogs and burgers at a barbecue on the first day of February. While most other parts of the country were buried under several feet of snow, Los Banos was feeling the promise of spring—thanks to a high-pressure system off the Pacific that had given the citizens an uncharacteristic reprieve from the usual rain and wind. Everyone knew it wouldn't last, that the fog would sock them in or the high clouds would obliterate all sunlight, but now, folks had broken out their shorts and reveled in the weather. The barren trees and dormant flower beds, however, were reminders of the season.

Patty always did take advantage of the unexpected.

Faith's hand clutched the bird, the frost sticking to her palm. She forced herself to relax, slightly alarmed at how good it felt to throw things, to mar her sister's compulsive perfection.

''You haven't lost it, Faith,'' one guest shouted.

Patty's distinctive laugh startled them all, and Faith

automatically put the bird back in the row. Someone tossed her the other bird and she deftly caught it with one hand and placed it beside its companions, the packaging around the bird none the worse for its high-velocity travel. The throw pillow, unfortunately, was a casualty. Patty's pride in her pristinely white house meant she had to have an arctic-white couch. The throw pillow was an even whiter white—except for the distinctive beige splotch in the middle.

A friendly guest quickly turned the pillow, before plumping it up, and small talk resumed. Faith would get it dry-cleaned tomorrow when her sister was house-hunting with her clients. For an informal bar-becue, Patty was beautifully dressed in a white linen shorts set. She stopped mid-stride before looking around suspiciously.

"What have you done?" Her voice was accusing, and Faith licked her lips, feeling as if she were twelve. Committee members chuckled uneasily, shifting away from the pair of sisters, as different as sand and silk. "I swear, Faith, you don't take anything seriously." Her tongue clicked with impatience and she said under her breath, "I don't know why you even came back."

Faith swallowed hard. "I thought it was to help plan Mom and Dad's anniversary," she said lightly.

"As if I'd let you ruin that as well," Patty muttered fiercely. But Faith heard it and tried not to feel the sting of the words. Patty's ice-blue eyes darted around the room, searching for evidence. Another guest ac-tually sat down and leaned back on the pillow. An unidentified person tittered and the small talk got louder to cover the slip.

Faith was ashamed of herself.

She was acting more like one of her young charges than the adult she claimed she was. But as she avoided Patty's pinched expression, she knew why she didn't want to live with her sister. She'd come back thinking she could reintegrate herself into her family, find home again, but instead, Patty treated Faith the way she'd always treated her. Eighteen years hadn't erased memories. Eighteen years hadn't altered her mother or softened her sister.

"I know you've done something," Patty said in Faith's ear, bringing her back to the present.

Faith looked at her older sister, fixated on the layers of pancake makeup obscuring Patty's beautiful skin. Faith gave her the same neutral smile she reserved for police officers and suspicious children who didn't want to be left with a strange nanny and said pleasantly, "I don't know what you could mean. I've just been—"

"Look at the time!" Patty glanced at the wall clock and then stared at Faith as if it were her fault.

"It's quarter to five," Faith said.

"I promised Amanda that I'd deliver her casserole to Jay Whitfield before five. He's got a council meeting tonight."

Faith swallowed hard, feeling a lump lodge in her throat. Jay Whitfield.

It'd been ages since she'd last seen him.

"Would you like me to deliver it for you?" Faith asked faintly. "That way you don't have to hold up your meet—"

"No." Patty cut Faith off with a crisp shake of her

head. "I don't. I don't want you anywhere near Jay. He and Amanda are a very happy couple."

Just by Patty's tone, Faith knew her sister was fudging the truth. Not that it mattered whether he was part of a couple or not. Much water had passed under that bridge as well.

"If they're so happy, there'd be no reason I couldn't deliver her casserole to him."

Patty was silent.

"Or you can make your committee members wait while you deliver it yourself," Faith pointed out.

After a brief hesitation, Patty opened the refrigerator and took out the glass dish, passing it to Faith, who grunted under its weight. Patty hastily scrawled an address on the back of an envelope. "Remember. He's taken."

BROWN BRIEFCASE IN HAND, a dark blue jacket slung over one forearm, his burgundy tie loosened and the cuffs of his white dress shirt rolled, Jay Whitfield stopped at the front door of his single-story ranch home, hoping, no, praying, that when he opened the door he would find his two sons, ten and seven, quietly doing their homework at the kitchen table while the nanny cooked a wholesome, nourishing dinner.

"Get *out* of my way, you puke chunk."

Jay winced at the dull thunk that followed.

"I was watching first."

"I don't care. I'm the oldest. *Move!*"

"*Ooooow!* I'm going to tell Dad."

"I'm going to tell Da-ad," mimicked the voice of his eldest son, Andy, a pre-preadolescent pain in the—

"Stop it!"

"Stop it!" the mimic singsonged.

"Quit that!" The seven-year-old voice bordered on the whiny.

"Quit that!"

"Andy!"

Sighing, Jay rattled the handle loudly and pushed the door open. He observed his two boys wrestling over the remote control to the television set and cleared his throat loudly. They stopped and looked up.

"Da-a-ad!" Sam, his youngest, hollered. "I was here first and Andy won't—"

"No, I didn't. You're a—"

"No TV," Jay said as he turned it off and walked toward the kitchen. "Andy, don't hit your brother," he added as the sounds of scuffling continued behind him. "Where's Marguerite?"

"She's gone," Andy said, letting loose a final punch that Sam ducked.

"What do you mean she's gone?" Jay stopped in the hall and looked at his sons in horror.

"Sam did it again."

Jay grimaced but asked, anyway. "Did what?"

"He threw up all over her."

"I did not."

"You did, too. *You* are a puke chunk."

"Andy. Stop that." Jay turned his attention to his youngest son. "Did you eat something bad for lunch?"

Sam, his eyes very round, shook his head.

"Then what made you throw up?"

"She wouldn't let him watch cartoons, so he threw up on her."

"I couldn't help it!" Sam wailed. "I just got upset."

Jay felt a sting of guilt. As competent as Marguerite might be, she wasn't Granny Doris, and Sam had never gotten over the fact that his beloved nanny could no longer care for him. They'd gone through several nannies in the past few months; Jay just couldn't find one who understood Andy and Sam's unique circumstances or his own sometimes frenetic schedule, especially during tax season.

He'd spent all morning and most of the afternoon calling and visiting various dairies to remind them that the March 1 filing date, the deadline for farm taxes, was quickly approaching, and to see if they'd received all the tax-related documents from their cooperatives. If he hadn't had an important subcommittee meeting at seven-thirty that morning and hadn't been the guest speaker at a local luncheon, he wouldn't have felt like such a fool, walking through the dairies dressed as if he were an outsider, rather than a fourth-generation Los Banian.

His muttered response, alternating between "council work" and "ladies' luncheon," seemed to bridge unasked questions about his mode of dress. In retrospect, his pride and his feet would have felt much better if he had just taken twenty minutes to drive home and change into a flannel shirt, his jeans and work boots, the familiar and expected uniform of the farmers for whom he worked.

His office manager, Debbie, had called them all in

late January, but he liked to meet with his clients in person to make sure there were no problems lurking in the shadows. They expected that kind of service since most of them had known him since he was a barefoot farm kid tagging along with his father. He tried to make himself friendly and accessible so they felt free enough to divulge any gnawing fiscal secret they might have held back the year before. When he'd returned to his office, he'd ignored the pile of messages Debbie had left before she went to pick up her children, plunging into a stack of documents he needed to be familiar with before the closed-session council meeting that evening.

"Marguerite called but you were out of the office. I'm old enough to take care of Sam and me," Andy said as he drew himself up to his full height. His head came to the middle of Jay's ribs.

"When did she leave?"

"About an hour ago. I told her I could handle things. She wanted to interview the Pollocks but had to go home and change."

Jay shook his head, still kicking himself, walked through to the kitchen and stopped. The kitchen was a mess. The boys had obviously made themselves snacks as soon as Marguerite left. He frowned at the peanut butter and several jam lids left upside down on the counter. Puddles of milk and soda mingled together. The bread bag yawned wide open, the boys apparently having rifled through the loaf for the softest pieces. Seven, count 'em, seven table knives were stuck to the counter tiles, dusted with crumbs of various origins. Cookies. Fruit Loops. Potato chips.

He took a deep breath and said, his voice sharp, "If you're old enough to stay home alone then you should be old enough to clean up after yourselves." He stared pointedly at the counter, knowing full well it was his irritation with himself that caused him to snap.

The boys weren't fazed at all.

"Sam was the last one to use the knives," Andy said accusingly. "He was supposed to wash them and put them away."

"I didn't open up all those jellies," Sam said.

"But you used them," Andy shot back.

"I don't care!" Jay said, the snap back in his voice. "I want the jars put away, the bread wrapped up, the crumbs wiped up—and not onto the floor—by the time I change. And you boys go wash. Since there's no Marguerite, you're going to the council meeting with me tonight."

"Da-a-ad!" Both boys whined in unison.

"We've got no choice," Jay said quietly. "There isn't time to get a sitter for tonight—"

"I'm big enough to look after Sam," Andy said, his blue eyes glittering with hurt.

Jay stared down at his eldest son. Everyone said his sons looked just like him, but he saw Becky all over them, in the shapes of their faces, their giggles, and in more subtle ways. Their eyebrows were Becky's—a little bushy for a woman, she'd often lamented, but perfect for two boys.

"I know you are, Andy." Jay rested his hand on his shoulder and squeezed lightly. Andy leaned in but didn't touch him. That was the closest they got to a hug these days. Sam didn't mind hugging, but Andy took his role as second in command seriously. "But not tonight. So, get cleaned up for the meeting." He gave a quick glance around the kitchen. "But first clean up this mess."

When both boys looked at him blankly, he added a bark to his voice. *"Now!"*

"But—"

"I don't care. Work together."

"He—"

"I don't care. I want this place in order or heads are going to roll," Jay repeated. He didn't feel nearly as stern as he probably sounded. After the day he had, he couldn't even imagine—

He caught the blinking light of the answering machine. He pressed the button and the digital voice said to him, "You have forty-three messages."

Well, at least it wasn't fifty.

It was on days like this that he missed Becky the most. He missed that Becky wasn't around to mediate their sons' fights. Becky was so patient, her laughter so pure. She'd probably never lose her temper with Andy and Sam.

It'd been five years now. Andy had been five, Sam, just two, when she'd died after a surprisingly brief battle with cancer. One day she was fine, though struggling with the sleep deprivation caused by having a two-year-old, the next she was undergoing a routine lumpectomy. Then the doctor was solemnly telling them it was stage-four cancer that had metastasized to her major organs. They had given her seven months with chemotherapy and radiation and seven weeks without. She'd chosen to forego the chemo and cheerfully took enormous amounts of morphine so her boys wouldn't see her sick all the time. She lasted eleven weeks—four weeks longer than the doctors had given her—and died in Jay's arms.

Since then, they'd gotten along. Just the three of them. Andy and Sam were good boys. Most of the time. They had fine hearts even though they didn't often show it. Jay had often wondered how much that had to do with the fact that the boys had no real connection to their mother. Sam didn't even have memories of Becky, except the ones Jay made for him, and although Andy liked to claim he had full recognition, Jay couldn't believe it. To Andy, Becky was probably just a warm, blurry image of someone he used to call "Mommy." With new dissatisfaction, he surveyed his bedroom as he unloosened his tie. The room had a just-moved-in feel, even though he'd been there for nearly five years. It was when they'd moved to town, shortly after Becky's death, that he'd decided to run for city council. It was a perfect solution for his grief.

He knew his father didn't approve of either the move or his decision to throw himself into council life on top of his job, but he preferred that to his father's incessant reminiscence of how things used to be— when his mother was alive, when Becky was alive. He just couldn't stay in that little cottage on the edge of his father's property, the little cottage Becky had lovingly restored when they were first married and were too poor to get a place of their own.

He'd still been in school then, spending his weekdays commuting to Santa Clara to attend his MBA classes and his weekends working on the dairy and being with Becky. She'd immediately fit into his all-male family, providing the feminine touches that had been missing since his mother had died. Becky had gotten pregnant a lot faster than he'd wanted, but the little cottage had had two bedrooms and Andy was a good baby. Two years later, after he'd passed the CPA exam and started his practice in town, the cottage had become a little tighter when she was pregnant again. As his small accounting firm grew, it became a tough topic of conversation between them of whether to stay on Gil Whitfield's dairy or move to town, especially once Gil had refused to use Jay's accounting services, preferring to hire Bruce Young.

Then it was a slap in the face. Now, as he stripped off his shirt, inspecting it for any leftover spaghetti from the University Women's Auxiliary luncheon before throwing it into the growing pile of laundry in one corner of the room, Jay admitted it was probably for the best. He loved his father, but they'd never agree when it came to work. Gil had fully expected Jay, as the eldest son, to take over one of the most lucrative dairies in Merced County. Jay had no such aspirations. He didn't want the dairy hours, the never-ending chores, the constant headaches. He had fully intended to participate in the family business, but only from the business side.

Thank goodness his younger brother, Lee, affectionately called Stinky by old friends and family, had wanted the dairy life from the time he was old enough to immunize his first calf. After a brief stint working in a pizza parlor, Stink had decided he'd much rather be his own employer. That was enough to keep the family peace, but it was hard to see the disappointment in his father's eyes every time Jay climbed into his mid-size sedan to head to his office job in town.

Becky, however, had wanted to stay on at the dairy and expand the cottage. She liked the fresh air and the wide-open space. She wanted her boys to know the freedom of growing up with acres to roam and call their own. While Los Banos, with only twenty-two thousand residents, was not necessarily a congested metropolis, it was different enough from the dairy. Having grown up in town, Becky craved the country stillness, the stark black nights glittering with stars. When Jay asked Patty Young to help them find a place in town, Becky halfheartedly made the rounds. Then Sam was born, and she got sick and he couldn't bear to do anything that would disrupt their lives more than the cancer had done. After she died, moving was no longer a question.

The tiny cottage was too painful to be in.

Everything about the cottage reminded Jay of Becky, from the draperies to Becky's lovingly restored antiques. One month after her funeral, much to his father's vigorous protestations, he moved his two boys to a nice ranch-style house on a heavily shaded street, named after an American president, just south of Pacheco Boulevard.

Jay laughed at the irony as he pulled on a pair of well-worn jeans and sighed with pure comfort. He didn't have the dairy hours, but being a city councilman-accountant single father was a 24/7 proposition. After dinner, he would need to don the suit again for the redevelopment meeting. Later, he'd comb through those forty-three phone messages to rank them in order of urgency. It was a chore he enjoyed doing. He liked the fact that people felt comfortable enough to call him, to let him know what was happening in the city.

Sam and Andy, however, weren't so sure about his value to the community. To them the phone messages and the council meetings were merely things that took him away from them. They weren't going to be thrilled with having to sit through another session. While he didn't regret running for public office one bit—the connection to the city and its people helped him through his grief—he did realize that Andy and Sam were growing up without him and that without a good nanny—

Ding dong!

Jay tugged on a Wild on the Wetlands T-shirt, glanced at the clock and sighed.

Dinnertime.

A doorbell ringing at dinnertime meant only one thing to the boys. Company. Since his election to office, three or four times a month, a different eligible woman would come bearing lasagna, tuna casserole, stew or a chicken pot pie. She'd coo over Andy and Sam, who expressed their resentment of yet another intrusion on their time with their father with stiff monosyllabic responses to her inquiries about school, their activities, their friends. After a tense introduction, they'd all sit down to a casual dinner, as Jay kept a sympathetic eye on his sons, who'd learned to palm particularly nasty pieces into their napkins rather than rudely spit them onto their plate.

While he liked on some levels that women found

him attractive enough to want to feed his family, he worried they expected the casual dinners to turn into something more. There'd be subtle inquiries about whether he planned to take a date to the Lion's Club dinner. Lately Jay had realized he did indeed want to take a date, but he just didn't feel right about singling out one of the ladies who had so, er, persistently dined with him these past few years. So Jay continued to go stag to all city events.

"Who is it, Andy?" Jay asked in a hushed voice from the corner of the hall.

"I'll check," Andy whispered back.

They had the routine down.

Jay felt a small rush of pride at his son as he stood on tiptoe to reach the peephole. Andy turned back with a shrug. "Don't know who it is. I haven't ever seen her before. She's got a casserole, though." He made a descriptive face.

Jay chuckled, momentarily forgetting that he was the father.

"You sure?" Jay was hopeful. His plan for dinner was closer to the arena of peanut butter and Fruit Loop sandwiches. He could use a square meal even though Andy and Sam were convinced the main purpose of a casserole was to hide distasteful vegetables like cabbage or broccoli.

Andy looked again. He confirmed with a heavy sigh, "Yes, casserole."

The doorbell rang again.

"You want me to get it?" Andy looked down, obviously disappointed.

Jay hesitated. He only had two hours before the

meeting and he wanted to spend some time with his sons. He nodded but slipped around the corner just out of sight. "But tell her I'm in the shower."

When a big smile spread over his son's face, Jay knew he'd made the right decision.

FAITH WAITED PATIENTLY on Jay's front doorstep and glanced around the neighborhood. It was a far cry from the dairy. Very upscale. This was a neighborhood of doctors and lawyers. She'd only been back in town two weeks, but it hadn't taken her long to remember the old streets and become acquainted with the new ones. She had been surprised by the growth of the small town.

She had left about a decade after the state had finished the I-5 interchange, which had effectively cut off Los Banos from north-south traffic, plunging the business community into a severe recession. Eighteen years ago, the town had been a virtual ghost town, struggling to find a way to rebuild itself. But now it had found a new life, thanks to the unexpected boom of high-tech companies in Silicon Valley. With the cost of housing skyrocketing in the South Bay, workers had been forced to move east to Los Banos.

Faith now saw new parks and bigger strip malls, but somehow, despite its increase in population, Los Banos remained the friendly, isolated farming town she had once lived in. Although, Faith imagined that with the arrival of the commuters, or newcomers, as they were called, the dairy farmers, like Jay's dad, had already felt the pressure of encroachment. She had also heard talk of an impending highway bypass circumventing the main drag of Los Banos and wondered whether it would repeat the I-5's devastation on the small city's economy.

She rang the doorbell again, not willing to admit to the small flutter at seeing Jay Whitfield again. It'd been a long time. She could count the times she'd been back in town on one hand, and each visit had been clandestine, quick, nothing more than a fleeting weekend. Even though she thought about him as she passed by the canals they had parked by, she hadn't seen him. Not since—

When she found out he'd married little Becky Turner, then had first one child, then another, any desire to see him fluttered away, fueled only by old memories and unfinished business. When Patty told her about Becky's death, Faith was heartbroken, not because she had known Becky, but because Jay would have to raise his boys alone. Even though it went against her vow to disappear from his life, she'd sent him a card, careful not to put a return address, expressing her sorrow at his loss.

Now she tried not to feel self-conscious as she waited to deliver Amanda Perkins's casserole—which from the smell of it, was not a culinary work of art.

Jay Whitfield.

When Patty had talked about him over the past two weeks, Faith had kept her face neutrally interested as if she didn't remember the shy smile, the furtive but passionate kisses in his father's truck, his sea-blue eyes sparkling with fun, or the way they'd talked about forever.

Or at least he had.

Forever seemed to be a long time to Faith then, and as their senior year drew closer to the end and Jay fumbled with a ring he couldn't afford—

Faith studied the elegant stained glass border on top of Jay's door and waited. It looked like he could afford considerably more than a diamonette, the carat weight equivalent to a grain of sand. She knew someone was home because she could hear scrambling on the other side of the door. She shifted the casserole from one hand to the other. She frowned at the brussels sprouts. Surely if Amanda was intent on snaring a man with two boys, it would be wise to fix a dinner more child-friendly. She rang the doorbell again. If no one answered soon, she would leave the casserole on the step and let him figure out whom it was from.

As she was turning to leave, the door opened just a crack and a pair of the bluest eyes Faith had ever seen peered out at her. Faith smiled. No mistaking this child's identity. He looked just like Jay. She felt a little twinge. How odd that she didn't even know his name.

"Hi," Faith said quickly.

"Hi." The boy was polite, unsmiling.

"Is your dad home?"

"He's in the shower."

Faith didn't know whether to be relieved or disappointed. But since he was dating Amanda, relief was probably the more productive feeling, so she chose that.

"Okay," she said agreeably, holding out the casserole, "This is for you and him from Amanda Perkins, who gave it to my sister, Patty Young, who gave it to me to deliver."

"I'll take it."

"Be careful, it's heavy."

"I've got it." He gave her a look of disdain, though he braced himself when she carefully deposited it in his arms.

"Yes, you do look strong," Faith said, backtracking, and was rewarded with a wary stare.

"I'm ten."

"I'd have put you at at least eleven."

There was a drawn silence.

"So," Faith said, "you'll tell your dad that it's from Amanda?" She laughed. "My sister told me very specifically I was to let your dad know."

The sullen lips twisted into a half smile. "Yeah." The boy sniffed at the casserole. "Brussels sprouts. Mrs. Perkins. He'll know."

"Okay."

Faith stood on the doorstep as the boy closed the door and realized that after all this time, she wanted to see Jay, see what kind of a man he had grown into.

She wasn't relieved at all.

She was disappointed.

JAY STOOD IN THE HALL, his stocking feet stuck to the hardwood floor, his heart accelerating, as conditioned to the timbres of that low, throaty voice as Pavlov's dogs were to the dinner bell. It had been ages. Too many years to count. He peered around the corner to see if the face matched the voice, but Andy and the door both blocked his view. Andy walked down the hall, gingerly holding the casserole. He wrinkled his nose. "Can we get pizza, Dad? This doesn't smell too good."

"Who was that?" Jay asked.

Andy shrugged. "She said to tell you her sister told her this is from Mrs. Perkins."

"Who's her sister?" Jay didn't dare think it.

"Mrs. Young."

In three quick strides, he was at the door, witnessing a slim strong back and tantalizing curve of hips, a woman's hips, not those of a slender teenager, retreating down the walkway.

He couldn't believe it.

It *was* her.

Not the apparition he sometimes saw in the hazy space between sleep and wakefulness or in reverse, from wakefulness to sleep. He'd often wondered what had happened to her.

"Faith!" he called quickly.

His heart thumped harder when she stopped.

She stood still a long time, as if debating whether or not to turn. Finally, after what seemed to be an eternity, she slowly wheeled around, an abashed expression on her face, part guilt, part pleasure. She tilted her head, the colorful beads strung in her hair softly rattling. Then she sent him a megawatt grin and said teasingly, "That was a damn quick shower, Whitfield."

CHAPTER TWO

WHITFIELD. MEMORIES CAME flooding back to him. Always a tad disrespectful, Faith had rarely called him by his first name. Jay stared at her. She hadn't changed one bit. Her hair was still a wild honey brown, but with several skinny braids held tight with glass beads down one side. She was darker, her face tanned so her light brown eyes seemed even lighter. Her clothes were gypsy bright, a combination of a flowing white blouse and a patchwork skirt. On anyone else it'd look ridiculous, on Faith it looked perfect.

''I didn't know you were bosom buddies with Amanda,'' he returned.

He leaned up against the door frame, his arms crossed casually across his wide chest.

She laughed and his heart fluttered at the pure alto, low bells ringing simultaneously. He couldn't stop smiling at the sound.

''No, not me, but Patty seems to have fulfilled a teenage ambition.'' She winked at him.

''In town for your parents' big bash?'' It wasn't creative, but it was conversation.

She pulled a face, finishing it off with a wry smile. ''If I last that long. Patty has different ways of doing things. I think a picnic or barbecue and a couple of rousing games of co-ed softball ought to do the trick. Patty's got something else entirely in mind.''

"How long you staying?" It didn't hurt to ask.

She paused before answering, her eyes cautious. "Until April 10, until the party."

FAITH WAS MESMERIZED by Jay's expression, which in an instant tenderly rubbed some small, vulnerable part of her. She would have thought his gentle, unspoken probing would be painful, but surprisingly it wasn't. There was no censure or judgment in his eyes, merely open interest. She shook herself, trying not to be flustered by his frank, head-to-toe appraisal of her.

He looked very different than she had remembered him. He had been a lanky teenager, mostly skin pulled tight over bones, no facial hair to speak of. Now he had filled in. Lankiness had been replaced by impressive breadth, and the day's growth of stubble made him appear even more masculine. Intelligence, an active curiosity, burned behind those bright blue eyes. His natural aura of assurance had matured and been refined. He hardly looked crushed that she hadn't agreed to marry him all those years ago. In fact, it appeared as if he had thrived.

Jay, even as a teenager, knew where he was going, knew what he wanted. And he went after what he wanted with charm and persistence. To Faith, he seemed capable of controlling the rotation of the earth. Except he couldn't keep her from leaving and he couldn't keep his wife from dying.

"I'm really sorry about Becky," she said gently.

His face lost the smile. He looked down to the

ground and shoved his hands in his pockets. He then looked up at the sky, almost as if he were seeking his wife behind the high clouds. After a moment, he nodded. "Thanks. We miss her, but we're doing okay. It was five years ago."

Faith felt slightly snubbed and was quiet, then ventured, "You have sons?"

The smile was back, this time bursting with pride. "Yes. Two sons. Andy's ten and Sam's six—no, he just turned seven."

Faith didn't know what else to say.

She shifted from one foot to the next. "Well, it was nice seeing you. You look great. I guess I should be getting back to Patty's. She's got a houseful of very important people. Charity drive, I believe," she finished lamely as she felt her arm make a gesture in the general direction of the car. "You know how she is." Faith was struck that he probably did know how she was. Better than she, herself, did. She added, "Speaking of which, why aren't you there?"

"Was invited. But I've got a council meeting tonight." He glanced at his watch. "In fact, I need to get the boys fed and dressed. We're due soon."

Faith nodded. "You're a very important person, too."

He shook his head with an embarrassed laugh. "No one person is that important."

THEY STOOD AWKWARDLY in silence. Jay couldn't think of a thing to say. Finally, Faith smiled as she moved to leave. "Well, I guess I better go."

"Want to meet the kids?" Jay blurted out before remembering the mess in the kitchen.

Faith shifted uncertainly. "You have a meeting."

"It'll just take a second."

"Well—"

"Come on," Jay cajoled, wondering why he was trying so hard. "For old times' sake."

Yes, that was what it was about.

For old times. Nothing more, nothing less.

Faith still hesitated. Then she smiled again, her eyes full of mischief. "Patty told me to keep my hands off because Amanda's in the running for your affections."

Jay started because he had forgotten about Amanda, and then he laughed out loud.

Who but Faith would say something so blunt?

"My affections aren't on the ballot yet," he said lightly. "Come in and meet my kids."

Faith knew with every ounce of her being she should get into her rattletrap of a car and go right home, run as fast as she could away from Jay's smiling face, right back to...what?

Patty's charity planning committee?

She glanced at Jay's watch, a tasteful silver analog. It was nearly five-thirty. Bruce would be getting back to the house soon, and even though he'd been nothing but nice and even overly solicitous since she first arrived, she just couldn't let her guard down around him, no matter how much everyone wanted to pretend that nothing had happened. What was it her mother had said on the phone during the Christmas holidays? *It was a long time ago. You've been forgiven.* Faith couldn't quite accept the irony of the situation. She'd been the victim and she was the one being forgiven. Two and a half months until her parents' party. What had she done to herself?

Suddenly, as if pulled by a magnetic force she was unable to resist, she was heading toward Jay, up the walkway, into the foyer of his house, standing on the plush light brown carpet. Once inside, she stood waiting for Jay to give her some cue.

"Please ignore the mess in the kitchen," Jay said hurriedly. "I just found out my nanny defected for some better children. Andy! Sam! Get in here and clean up this kitchen. Now!"

No children appeared.

Apparently, they had gotten good at laying low.

Jay grunted with good-natured frustration. "I guess I'll have to go find them."

While he was gone, she surveyed the kitchen, noting that what Jay called a mess wasn't really a mess at all. There were a few jars open and some sticky stuff on the white tile counter, several knives and dirty plates were strewn about and assorted bits of cereal were floating in puddles of milk and soda. Nothing she couldn't take care of in a minute. She closed up the bread, gathered up the utensils and the plates and ran the water, impressed by the gleaming brass fixtures.

Quiet opulence.

She had lived in one such place in Oregon, when she'd looked after the four children of a pediatrician whose husband had been recovering from a triple bypass. It was exactly the kind of nanny job she preferred, short-term, emergency-related, and over the years she had developed a good reputation and had not wanted for work, her employers developing an intricate network of word-of-mouth referrals up and down the West Coast. As one position began winding down, she'd just put out feelers for another, which never was too far away. Lately, she'd been opting to live out rather than in the household, and when her last job ended right after Thanksgiving, a peculiar restlessness had come over her. It was the first holiday she'd actually spent alone. After her mother's call, even though she had serious misgivings about what she was about to do, she had made the decision to head home.

She looked down, surprised to see she'd already done the dishes. She glanced at the counter. It would be just a small thing to wipe it down. She found a stack of sponges under the sink. A clean kitchen would be one less thing for Jay to worry about, especially if he had to go to a meeting. That task finished, Faith wandered out to the hall to study a row of pictures hanging haphazardly on the wall, at waist height.

One large eight-by-ten was hung so low, Faith had to bend over to look at it. She smiled when she saw the small fingerprints all over the face, especially by the smile and the eyes. Lip prints on the cheeks. She barely recognized Becky Turner, who had been three years behind her in high school. Since she and Jay had been in the same class, it seemed amazing that the two would ever meet. But a three years' age difference in high school wasn't as important when one became an adult.

As she studied each of the pictures—Becky with what Faith supposed was Andy as an infant; another outside on Jay's dad's dairy with the two boys; Becky emaciated, a wistful smile on her face as her two boys hugged her—Faith straightened them, even though she suspected they'd soon be crooked again.

JAY SAT IN THE BOYS' ROOM on the edge of the bunk bed and stared at his offspring. Andy was at his desk pretending to be absorbed in homework and Sam sat on the floor digging his way through a pail of lifelike plastic bugs. Jay, a little desperate, hoped that if he gave them a stern-enough stare, he could actually will these children to be cooperative.

It wasn't working.

It just made Andy more stony and Sam fidget as he lined up spiders and cockroaches according to size and color.

"Okay, Dad. I'll go meet her." Sam, always the pleaser, capitulated first. "But I'm not going to like her."

"If we go meet her, do we have to go to the stupid meeting?" Andy, always the bargainer, dickered, then complained loudly, "And how come we can't just order pizza? Why do we have to eat what they bring?"

"Because if someone took the time to make a casserole, we should be gracious enough to eat it." Andy looked unconvinced, so Jay added, "I *like* Mrs. Perkins's cooking. It's very nice that she did that for us. Besides, I didn't make anything for dinner."

"So let's order pizza," Andy said reasonably.

Jay shook his head. "No, we'll have casserole. I want you to come meet this other lady."

Both boys pulled back, their distaste for this chore obvious.

"No," Andy said, his voice sullen. He crossed his arms and Jay could feel his soul withdraw. That was new. While not the most social of children, Andy wasn't ever that closed.

Jay put his hand on his son's thin shoulder and squeezed gently. He felt Andy stiffen, but said, anyway, "Andy, sitting in your room sulking isn't going to change the dinner menu. End of discussion. Move. You have a kitchen to clean up."

Andy wouldn't meet his eyes, and Jay felt a small jab of guilt.

"For me, please," Jay added, and breathed a sigh of relief as Andy rose slowly.

With his hands on the boys' shoulders, he walked them down the hall to the kitchen. When they saw Faith, a picture of hedonistic color, casually flipping through *Know Los Banos*, a local publication, her beaded earrings nearly sweeping against the tile as she leaned against a sparkling counter, the boys brightened immediately.

"Faith, you didn't have—" Jay protested. He felt his cheeks grow hot with embarrassment.

"No problem," she said breezily, with a dazzling smile at Sam and a quick wink at Andy. "It was a snap." She regarded his sons with a frank stare.

Sam stared at her and then up at his father. "She's not like—" he said loudly, before Andy hit him. "Ow!"

"Andy. Sam. This is Faith, er—" He realized suddenly he didn't know whether she had ever married.

He looked to see if she was wearing a wedding band.
She wasn't.

"Weaver," she supplied.

"Weaver. We went to school together," Jay added,
wondering why he was so pleased. No wedding ring.
No new last name. Did that mean she'd never married?
Or did it mean that she'd married and divorced and
was back to her old name? Did it matter?

Andy looked at her skeptically. "You're as old as
my dad?"

Faith nodded solemnly. "Actually, I think I'm
older."

"You're not older than my dad?" Sam asked as if
he couldn't imagine anyone being older than his dad.

"How old are you?" Andy asked Faith point blank.

"Andy!" Jay said reproachfully.

"Thirty-six," Faith replied just as bluntly.

Andy shot Jay a smug look.

"It's not polite to ask a lady's age." Jay walked
across the room and opened the refrigerator door.

"She's *not* a lady," Sam almost shouted, his gaze
fixed on Faith, a broad smile growing on his face.

"*Sam!*" Jay couldn't control the edge in his tone,
and Sam's head snapped back from the reproof he
heard.

Sam stared at him, eyes round, his chin trembling.

"She's not a lady," he repeated in a small voice.
"She's a mom."

FAITH FELT AN INDEFINABLE emotion press against her
heart, her eyes on the small boy in front of her. She
instantly saw the remorse in Jay's expression, the ten-

uous control of Sam's bottom lip as he tried to not cry in front of company. She had long given up the notion she would ever have children of her own. She had built a career around caring for other people's children, borrowing them temporarily.

Faith bent over so she was nose-to-nose with Sam and said with a cheerful smile, as she tilted up his chin, "Well, thank you so much for the compliment. I'd much rather be a mom than a lady. I think that's the best thing in the world to be taken for."

As much as she wanted to plant a sound kiss on his forehead, she resisted. She looked up at Jay, who thanked her with a quick nod and distinct gratitude in his lovely eyes.

But Sam avoided looking at her.

The damage of Jay's reprimand had already been done.

Andy said, his voice rough, "She's not a mom, stupid—"

"Don't call your brother stupid—" interrupted Jay.

Sam defended himself. "I didn't say she was *my* mom—"

"Well, moms can come in all sorts of shapes and sizes," Faith said reasonably. "Sam's comment was very wise."

"She looks like *a* mom." Sam smiled up at her, his little arms crossed defiantly. "Are you one?" he asked hopefully.

She shook her head and he sighed regretfully.

"Are you going to stay for casserole?" Andy asked, a special glint in his eye.

"I don't think Faith has time—" Jay began, as he

moved behind the counter to fiddle with the casserole that had taken on the smell of a wet, unwashed sock. He turned on the oven, his intent obvious.

"I wouldn't mind a pizza," she said casually, her eyes on Andy.

Andy didn't say a word, but both he and Sam looked at Jay.

Jay stared at the casserole. Faith hid a smile. The sock smell was almost overpowering. He glanced up at the clock. Then Faith realized her error. He didn't have time. He had the council meeting.

"We can pretend to eat it," Andy suggested, mistaking his father's hesitation for capitulation, then added for clarity, "And then tell Mrs. Perkins we liked it very much."

"Andy." There was a distinct warning in Jay's voice. Andy's mouth pulled tight and Faith realized she had just overstepped her bounds. So much for trying to win a popularity contest. Jay said brusquely, "No pizza tonight. This casserole will have to do. We have to be at City Hall by six-thirty."

Both boys shot accusing glances at Faith and she felt awful.

"I'm sorry, I feel like this is my fault," Faith said in a low voice.

Jay shrugged with defeat, a gesture Faith didn't find familiar, but which made her realize Jay was essentially a stranger, even if he could still caress her soul with just a look. "It's no one's fault. It's the way it is."

"I don't want to go to the stupid council meeting," Andy burst out.

"Me, neither!" echoed Sam.

"If Marguerite hadn't quit..." Jay said pointedly. Both boys looked away, not able to quite meet his gaze.

"That was his fault." Andy eyed his younger brother.

"It was not!"

"If you hadn't throw up on her—"

"I didn't throw up *on* her—"

"I don't care!" Jay was clearly at the end of his rope. He began pulling plates out of the cabinet and set them on the counter, along with glasses and silverware. "Set the table! We're going to eat the casserole and go to the meeting."

Faith noticed he put out three plates and three glasses and cleared her throat to make her exit.

Jay looked down at the plates, then back at her.

Obviously, he didn't intend for her to eat with them, but he took time to say politely, "You're welcome to stay."

Faith didn't hear any welcome in his tone but saw the spark of hope in Sam's eyes. "Thank you for the kind offer. But I better get back." She smiled and leaned forward toward the face that had fallen with her response. "It was a pleasure meeting you both." She gave a special smile to Sam and another wink to Andy.

Neither answered, but Sam whispered to Andy, "She still looks like a mom."

"Why can't she sit for us if you don't trust me?" Andy asked loudly.

JAY HAD A THOUSAND REASONS why Faith couldn't sit with the boys. Most of them had to do with the fact that he was suddenly uncomfortable with vivid details about her, like what she smelled like, how soft her wavy brown hair was. First love was always powerful.

"I'm sure Faith has better things to do with her time," Jay said hastily.

"No, I don't." The words were matter-of-fact.

"Patty's charity committee."

"You have a phone."

"I can't—"

"Sure you can. I'm certified in both adult and child CPR. First aid, too. I'm also a professional caretaker, nanny, if you want to call me that, among other things."

He couldn't conceal his surprise. It hadn't occurred to him that Faith would actually have a profession. Come to think of it, he didn't know a thing about her. She could be a lawyer or a stockbroker for all he knew.

"What do you think I've been doing with myself for the past eighteen years? A girl's got to make a living somehow."

"I just never thought you'd be the type to take care of children."

"Really? Why'd you think that?" Her voice was casual but she had fixed those attentive eyes on him again, almost probing to see if he remembered. "I like children."

It took him several seconds to recover that mental file, a file he'd deliberately buried under all the new memories he'd acquired—fun memories of dancing with Becky on their wedding day, making love in the cottage, the birth of their children. But once he found his Faith Weaver file, he realized that it came attached with an unexpected wave of pain and confusion, and he knew why he'd buried it in the first place. Buried, but not deleted.

How could he have forgotten her amazing skill with his little brother? Their senior year in high school, Faith had pitched in big time right after his mother's death, helping with Lee, then only a year old. Suddenly, Jay remembered that year—how painful it had been without his mother, how close he and Faith had gotten because they were always together, trying to cope with the massive hole that Michelle Whitfield's death in a one-car accident had left in their lives. Then prom night, an awkward proposal, a tearful fight, a rejection he hadn't allowed himself to think about in almost two decades. *I don't want to go to college. I don't want to get married, Whitfield. I'm sick of being a mother. I just want to be free!*

He'd been devastated because it had never occurred to him that after graduation Faith wouldn't want to stay. When their relationship abruptly ended, it felt like his mother's death all over again. Jay sucked in a deep breath, tucking that memory back in a safe place. It had all worked out. He'd gotten on with his life.

"I'd gotten the impression that you didn't care for children—" he said carefully.

"I was a child myself. I'm not that anymore." Faith's voice was clipped. "If you'd rather take them to the meeting, that's fine. However, if you'd like to leave them home with me, that would be fine also."

Jay stood still.

He leaned over and checked the casserole in the oven. It was bubbling, but the smell was filling the kitchen. He surveyed his children, who were holding their breath.

"Okay."

"Then we can have pizza instead," Andy said quickly, as the cheering subsided.

"No—"

"You can have casserole, Whitfield," Faith said, backing Andy up. "But the boys and I are ordering a pizza."

Jay didn't like that, either. He didn't mind casserole, but he didn't want to be left out of the fun.

"Please, Dad?"

"Please, Dad?" the echo came. Sam went one step further and gave Jay a big hug, pressing his forehead into Jay's stomach. That easy forgiveness for a parental faux pas almost undid Jay as he returned the hug, his squeeze tight.

"All right."

More cheering as the boys high-fived each other.

"What should we order?" Jay asked.

"Pepperoni!" both boys shouted in unison.

Faith frowned and then asked tentatively, "Can we make it half and half?"

"Sure. What do you want on your half?"

"Veggie."

"*Veggie?*" The boys looked at her aghast. Their expressions spoke volumes. Why in the world would someone ruin a perfectly good pizza with vegetables? Jay knew he had the same look on his face.

"Something you not telling me, Weaver?" he asked.

Faith shook her head. "Nope. Just feeling like having a little roughage. You know how it is for us older folks."

Jay called the pizza parlor and ordered two pizzas, a large pepperoni and a small vegetarian pizza, listening with one ear as Andy and Sam explained the intricacies of a new electronic game Andy had received as a birthday present from his Uncle Lee. Faith seemed suitably impressed and eagerly took control of the opposing joystick. When she beat Andy the first time, he looked at her accusingly.

"You've done this before," Jay observed.

"Do you know that for a fact?" Faith asked, her voice low and teasing.

The laughter followed him as he went to change for the meeting. He found a fresh shirt but put on the same slacks, jacket and tie from the day. He peered in the mirror, trying to see himself as a seventeen-year-old, but couldn't. Maybe he'd been thinner, with not as much facial hair.

Do you know that for a fact?

A fourteen-year-old Faith had asked him the exact same question when, on a dare, he'd boldly told her she was wearing an undershirt instead of a bra. Jay, truth be told, wasn't quite sure of the difference between the two. Then she'd asked if he wanted to see and he'd fled, his face burning, his heart pounding in his ears. The next day, he'd taken the long way around to get to his classes just so he wouldn't have to face her.

He'd tried to avoid her for the next full year, but every time she saw him, when he least expected it, she winked at him in the halls. Then through some fluke of scheduling, they ended up with five out of six classes together—even P.E., where she'd humiliated him when she got past him twice to score for the girls during a co-ed soccer match. And he'd spent most of the time, because of their last names—Weaver and Whitfield—looking at the back of her hair, studying the wild waves she mostly let fall where they may, the depth and variation of color, some strands like gold thread, others the deep, rich color of a milk chocolate bar.

He remembered one time, when he thought she wouldn't notice, reaching out and touching a lock, surprised at how soft it was. He thought it would feel wiry and coarse, like touching the nose of a calf. But it wasn't. It was as soft and fine as his mother's silk robe.

"Dad!" Sam came up to him, hopping from one foot to the other, watching him tie his tie. "Mrs. Weaver just beat Andy again! Nobody beats Andy."

Jay straightened the tie. "You want to pick out the tie tack?"

Sam nodded eagerly and climbed up on a chair so he could see the top of Jay's tall dresser. Sam carefully slid out the bottom drawer of the handsome jewelry case that Becky had given Jay for their first anniversary. He meticulously looked at all of them and finally chose a large pearl.

"That one?" Jay asked—it wasn't a favorite.

Sam's affirmation was vigorous. "I like that one."

"Then this is the one that I'll wear." Jay carefully tacked it through the silk and then smoothed the tie as he put his jacket on. "How's that look?"

"Good." Sam nodded with approval.

Jay followed Sam into the living room and watched Andy and Faith furiously manipulating their joysticks. Andy had faster reflexes, but Faith had much better aim and accuracy and the fierce demeanor of a serious competitor. When Faith looked up, Andy took her out.

"There, I beat you!" Andy said triumphantly.

"That you did," Faith replied with an appropriate amount of loser's remorse.

"But you're still ahead. We need to play another game," Andy reminded her.

"Maybe later."

"I'll play you, Andy," Sam offered.

Andy opened his mouth but glanced up at Faith and then reconsidered.

"I think that's a great idea," she remarked as she handed her joystick to Sam. "Then your dad and I can catch up on old times."

Faith rose easily from the floor, her floral skirt swirling around her as she looked around the room for a place to sit, obviously debating whether she should sit next to him on the couch or choose the easy chair across the room. When she chose the easy chair, he couldn't squelch the disappointment.

"So you're a councilman now," Faith said, her eyes traveling up and down his attire. "You clean up nicely, Whitfield."

"Dress code."

She smiled. "How long have you been on the council?"

"It's my second term."

Faith nodded again and then cocked her head. "Aren't you a little young for that line of work?"

Jay grinned. Faith never took long to ask what she wanted to know. He nodded. "Yes. Very young. I think people felt sorry for me after Becky, so they voted me in."

"Just the first time," Faith observed. "You must have earned it the second time. You like it?"

Jay stared at her for a long time, noting the true interest that shone in her maple-colored eyes. Her gaze wasn't speculative like Amanda's and the others', almost as if they were searching for just the right question to unlock him, to make him interested in them. Faith just wanted to know.

So he told the truth. "I love it."

"Love it." Faith thought about that for a moment and then asked, "Why?"

Jay laughed. He had his pat answer for why he liked being a council member, the answer he reserved for reporters and speaking engagements. He was used to probing questions about his youth, about his commitment to the city. But now with Faith watching him so intently, he searched for the real answer.

"Because," he said slowly, "I think I can make a difference. At first, I was only going to serve one term, but at the end of it, I was in the middle of three projects that I felt strongly about, and I realized if I weren't on the committee, they wouldn't have the necessary support. I love this town, I like the people in the community, and I think they deserve the kind of representation I can give them.''

''And who takes care of your kids?''

Jay held back a wince.

''We had a very good grandmother substitute who took care of Sam from the time Becky died to about a year ago. Becky arranged it herself. She interviewed people and decided on Granny Doris. Granny Doris didn't take her promise to take care of Becky's kids lightly.''

Faith just looked at him compassionately. ''No,'' she said slowly. ''I don't imagine she would.''

''Do you remember Becky?''

Faith shook her head. ''Not really. She was a couple years behind us, wasn't she?''

Jay nodded. He couldn't help looking over to one of her pictures. Odd that he never thought of Becky as younger. In fact, she always seemed old and wise to him. His sounding board, his voice of reason. She smiled at him from their wedding photo.

''So what happened a year ago?''

''Granny Doris just pooped out. She had a mild stroke, and even though she wanted to continue to take care of the boys, she really couldn't anymore. She moved to San Luis Obispo to stay with her daughter.''

''So you've been searching ever since?''

Jay snorted. ''Let's just say, we're past the searching stage. We're now desperate. We only had Marguerite for a few weeks. Her English wasn't great, but she was a good cook. The boys—'' he looked meaningfully at his sons, but absorbed in the game, they didn't know they were being talked about ''—put whoever stays through the paces. Sam has been going through a little separation anxiety from Granny Doris, so he's got a tricky stomach. It was actually easier being on the council four years ago than this last six months. I got a few months' grace period of good behavior after Granny Doris left, but now they're just bad.''

Faith stared at his sons thoughtfully. "They don't look bad."

Jay grinned. "They're being good because they'd rather stay home than sit quietly at a council meeting. Pizza is also a wonderful incentive, no offense."

"None taken."

"So where are you staying? With your folks?" He was trying to make the conversation light, but he saw her withdraw almost imperceptibly.

"I'm sure you know, but my parents' place is a little crowded. Mom's crafts," she said by way of explanation. "I thought it'd be nice to spend some time with Patty and Bruce."

"Really?" Jay lifted an eyebrow. He found that surprising, not at all at ease with the uncomfortable feeling that news revealed.

She gave him a wry smile. "People change, Whitfield."

"Have you changed?"

HAVE YOU CHANGED?
    It was such an innocent question, but it seemed to speak volumes to Faith. Suddenly, there was tension in the room that hadn't existed before he'd asked the question.

Faith was silent. She looked away, slightly disturbed by a fluttering in her chest that led to an eerie reminiscence of high school. She didn't want to go that way with him. She didn't want to relive the hours talking and talking and talking. One night they spent the whole night outside of her house just talking in his father's truck. They had both gotten into big trouble. He'd gotten grounded for a month, mostly because Jay's father, Gil, was furious that his son hadn't bothered to think about Faith's reputation. But those things never mattered to Jay as much as they did to the people around him. Faith didn't know how, but Jay seemed sure from the moment he touched her hair that he would marry her. The sooner the better. Faith was never that sure about anything.

"You don't really want to know," she said, her voice curt.

He was made silent by her tone, like a candle blown out by a puff of breath.

"Change really isn't what it's cut out to be," she added, trying to make it better.

Jay nodded and looked away, staring at his sons playing. As much as Andy seemed to be merciless on Sam, beating him to a pulp, Faith could tell that Andy was holding back, enough so Sam could play, but not so much that Sam would beat him. Every so often Sam would get in a lucky shot, more by the strategy of constant shooting than any real skill. Despite what Jay said, Andy showed signs of having a big heart. Faith didn't know why she suddenly felt a swell of affection for Andy. Was it because he looked just like his father?

"Your kids are great," Faith commented, and then shot him an apologetic smile as she tried to make right whatever had just gone wrong. Kids were always a safe topic, right?

Jay smiled directly at her and she felt her chest expand with her relief.

"They are when they're like this. I think you've got them on a good evening."

Faith nodded again and they lapsed into silence to watch the boys play, then squabble, then resolve the disagreement, just as Jay leaned forward to intervene. She smiled at him when he sat back. He smiled briefly, his eyes darting to the clock on the mantel. The silence lengthened awkwardly, but try as she might, she could think of nothing else to say.

CHAPTER THREE

JAY SHIFTED AWKWARDLY on the couch, feeling the quiet stretch from wall to wall. He needed to leave in ten minutes, and even then he'd arrive at the council chambers a few minutes later than he normally liked to be. Luckily, Faith had directed her attention to the boys rather than at him. He appreciated how Faith listened with her whole being, her light brown eyes flickering back and forth between the two boys. She chuckled, a delighted, joyful sound, in response to one of Andy's colorful-but-hardly-appropriate-for-mixed-company jokes. He gave his dad a furtive glance, but Jay didn't have the heart to reprimand him. This was one of the few times that Andy actually conversed with an adult, rather than drooping into an oppressive silence or responding to questions with rude, mono-syllabic nonanswers. When the doorbell rang, he popped up, relieved, even though Andy, who'd been given the money, went and answered it. After they set themselves up at the kitchen table, he leaned over Sam and took a slice, juggling it and a briefcase, deciding he'd have to eat on the run.

Faith walked him to the front door, opening it for him, then stuffing a napkin in the crook between his palm and the pizza.

"Uh, thanks." He was as conversant as Andy. He looked meaningfully in the direction of the kitchen. "For everything."

Faith shrugged, her eyes matter-of-fact. "I'm happy to do this. I feel a little responsible, anyway."

He was surprised. "Why?"

"If I hadn't mentioned pizza—"

He cut her off. "You just contributed to something already brewing. The boys didn't want to go, anyway."

"Do you care?"

It was an interesting question. "Sort of. I'd like them to appreciate what my involvement in the city council means, but I'm afraid they just see it as one more thing that takes me away from them."

"Maybe it is," Faith said.

He looked for censure in her expression, but there was none. It was just Faith, a few years older, more lines etched under her eyes, the corners of her lips still tilted upward in a permanent smile.

"It's good to see you, Weaver."

"Right back at you, Whitfield." She angled her head toward the mantel clock. "You'll be late."

"I'll be home about nine."

"And bedtime?"

"Bedtime?" he asked as he bit the tip off the pizza.

"Yes. What time do your kids go to bed?"

He chewed and then swallowed before he said, "When I do."

Faith gave him a look of surprise, but then observed mildly, "It must be hard to get them up in the morning for school."

"Sometimes," Jay replied, dampening a small, unexpected cinder of defensiveness.

Faith nodded. "Maybe it's better if I try to get them in bed by nine."

Jay laughed. He knew his boys. If she could get them in their pajamas by nine, she'd be lucky. "Try your best." As he left, he felt something stir under his breastbone, something resembling a combination of foreboding and anticipation.

AT QUARTER TO ELEVEN, Jay pulled into his subdivision. The closed session of the council meeting had actually finished early, but an impromptu discussion with two worried business owners about a large tree whose roots were tearing through the sidewalk in front of their adjacent properties, making it unsafe for their customers, had taken up the extra time. The mayor, his mentor, had given Jay an approving nod, her coronet case in hand, as she made her way to a late rehearsal. He had walked the pair out of the building to the parking lot, and felt the chill of the February night on his face. It might have been a warm day, but the nights still dipped into the low thirties, cold for California.

The three of them had spent another twenty minutes knocking around ideas, their breath visible under the glow of the parking lot light. The door of Jay's sedan was open, his foot resting comfortably on the edge. With the promise of some research and a follow-up call the next week, he had felt a deep sense of satisfaction run through him as they nodded agreeably. This was exactly why he'd become a council member.

It was only when he started for home that he remembered something was different. Something pleasant. His heart thumped loudly, the unfamiliar eagerness to see Faith creeping up his shoulder blades as he thought about her, about seeing her, about seeing her with the boys. There was no way Faith could have put them to bed by nine o'clock. But…if she had been successful, that would mean he could steal a few moments alone with her. Catch up on old times, not the painful old times, but the good ones. They had shared a lot of those. That's all. Nothing more than that. He could look into those light brown eyes and see if her irises were still flecked with gold.

As he turned the corner on his street, Jay groaned out loud at the sight of a familiar white truck parked behind Faith's beat-up hatchback. Damn. What could his father want at this time of night? He realized he was going to have some explaining to do about some decisions completely unrelated to Faith and he didn't want to do it—especially to his father. Faith would just give his father that much more fodder to graze on.

He sat in his driveway for a full five minutes before finally, slowly getting out of the car. The adrenaline from the evening had departed quickly, leaving him feeling flat and tired. He let himself into the house— this time hoping the boys would be wide awake, allowing chaos to reign and preventing him from having to have one more discussion. However, if he expected chaos, he was disappointed. The house was dimly lit and very quiet except for the hum of the television in the family room behind the kitchen.

"Hello!" he called.

"Back here," Gil Whitfield responded. Jay stiffened at the sound of his father's voice. It wasn't that Gil had been a bad father. In fact, it was quite the opposite. Jay had been Gil's shadow for the first seventeen years of his life. But when his mother died, he discovered he and his father had very different ways of dealing with grief. Jay didn't want to talk about it; Gil couldn't do anything but talk about it, over and over and over again. Faith had served as a wonderful mediator between the two of them, but then she was gone and Gil wanted him to work on the farm and help raise Stinky.

Even though he knew he should, he couldn't. He'd fled to college.

He and his father had never really recovered from that. Marrying Becky and moving into the cottage had helped. But again, someone else, Becky, had served as the go-between, the glue that held their family together. And she was gone, too.

Jay slowly walked to the family room, where he found his father and Faith sitting amiably across from each other, the television providing background noise rather than entertainment. Both looked relaxed, happy, and as if they were just coming out of a deep, enjoyable conversation. Jay found this situation even more disconcerting. Faith appeared more at home with his father, more comfortable in his house, than he'd felt about either since he moved in without Becky.

"Where are the boys?" he asked. He could feel his own tension mounting, and the words came out more clipped than he intended. He tried to tack on a smile at the end, but it didn't fool Faith, who cocked her head, seeming to take inventory of his face, her bright eyes calling his attempt at a smile a lie.

His father gave him an enlightened stare. "In bed."

If Gil's tone had been light talking with Faith, it was now equally abrupt.

"You're kidding." Jay shot a quick look at Faith and then back at his father. "How long have you been here?"

Gil shook his head and asked Faith, "How long have I been here?"

"About two and a half hours. You got soundly beaten at checkers and World Warriors Part Two. Not by me, I might add."

"What did you want, Dad?" Jay couldn't curb the impatience in his voice.

"Can't a fellow see his grandsons?"

"You see them enough."

"I heard you lost another nanny," Gil said, changing the subject.

"I'll find another."

"The boys can stay out on the farm with us. You know how much Bess likes to have them around."

"Bess is busy enough with her own grandchildren—"

"*Our* grandchildren," Gil corrected him. "We've been married for over a year."

Jay had nothing against Bess, his father's new wife. In fact, he liked her a lot and felt that her no-nonsense personality was beneficial to his father and the dairy. Both widowed, they had a lot in common. He'd grown up with her son, Mitch Hawkins, and Stink had nurtured a major crush on Mitch's little sister, Katie. But he certainly hadn't expected Mitch to become his brother by marriage or how much it bothered him that after nineteen years of being alone, his father had replaced his mother.

The rational side of him knew it was good for both of them. He'd stood up for his father at the wedding, helped Mitch move Bess in with Gil. Katie, Bess's daughter, who had been back east attending her third year at Columbia University, had flown in unexpectedly for the small ceremony. But even as they said their vows, the teenager in him, who'd lost his mother at seventeen, was resentful for two reasons. One, he still felt raw from Becky's death and couldn't imagine ever making those same vows to someone new, and two, he didn't think his father should even after nineteen years. The deaths of their wives should have brought them closer, but instead it merely accentuated how very different they were.

"Isn't Phoebe expecting again?" Jay asked pointedly. "I'm sure—"

"So what are you going to do about child care?" Gil cut him off with the direct question.

"I'll find another nanny."

"Well, we think we've come up with a solution to your nanny problem," Faith ventured. She'd been so silent, Jay'd forgotten she was there. She watched him carefully though, and Jay didn't like the fact he had just exposed to her the long, unhealed resentment he felt toward his father.

FAITH WAS NO shrinking violet, but the stare Jay sent her way was hard and closed, despite the pleasant smile curving the corners of his mouth upward.

"You have, have you?" Jay asked agreeably, the skeptical arching of his brow screaming his impatience. It was such a nice brow to be looking so hostile.

"I can watch them," Faith replied practically. "I do have a lot of experience...."

Jay made an impatient noise that originated somewhere in the back of his throat. He shifted his gaze between his father and her, until he finally settled on her, his eyes not able to cover his irritation. However, when he spoke, his voice was even. "Stay out of this, Faith. You don't know—"

Time to drop another bomb on the councilman.

She said in an equally cheerful voice, "Well, since I'm going to be living on your dad's farm—"

"You're what?"

Eyes can burn, Faith discovered, convinced the tips of her eyelashes were scorched.

"Faith mentioned she'd be interested in a place of her own," Gil put in.

"Is that so?"

"So I offered her the cottage."

Faith watched Jay's eyes darken and said quickly, "It seems like a good compromise—the cottage in exchange for my nanny services. Gil tells me you're moving into tax season and you need help with the children."

Jay said nothing and Faith held her breath, searching his face for some indication of his feelings. He'd mastered the poker face.

"I'm going to check on the boys," he said politely, and then added, "Thank you, Faith, for filling in tonight. I really appreciate it. Drive safely.'' Then he walked quietly out of the room.

Faith exchanged glances with Gil Whitfield, the rugged planes of his face so familiar, so much like Jay's that it felt as if she were seeing what Jay would look like in the future. When she was a teenager, she'd found Gil intimidating and shyly skirted past him as he greeted her in a loud, booming voice. Jay's mother had been gentle, cheerful, bringing them just-baked cookies as they worked on their homework at the kitchen table, holding baby Lee away from them because he had become their favorite procrastination device. After she died, Faith and Gil had done a lot of talking because there was no one else for him to talk to, especially not Jay, who would snatch Lee up and walk outside every time Gil mentioned his wife's name or rehashed the senselessness of her death.

Gil still had an intimidating carriage, as she'd seen when he had found her that evening with his grandsons, but Faith saw his gruff manner in a different light and had met him with a big hug. As his bushy brow unfurled with recognition, he'd hugged her back tightly and she felt something warm spread through her soul. Since she'd arrived back in Los Banos, Gil Whitfield's firm squeeze was the first hug that felt genuine.

''Jay's used to being in charge of all great ideas,'' Gil said in a conspiratorial whisper, lightening the effect of Jay's abrupt departure from the room. ''Don't take it personally.''

''I guess that's my cue,'' Faith said as she stood up, looking around for her car keys.

"Why don't you check out the cottage tomorrow morning?" It was more of a command than a request. "I'll leave the keys with Stink and have him keep an eye out for you."

"I don't think so." Faith glanced in the direction of the bedrooms. It seemed better to let Jay and his father work out whatever problems they had with each other.

Gil made an impatient noise. "He doesn't hold any love for the cottage. He left it a long time ago. Right after Becky died."

"No." Faith shook her head resolutely. After a moment's hesitation, she leaned over and planted a small peck on the older man's rough cheek and whispered, "It was great seeing you again."

"Trust me. It'll be nice to know it's being used. Becky would have liked that. You can have it for as long as you're in town. You'll have to clean out a few cobwebs, but I think most of the furniture is still intact. Becky was a big one for antiques." Gil wasn't easily put off.

Funny, Faith thought as she walked slowly through the house on her way out. There wasn't anything in Jay's house that even remotely suggested that Becky liked antiques.

JAY WATCHED HIS SONS SLEEP. Andy was in the top bunk, on his stomach, his face buried in the pillow, his arm hanging down. Sam was in the bottom, curled in the fetal position, his face smashed up against the wall. Both were out for the count, sleeping the way only children could, as if heavily sedated. He gently tucked in Andy's arm and then pulled Sam away from the wall. Amazing. Who would have thought his children would be asleep before midnight?

Faith had.

He started.

What was his father up to?

He knew Gil still resented the fact that after Becky died, Jay'd taken his grandsons away from him. At a time when Gil felt the family should pull together, Jay felt claustrophobic. He didn't want to be engulfed in a family unit without Becky. His father talked about Becky incessantly, just as he had talked about his wife for years after her death. It was as if she was alive, sitting in the next room. Jay couldn't deal with Gil's chatter, because he was painfully aware that Becky was not alive, that she wasn't ever going to sit in the next room.

While he adjusted the covers over the boys, the sputtering of an engine cut into the silence of the night. He glanced out the window to see the hatchback's red taillights disappear down the street. However, his father's truck stayed solidly parked. He couldn't curb his disappointment. The wrong vehicle left. After a few minutes more of watching his sons sleep, he couldn't stall any longer. His father could wait out molasses.

"Any coffee left?" he asked as he rounded the corner.

"Sure. Faith made a pot for me." Gil gestured to the kitchen.

"Do you want a refill?"

"Nope. I'm done."

"How about Faith?" Jay looked around the room even though he knew perfectly well he wouldn't find her.

"She's left already and you get extra points for being rude." The reproof in his father's tone scraped against Jay's every nerve. His father held up his hand. "Before you get your shorts in a knot, I offered her the cottage. She didn't ask. And I'm not going to un-offer it."

Jay felt the blood drain from his face and he sat down. "You can't do that. It's Becky's."

"You can move back in if you'd like—"

Jay shook his head impatiently. "You know I won't do that—"

"Faith needs a place to stay until her parents' party in April—"

"No, she doesn't. She's with Patty and Bruce."

"The cottage is perfect—"

"No. It's not perfect. This is unacceptable." Jay couldn't imagine Faith in the cottage, didn't want to imagine Faith in it. What could his father be thinking?

Gil grunted, indicating that that particular conversation was over. He swallowed the last of his coffee before he launched into what Jay suspected was the real reason for his visit.

"Jay," his father began with no preamble. "What's this I hear about you chairing the committee on encroachment and agricultural concerns for the county?"

"Now, where'd you hear that, Dad?" Jay leaned against the wall and crossed his arms. He should have known. It was all business with Gil, except when it came to his grandsons and now, surprisingly, Faith. Jay frowned, wondering what Faith and his father had discussed.

"A little birdie. Is it true?"

Jay sighed. The committee wasn't going to be announced until the next council meeting in two weeks. In fact, they had just finished discussing the purpose of the committee tonight. "I can't say, Dad."

"Why not? It's not like it's a secret."

"I just can't. You'll find out in two weeks."

"It's going to put you at odds with the farmers."

Jay kept his response neutral. "It doesn't have to, Dad. There are a thousand ways to compromise."

Gil Whitfield snorted. "Agriculture built this town, and if council would only get their heads out of their asses, they'd realize the more they let them build, the less agriculture there's going to be. Not to mention water."

Jay nodded, taking his father's words very seriously. He would never voluntarily mention water, unless he was on official council business. It was too volatile a topic. For most people, water was simply what came out when they turned on the tap. Water was the lifeblood for an agricultural area, and the farmers were afraid the city wells would dry up their shallower wells, leaving them with *no* water unless they were in a district where they could access surface water.

Bruce Young, Patty's husband, had become a very important ally to help negotiate these complex matters. As the financial manager of the Whitfield Dairy, Bruce had been instrumental in bringing Gil into the twenty-first century. Because of his work on the Whitfield Dairy, Bruce enjoyed quite a bit of respect from the local industry, and Jay relied on him to help with the conversations, which would eventually benefit both the city and agriculture.

"Dad," Jay said. "It's long-range. We'll have plenty of opportunities to talk about this later."

"I just wanted to warn you." Gil stopped and stared at Jay in a way that made him feel like he was a teenager again. "So, what are you going to do about your two boys?"

"What do you mean?" Jay asked, suspicious.

"Tomorrow. What are you going to do about them?"

Tomorrow. Damn. Tomorrow. He hadn't had time to even think about tomorrow. He was booked through the afternoon and he had no care for his kids. Gil stared at him expectantly.

Jay didn't want to ask, but said, anyway, "You're sure Bess won't mind?"

A large smile broke over Gil's face. "She'll love it. The twins will be there in the afternoon. The boys can see their cousins."

"Thanks, Dad." Jay felt his pride stick in his throat. "I owe you one."

"Well, remember that when you're chairing that committee," his father said as he stood up to leave.

"I will." Jay straightened as Gil walked past him. "And, Dad?"

"Yes."

"Don't let Faith have the cottage."

FAITH WALKED QUICKLY up the front stairs to her sister's house because the night had turned chilly and she'd neglected to bring a jacket since the day had been so warm. As she fumbled to insert the key in the door, the porch light snapped on and the door swung open. Startled, Faith took a step back.

"Faith!" Bruce smiled eagerly as if he was expecting her. "We missed you tonight at the meeting. We sure could have used some of your great ideas."

"Hi, Bruce," Faith greeted him.

He stared at her for a full twenty seconds, his dark eyes made abnormally large by thick glasses. He was the only son of one of the wealthiest families in the area, a fourth-generation Los Banian and well-liked by all for his impeccable manners. He hadn't changed much since he first started dating Patty during their final months of high school; he still looked very much like the pale, intellectual type—slightly built, medium height, wheat-colored blond hair, youthful face, and skin so fair Faith could make out the thin blue veins in his neck and forehead.

Back then, Patty had been all aflutter when Bruce had asked her out, and Dearie had been delighted. She'd always wanted to have her daughters make "good" matches, and Bruce Young was an even bigger catch than Dearie had imagined. She was also relieved that the expense and the thousands of man-hours needed to keep Patty on the beauty queen circuit had finally netted a tangible payout.

Faith had been just a freshman then, impressed by Bruce and the fact that he didn't mind if she tagged along with them to the movies or the Detention Dam, by the San Luis Reservoir, a favorite hangout among the bolder high school students. He'd always made her feel comfortable, teasing her like the older brother she didn't have. Patty and Dearie quickly cut those three-somes short and Faith had been crushed, but the summer after their graduation, Bruce quickly became a frequent member at the dinner table and Faith had liked that. In fact, the Weavers felt more like a family with Bruce than without him. And she supposed, if she were honest, she had been envious of Patty and had developed a small crush on Bruce.

Faith fought to control a shiver.

"Uh, can I come in?" Faith asked, rubbing her arms and stamping her feet to keep warm. "It's kind of cold out."

Bruce seemed to wake up, the smile never leaving his face, and quickly opened the door wide for her.

"Out late, aren't you?" he asked conversationally as Faith brushed past him and headed for the staircase. "Patty's been worried."

Faith didn't think so, but replied briefly over her shoulder, "Jay had a council meeting that ran late."

"I guess I'm not surprised."

Faith wasn't sure what he was getting at and stopped at the foot of the stairs, her hand resting on the railing. "Surprised at what?"

"That you and Jay would hook up again." He tilted his head, his expression almost hopeful. "Do you think there's something there?"

She shook her head. Even if she did, she certainly wouldn't confide in Bruce.

He looked down as if he knew what she was thinking.

"Look, Faith. I know that we've got, uh, history together, but it shouldn't have to ruin your stay here. I'd like to help make your stay as enjoyable as possible." He walked right up to her, standing a little closer than a brother-in-law should. As she backed up a step, he reached out and with a hand that trembled slightly tugged on one of her braids, his fingers caressing a strand of beads before he let go. "I like those."

Faith felt her heart pound in her chest. "Bruce, you know that we don't have history," she said, her voice quiet. "We have something else entirely."

He appeared hurt, his pale skin flushing, and said, "We were children, Faith."

"No, Bruce. You were an adult. I was still a kid."

Bruce went still. Then he said carefully, "No, you were very much a woman. I remember very clearly."

"Well, I remember, too," Faith retorted. Her voice felt tight, her throat dry.

"It was a long time ago." Bruce sighed heavily. "Can't we just start over? Can't we be friends again?"

Faith couldn't even look at him. "I appreciate the fact that you and Patty have opened your home to me. But I just can't imagine ever being friends with you—"

"We were friends, Faith," Bruce said, his large eyes sad.

"*Were*. Let's just leave it like that. Good night, Bruce." She turned to walk up the stairs and tensed when she felt him gently grip her arm. "Let go of my arm, Bruce."

He didn't let go, but Faith could tell he was very careful not to hurt her, and he pulled her close to him. She could feel his breath by her temple and heard him inhale. She didn't want to scream but felt one building. With a desperation she hadn't felt in years, she tugged her arm out of his grasp and whirled around only to see Patty standing at the top of the stairs.

Faith met her sister's ice-blue stare before hurrying up the stairs. Patty stepped out of the way, her mouth held in a rigid line. Faith needed to get out of this house as soon as possible. Gil's offer was a gift.

"I ABSOLUTELY FORBID IT," Patty Young stated early the next morning, her thin face drawn, her lips pulled tight. Faith had to admit that her sister, even angry, looked fabulous. Early in her stay, she'd come to admit Patty was a well-respected, highly successful real estate agent. With the boom in refugees fleeing from the exorbitant housing prices in Silicon Valley, Patty was having yet another record-breaking year. From the reports Faith heard, Patty was in the running for agent of the year. Her sister continued, her voice brusque, "You'll have to call Gil Whitfield and tell him you've got other plans."

"I told him I wasn't going to take the cottage," Faith said mildly.

"But you're thinking about it." Patty shot her a piercing stare.

Faith was silent. She *had* spent the night thinking about it. She didn't like the way she felt in this house, the way her sister made her feel, the way Bruce made her feel. Gil's cottage was a perfect solution to the problem. She could still be reasonably close to the family, but she wouldn't have to be suffocated by them. She could help with the planning, but she didn't have to breathe the planning the way Patty did. She could be cordial to her brother-in-law, but she wouldn't have to dance around his unwanted attention.

Faith flipped through one of Patty's upscale home magazines, studying the images the advertisements projected, aware that she'd just lied. She wasn't just thinking about it; she *was* going to take the cottage. She knew that when she saw a twin of Jay's white kitchen, right down to the gleaming brass fixtures, and flipped past it, ignoring the feeling of displacement, as if the life portrayed in the magazine was as unreachable as living on Pennsylvania Avenue in a large white mansion. She stared at another advertisement, studied the play of light on a kitchen nook. It looked peaceful. Sitting with Jay's kids had felt peaceful—even when they were throwing punches at each other. Sitting in the family room with Gil had felt peaceful. Patty's house felt as if the whole foundation would shatter with a high-pitched noise.

"I'm a little old to be forbidden to do anything," Faith remarked before glancing up at her sister, who was stabbing an elegant gold hoop into one ear. If Patty's face got any redder, she would probably pop a vein. "And it's not like I'm leaving the area," Faith said reasonably. "I'll be around to help plan the anniversary party."

Patty didn't say anything. She just put the other

hoop in. Then she set a shoe on the counter, readjusted her pantyhose and put the shoe on.

"So what's this about?" Faith leaned over the tile island to grab herself an apple. "If I were to move into the cottage, would I be stepping on someone's toes?"

"I told you Jay and Amanda have an, uh, understanding."

"That's not what he told me."

"So what happened?" Patty looked sharply at Faith as she bit into the apple with a loud crunch. "You deliver a casserole and suddenly you and Jay are the best friends in the world?"

Faith shook her head. "No, that's not it at all. He simply lost his nanny and needed a sitter for his kids."

"And?"

"And I was there," Faith informed her. "I'm not sure why this is a problem. It'll be better for everyone. You and Bruce get your place back. I know it hasn't been easy having me here."

Patty sent her a pinched smile. "We're different people, Faith." Patty sucked in a deep breath. "I love this town. You can't stay in one place for more than a few months. Amanda and Jay are our friends. I know you and he were once an item, but you chose another life over him. Now you want to move to his old cottage?"

"This has nothing to do with Jay." Faith knew her voice was defensive. She could feel it welling up inside her.

Patty shook her head and said emphatically, "Under no circumstances am I going to let you blow into town, shake it up and then—when nothing can ever be the same—blow out again. If I've got you under my roof, at least I can contain the damage you'll do to all of us.''

Faith kept her face completely neutral, pretending she could ignore the hurtful words, which stung more because of the residual truth in them. The saddest thing was she knew exactly what Patty meant.

''Like last time?'' Faith asked, her voice low, her eyebrow cocked.

''We've forgiven you for that.''

''Forgiven me for what?'' Faith could feel her ears burn with a mixture of humiliation and resentment. Patty sounded too much like Dearie. The tension in the kitchen throbbed like a newly plucked scab.

''For sleeping with Bruce and not having the guts to stick around and face the consequences. You devastated everyone, Mom, Dad, me, Bruce, Jay—''

''Let's not go there,'' Faith interrupted her sister. She tried to will her hand to stop shaking as she took another bite of apple. She met Patty's eyes. ''And I did not sleep with Bruce.''

Patty gave a bitter laugh. ''Don't start the lies again. I saw you, Faith. I saw you get out of Bruce's truck. He told me what happened.''

''That's all you know.'' Faith felt her cheeks burn.

''I saw—''

''You don't know what you saw. I tried to tell you—''

Patty's mouth was pinched. ''Tell me what? That Bruce forced you? Like he forced you to get in the car? He forced you to cry on his shoulder? He forced you to drink? He forced you to kiss him? He forced you to undo his pants?'' Patty snorted. ''You were practically engaged to Jay.''

''I was never engaged to Jay. That was Jay. That was Bruce. That was you. It was Mom and Dad and college and everything. None of it was ever about me at all.'' Faith took a deep breath and then opened the magazine and started to flip the pages, not really seeing anything. Patty's version of the truth scraped against the lining of her stomach.

''It's never your fault, is it, Faith?'' Patty walked across the kitchen, her heels clicking on the tile. ''It's my fault, or Bruce's fault, or Jay's fault, or Mom's fault. Do one favor for me and call Gil and tell him you can't take the cottage.'' Patty rummaged through a pile of forms in her corner office.

''I'm sorry, Patty. I can't do that.''

''Not content to ruin our lives once?'' Patty's words were biting.

Faith flinched and then abandoned her vow to be neutral. ''Just by looking at you, I can see I didn't ruin your lives. You and Bruce are happily married, financially successful. Mom and Dad haven't changed one bit. I obviously didn't ruin Jay's life, either. He's a respected councilman, he's got a nice house, great kids. The only life that's been ruined is—''

Patty raised an elegant eyebrow as Faith cut herself off. ''Yes, exactly.'' Patty's tone was brisk. ''If you've ever had feelings for Jay, you'd leave him and his family, including his father, alone. You should have never come back, Faith. But now you're here, lay low. It's unpleasant, but it's the best we can do.''

CHAPTER FOUR

IF YOU'VE EVER HAD FEELINGS for Jay, you'd leave him alone. Patty's words echoed through Faith's mind as she drove out of town north on 165 in the direction of the Whitfield dairy. It wasn't as if she'd asked to move onto the farm. Jay's father had issued the invitation. And if taking care of his kids helped Jay out, then that was the least she could do for him. But her resolve almost failed when she turned onto the long driveway. So many memories.

Fortunately the main house was the only part of the dairy that hadn't changed. The pole barns around the house had been expanded enormously. They were brand-new and the large herd of Holsteins looked healthy and fat. She cautiously pulled into a well-groomed gravel courtyard and parked next to a row of trucks. As she got out, a young man on a tractor flagged her down.

"You must be Faith! I was told to expect you this morning." The man jumped down from the tractor he had just stopped. He pulled off his gloves and stuck them under his arm, eagerly walking to meet her.

"Lee," he said, introducing himself with a grin. "Lee Whitfield."

This tall, blond, strapping young man was a far cry

from the chubby toddler everyone had called Stinky, so named because he had once gleefully ventured into a fresh manure pile, smearing cow waste in his hair and every crevice of his body. It'd taken her nearly an hour and five tubs of water to get him clean.

"It's no longer Stinky?" Faith asked teasingly. She didn't know if the nickname had stuck or if he'd even remember the incident, but she sure remembered him. He'd been a constant part of her life for two years, especially the year after Jay's mother had been killed in that car accident, the year she was seventeen.

Lee's neck turned red and the blood worked its way up from his neck to the roots of his blond hair. "Only Dad and Jay call me that anymore. And Mitch, too."

"Gosh, you were no bigger than—"

"They all told me I was pretty pesky."

"You were cute." Faith had been with Jay in the hospital while his mother was in labor. She was the third person to hold Lee, Jay's mother smiling at her from the hospital bed.

"I don't remember you at all," Lee said honestly.

"You wouldn't. You were only two when I left."

"You knew my mom?"

Faith felt her throat tighten at the memory of Michelle Whitfield. "Yes, I did. She was a wonderful woman. She loved her family a lot. I'm sorry you didn't get a chance to know her."

Lee looked away and cleared his throat abruptly. Then he dug a key out of his pocket, which he flipped to her. When Faith caught it one-handed, Lee grinned in approval. "Dad told me to take you out to the cottage to see if you want it. It's been locked up for years now.''

"It must have been a sad time."

Lee's face was pensive as he opened up the passenger door of a beat-up farm truck. "It was. Did you know Becky?"

Faith shook her head as she accepted his help climbing up, feeling the strong hand on her elbow. God, he was young. Was that what Jay had looked like, was that what *she'd* looked like eighteen years ago?

He ran around to the other side of the truck and got in behind the steering wheel with youthful energy.

"So are you taking over the farm?" Faith asked as they bounced along the rough road.

"Looks like it." He shrugged casually. "Dad would like Jay to come back and run it, but that's not going to happen. Jay likes his job too much. He can't do all three things and be a dad, too. Dad's training me. I'm also working with Mr. Young, uh, your sister's husband—" Lee said awkwardly "—to learn the business side. Mitch helps me out all the time."

"Do you like it?"

"Love it," Lee confessed as he pulled up to the cottage. The glow in his eyes told her that Lee "Stinky" Whitfield was exactly where he belonged. Lee got out of the truck and came around to the passenger side to open the door for her. When she stopped to study the cottage, he looked at her apologetically. "Well, here we are. It isn't much."

"ISN'T MUCH" WAS AN understatement. The cottage Faith had assumed would be, as Patty would put it, in "move-in" condition was actually in a sad state of neglect, with zero curb appeal. It'd be a hard sell for even someone with Patty's talents. The paint on the outside had faded to a dust color, and what wasn't faded was peeling. It looked as if there had once been flower beds along the foundation, but they had long since grown over with weeds. The windows were so grimy that even when she pressed her face against a pane, she could barely see in. She felt her hope for a new home plunge to her feet. But this was merely the exterior, and a tiny flame of hope flared up again. Quite possibly, she only had to do as Gil had said the night before and "clean out a few cobwebs" inside.

"I guess it needs a little work," Lee said sheepishly.

"Is the interior still good?"

"I don't know," Lee said. "Try the key."

With a little fumbling, Faith inserted the key into the lock and was surprised when the door swung open easily, but as her eyes adjusted to the dimness of the cottage, even the tiny flame was doused. The inside was as depressing as the outside, with ghostly dust cloths—and layers of dust—draped over the furniture. Peculiar odors of wildlife and wildlife waste permeated the cottage.

Lee fumbled with the switch, and suddenly there was a flash of light, then a pop and a sizzle before the room went back into darkness.

"We might have to fix the wiring," he added.

The light couldn't have helped transform the inside one bit; the place remained dingy and dull, with old yellow-and-orange shag carpeting and heavy, dark, early sixties draperies. This wasn't exactly the refuge Faith had in mind. She'd imagined a cheery blue-and-white number, something that could be found in *Better Homes and Gardens* magazine, or if she couldn't have that, then a clean if unattractive cardboard box.

But if she squinted, perhaps she could see the remnants of life here: Andy crawling on a much cleaner carpet, family dinners around the small table set off from the kitchen.

Faith peered under one of the dust cloths—an antique chair peeked back at her.

"Why, you're beautiful," she told it. "You shouldn't be hiding under an ugly drop cloth."

"No one's been here for a long time," Lee said helpfully.

Faith nodded absently, wandering from one small room to the next. A whole family once lived in this house. In her mind's eye, she thought she could see Andy's tottering steps. This is where both boys were born. She entered the kitchen and turned on the faucet. It groaned so eerily she jumped back. Again, she felt her plan to move out of Patty's home fade. But then the plain stainless steel faucet sputtered and rust-brown liquid started to trickle and then gush and soon cleared.

Her heart leapt at the sight of clean water and she took that as a sign.

"Water still works," she called.

"Faith, I don't know if you want to stay here." Lee's tone was uncertain. "It'll take a lot of work to make it livable."

Faith, who would have agreed with him before she

saw the clear water, shook her head emphatically. "I don't know about that. It's not as bad as it looks."

"You haven't even seen the bedroom."

Faith followed Lee's voice to one of the bedrooms. "With a little elbow grease, this place could be—"

She carefully walked to where Lee was standing.

"Watch your step," Lee said as she stumbled. He caught her arm to steady her.

Faith looked down and realized that both bedrooms, doors side by side were up one slight step, giving the main room and kitchen the sensation of being sunken. She entered the room and tried not to gasp. Now she knew where the unpleasant smell came from. The carpet was heavily soiled with small-animal excrement. She saw a nest or two in the corners. The heavy brass double bed appeared dusty, but untouched, even though five years of cobwebs obscured the intricate filigree in the headboard. The drop cloths were strewn along the floor, and Lee gingerly picked one up, setting a swarm of woodchip-size crickets moving, their legs finding the yellow-and-orange shag carpet rough-going.

Faith, who wasn't really squeamish about animal life, stepped back to let them pass.

"Well, the bed looks okay," Faith said with false optimism.

"You'd need a new mattress." Lee shifted around, his arms crossed over his chest, and balanced back on his heels. "As excited as Dad was about having you live in this place, I don't think he had any idea of its condition."

Lee looked distinctly unhappy and Faith felt oddly

touched. He didn't even remember her, yet he wanted her to be in the cottage. But probably not as much as *she* wanted to be in the cottage. The thought of suffering through the next two and a half months at Patty and Bruce's was not pleasant, and she knew she wouldn't make it to her parents' anniversary—Bruce or Patty would chase her out long before that.

Faith stared reflectively at the ruins. It could be made habitable. In the end, that was all she needed. She wandered into the other bedroom, the decorative border still circling the four walls, indicating that this had been the nursery. The crib and a twin bed were pushed against the wall, but some rodent families had found refuge in both. She walked back into the bleak main room. It was dark and felt terribly claustrophobic, as if the beamed ceiling was pressing down on her. But somehow, this cottage, even in its disrepair, offered her a more welcoming option than Patty and Bruce.

Thirty minutes later, Lee was climbing back into the truck, shaking his head in amazement. "I can't believe you're going to take it," he said as they bumped toward the main house.

"I'll drive into town and see if I can get someone out here to tell me how much work it will take to make it livable." Faith's mind was whirling. "I think with the help of an exterminator and a good carpet layer, I could do the painting and the cleaning. I've done a little of this work before." Very little. "Would Gil trust me with a project like this?"

"I'm sure Dad would even finance it," Lee said practically, as he swerved to avoid a large pothole.

"He still dreams that Jay'll move back here with the boys."

"I don't think that will happen."

Lee nodded, his expression thoughtful. "I don't, either. But Dad can't help but hope."

"So you don't think he'll mind."

"Not at all."

"What about Jay?"

Lee gave her a puzzled look. "What about Jay?"

"Would Jay mind?"

Lee shrugged. "He might."

JAY WASN'T HAPPY when Lee called to tell him about the cottage or that right at that moment Faith had a contractor looking over it. He wasn't happy Faith was there looking at all of Becky's things, his things, their things. He wasn't happy at all. Then again, he reassured himself, there were plenty of things that could go wrong. The place might not have electricity or running water. Faith could decide not to take it. His father could decide not to let her have it. Since all the scenarios seemed remote, he found himself shuffling around appointments so he could take off an hour early, an hour he really couldn't afford, to see if he could dissuade Faith.

The cottage of all places. He had deliberately avoided the little house because it held too many memories, too much of Becky. The loss he felt was made more evident by everything he'd left there—her furniture, her decorating schemes. It felt as if Becky had touched every inch of the small space.

When he arrived, he saw one more thing to feel

guilty about. His stomach hurt just to look at the disrepair. The weeds had grown up beside the foundation, almost hiding the dingy windows and faded paint. Becky would have never allowed the cottage to deteriorate to such a level and wouldn't have wanted him to let it happen, either.

His father had assured him it was still in good condition, but now Jay realized that he'd simply meant *structurally*. He parked next to Faith's dinged and faded hatchback, which in some ways matched the cottage. The finish on her car must have been silver at one time. Not anymore. It was rusted out in several places, evidence of coastal life. Salt air was brutal on enamel. As he got out of the car, he noticed a large pile of weeds Faith had begun to clear from the back, along with an equally generous pile of familiar shag carpeting and heavy curtains.

Though he'd known she'd be there, Jay hadn't expected to see her dressed in grubby jeans and an old Cal State Northridge sweatshirt, as stained as her car was dinged. And he certainly hadn't expected to find her vigorously scrubbing the windows of the cottage, trying and actually succeeding in pulling out quite a shine from the old glass.

"You've just been sold some swampland in Florida," Jay said in as casual a voice as he could muster. He was close enough to see the sparkling streaks of gold buried in the brown of her hair. She smelled of sweat and soap and he was disturbed by how attractive that was.

She jumped and turned to look at him. Beads of perspiration were caught on her lashes. "You shouldn't sneak up on people.'' She swiped at her forehead, streaking grime across it.

''You mean you couldn't hear me coming down that road?''

She flushed and pushed a flyaway strand of hair out of her face. ''I thought you were Gil.'' She glanced up at the sun. ''Mitch was already here to drop off the twins with Bess.'' She pointed to the pile of carpet and drapes. ''He pulled those out for me, and Gil said he'd come by later to see if he can do anything about the wiring. An exterminator is scheduled to bag the place at the end of the week.'' She took a breath and then looked at him hard. ''You're off work early. Are you here to pick up the kids or do you want me to drop them off later this evening?''

''What?'' Jay was puzzled.

''They're up at the main house. Your dad picked them up this afternoon. He gave me their schedule, so I can start tomorrow.''

''Start what?''

''Watching your children.''

Jay felt like an avalanche had hit him. He stubbornly shook his head. ''I don't think so. It was nice of you to sit with them last night, but—''

Faith turned her back to him and picked up a small plastic brush. She scrubbed vigorously at the corners of the windows, finally revealing a straight edge of glass against the wood.

''So who's going to watch them?'' she asked casually.

''I've a got a few people lined up,'' Jay fibbed.

Faith rolled her eyes. ''You're so busy, I'd be surprised if you even had your clients fully lined up. You were right last night. Bess does have her hands full with the twins. They're cuties but active. Andy and Sam sure like them, though,'' she added thoughtfully. ''I think spending time here is good for them. But it'd be hard work for Bess and Gil if it were every day.''

''Why are you doing this?'' Jay asked, his voice low.

She glanced at the brush in her hand. ''It gets to the corners easier. Don't you think that window looks better?''

''You know what I mean.'' He turned away from the cottage, so he wouldn't see Becky blowing raspberries on Sam's chubby tummy, so he wouldn't see Becky laughing as Andy pantomimed his day at preschool.

Faith stopped what she was doing and said frankly, ''I have no idea what you're talking about, Whitfield.''

Jay didn't expect the jolt of defensiveness that struck him.

''Moving in here. Can't you get an apartment in town? Why do you want to live here, for heaven's sake?'' Jay asked impatiently. ''Look at this place. It's run-down. It's hardly someplace you'd want to live. This in exchange for taking care of my kids? I think you're getting robbed. You're not going to be able to move in for at least two more weeks.''

''Which means I'll have two months that I won't have to stay with Patty…'' Her voice trailed off as she scratched her neck without meeting his eyes.

''And Bruce,'' he added dryly. He'd heard the rumors. In fact, Patty had alluded to them on more than one occasion.

Her brown eyes widened, and she looked at him sharply.

"What do you mean by that?" Her face became guarded. "What are you talking about?"

Jay tried to make his tone light. "I just figured it would be awkward to live with someone you once cared for."

She was silent for a long time, her eyes studying the peeling paint. "I think it would be nice if we could duplicate this color. Don't you?" She pried a good-size chip off the exterior wall. "I wonder if I could get the paint store to match this."

"You did care for Bruce, didn't you?" Jay persisted.

Something flashed in her eyes. After a long, tense moment, she bent over to retrieve her bucket of soapy water and scrub brush. "No," she said succinctly. "I never cared for Bruce. Not really."

It was the answer Jay had hoped for, but her tone was unexpected.

Wanting to know more, he followed her to the next window. Faith scrubbed this one even harder.

"This cottage could use some life in it," Faith commented matter-of-factly, obviously not willing to give him more.

"It's a wreck."

She nodded. "Yes, it is. But some things are worth the trouble."

Jay was quiet, trying to sort his thoughts. Finally, he repeated, "Why are you doing all of this?"

She dropped her scrubber in the bucket and retrieved a squeegee. Rubber squeaked against glass.

"I don't know, Whitfield," she answered honestly, and then said, "Sometimes a girl's just got to have her own home."

"Just so you know," Jay said, half joking, "I don't come with it."

THE WORDS HIT FAITH like a blast of cold water and she didn't know whether she should laugh at his presumption or cry because there might be some part of her that wished he did.

Or not him, but the boy he'd been.

Certainly, she didn't expect Jay to come with the cottage, and she didn't have any illusions they could or would pick up where they left off in high school. But perhaps there had been something inside of her, hoping, just hoping. Faith pushed away the feeling and tightened her resolve.

"Why'd you think I'd want you to?" Faith chose to respond with teasing. He might be a council member, but that didn't mean he was irresistible, even with those pretty eyes.

Jay shrugged, his gesture arrogant. "You seem to be looking for something, and I just wanted to let you know it wasn't me. When Dad said you wanted to move in—"

"I'm not looking for anything you can give me," Faith interrupted evenly. "Just a little peace for the next couple of months until I'm on my way. Give me something to do with my time and that will make me even more happy."

"An apartment could give you peace."

"But it's not free," she reminded him.

"Nothing is free, Faith." Jay's voice held an edge of warning. "We pay for every decision we make, one way or another." The corners of his mouth twisted up to take the sting out of his words.

Faith plopped the scrub brush into the bucket, watching the dingy water wash over the side and onto her shoes. She wiggled her feet in her socks and felt the damp seep in between her toes. Thinking about her toes allowed Faith to ignore how much Jay had really changed. And even if he did come with the cottage, she would have to start again, as if they'd never met, because he in no way resembled the boy she had loved.

"Patty forbade me to move."

Jay showed no surprise, but he asked, "Why would she do that?"

"I guess she's under the same impression you are."

"Which is?"

Faith gave him a look of disbelief. "Which is—" She bent down and picked up the scrub brush again and attacked a particularly crusty area, feeling the push against her muscles, the familiar twitch of exertion in her lower back. "That I'm back in town to wreak havoc on those around me. Believe me—" she stopped and stared straight into Jay's sky-blue eyes "—I'm not. I would, however, be more than happy to take care of your kids in exchange for the use of this cottage, which was what your father and I talked about. To help you out and to help Gil and Bess out.

I think Gil realized this afternoon how big a handful both the twins and the boys are at the same time.''

"So what are your credentials? Do you have references?'' Jay asked, his tone all businesslike.

Faith shot him a surprised look and responded with an equally businesslike tone. "I've experience in practically everything and anything that has to do with children from the age of zero to sixteen, except the pain of childbirth. I've been a nanny for nearly twelve years. I've got a master's in psychology, emphasis in early childhood education from Northridge. I'm affiliated at both the state and national level with professional day-care organizations. And I'm good at it. And yes, Whitfield, I have a résumé and references. Five pages of them.''

JAY WAS FLOORED. "Good at what?'' he asked as his mind tried to connect Faith with a college education. Her decision to not go to college had been the beginning of the end. They had had plans together.

She met his eyes and looked away quickly. "Raising other people's children. I get attached, but not so attached that when the post ends, the children and I are torn apart. I can fill in until tax season ends and that should give you plenty of time to find a permanent nanny.''

"When did you get a degree?''

Faith shrugged. "A while ago.''

"I thought you didn't want to go to college,'' he said, his voice pensive. He couldn't help sounding betrayed. They had made a pact to attend the same college. That was yet another plan, another promise Faith had abandoned. In fact, he just now realized that he'd been counting on Faith's going to the same college, so they could face his father together. But she'd taken off, never looking back.

"I didn't want to go to college then," she corrected him gently. "I always planned on going. Just not right after high school. People do grow up, Whitfield."

Jay was silent.

"What do you say?" Faith broke into his thoughts. "Your children."

"How long could you take care of them during the evening? I have excessive hours sometimes," he asked, knowing that he had to do something, because Bess tended to pay for his father's exuberance. She couldn't keep Andy and Sam for as long as it would take for him to find a suitable nanny.

"For however long you need me to take care of them," Faith said matter-of-factly. "I'd like to spend some time working on the cottage over the next couple of weeks, but I can do that while the boys are in school."

She stood back and dumped the bucket before moving around to the front of the cottage. "I'm between jobs. I've given up my apartment. And I always feel better working than not working. Sitting your kids will get me out from under Patty's feet until I can move in here."

She paused, then opened the door to the cottage. "You coming?" she asked as Jay stopped at the front step.

Jay stood on the threshold of the cottage, his heart beating wildly as he peered in. It was larger and lighter than he remembered it being, but then again, it was practically empty with no curtains to obscure the light. No trace of an ever-fattening Becky as she grew large with Sam, no three-year-old Andy spinning and yakking wildly.

"You moved the furniture around," he observed from the door frame, stalling, not wanting to enter the house.

"Do you mind?" Faith looked back at the living room and surveyed her work.

"Yes. But I guess it's not my place to mind." He couldn't keep the undertone of bitterness out of his voice.

"It is your furniture, though," Faith conceded, then added with a tilt to her head, "These antiques are beautiful. I'm surprised you didn't take them with you. They would look lovely in your house."

"Different style. Besides, the boys are really rough on furniture," Jay ad-libbed. "I'd hate to see something this beautiful be shredded into bark."

"You can teach children to respect pieces like these," observed Faith. "You can come in, you know."

"I know."

There was a long silence and Faith met his eyes compassionately. Jay felt an unfamiliar stirring under his ribs, as if Faith had just reached into his chest and massaged his aching heart with a soothing, warm touch.

"There's nothing but good feelings here," she said softly. "These memories are wonderful, good things. Don't let the good memories cause you pain."

Jay grunted.

He had no use for Faith's compassion right now. He couldn't do anything with it. All it would accomplish was to topple years of careful construction. Avoidance and denial combined to make an excellent mortar. It was unbelievably hard to live without Becky. It was even harder to raise her two sons, their two sons, without her—without her behind him, her arms wrapped around his waist, her face pressed in the indention between his shoulder blades.

Jay stepped through the threshold and Faith abruptly turned, almost as if she was giving him privacy. He waited for the onslaught of pain to hit him, like a towering wave pulling him under the surf, crushing him so badly he forgot he even knew how to breathe.

But it didn't come.

All that washed over him was a small but not unpleasant tickle, like the gentle surf, pulling sand from under his feet on a particularly hot day. He ventured a little farther into the cottage, swearing he could hear the resonance of Becky's laughter coming from the bedroom.

"Is that where you're going to stay?" He didn't mean for the words to come out so sharply. It just unnerved him to think of Faith sleeping in the room he and Becky had shared.

Faith stiffened.

"No," she replied in a measured tone, quietly rebuking him. "I thought I'd take the small room. I like the way it feels."

"The mattresses are probably bad."

Faith nodded. "I'll replace both the mattresses. Gil

took the crib up to the main house as a spare for when Phoebe's baby is born. That way she can visit while the baby naps.''

''The bed won't fit in there.'' He jerked his head toward the boys' room while referring to Becky's oversize brass bed, with the white porcelain knobs, hand-painted with small pink posies. He knew. They had tried when they found out they were going to have Sam, wanting to give the boys the bigger room, laughing as it got stuck, trapping Jay inside Andy's room until Becky could get help from Gil.

''I didn't think it would,'' Faith said steadily, looking straight into him. The hand caressed his heart again. ''I don't mind sleeping in a twin bed. I've done it a lot in my lifetime.''

Jay had a hard time believing that. Faith hardly appeared to be someone who would sleep alone for any extended period of time. Surely, Faith was built for love, for spooning, for cuddling. He laughed in disbelief.

FAITH FELT THE SARCASM of Jay's laugh cut into her soul. She thought she was immune to hurt. She thought that after eighteen years, his opinion no longer mattered to her. But she discovered that it did.

''What's so funny?'' she asked, unable to fully mask the hurt.

''Surely you don't expect me to believe—''

''What?'' She cocked her head to the side, wondering if he would actually say what she thought he was going to say, wondering whether this could actually be the same person she'd spent every waking moment with from the time he'd first kissed her at the homecoming dance their sophomore year until their last prom.

"To believe..." He looked at her a little less certainly, as if it had just occurred to him that what he said might not have been flattering.

"To believe?" She arched an eyebrow at him.

"To believe you've been, uh, celibate all these years."

There was a long pause and Faith wondered what it was that he really wanted to know.

"Why would that be so difficult?" Her voice sounded strained to her. She stared at the floor.

"I know you, Faith." He said it like a statement.

Faith shook her head. "Can't imagine how you can. I've just been trying to adjust to the fact that you're nothing like the boy I knew in high school. I'm not the girl you knew, either."

"I discovered that right before you left."

Faith recoiled again. His voice was so mild that one would almost have to be clairvoyant to hear the reproof, the bitterness, but Faith heard it as if he had spoken. So she said the only thing she could think of.

Nothing.

JAY STARTED TO FIDGET once the pause extended beyond the two-minute mark. Those tax forms in his briefcase really needed to be processed as quickly as possible. He hadn't spoken anything but the truth, but for some reason, he seemed to have said something wrong.

Perhaps not wrong, but not right.

He felt awful.

He could hear Becky chiding him. Becky had never been jealous of Faith. She had responded to his story about her with compassion. Now she was telling him to react the same way. He certainly couldn't know what roads Faith had traveled in the past two decades. So he extended to her the most precious peace offering he possessed.

"Can you pick up the boys after school tomorrow?"

Faith shot him a look he couldn't fathom. Hurt mingled with a desperate determination. She gave a small smile and shrugged, then accepted his offer with a gracious "Yes."

"Sam gets out at 2:45 and Andy gets out at 3:15."

"Easily done."

"Do you have a car?"

Faith nodded to the car outside the cottage.

Jay blinked at the dilapidated heap. "A different car?"

She shook her head.

"That's hardly safe," Jay observed.

"Well, I'm a safe driver."

"That's not going to protect you against the idiots who are driving these days." He paused and then plunged into the deep end. "You can borrow the station wagon while you're transporting the kids. I hardly use it, anyway."

"So you want me to start tomorrow?"

"Tomorrow," Jay confirmed. "I'll call the school and let them know that you'll be picking them up." He took the key to the station wagon off his key ring and offered it to her. She took it slowly, and then pushed it into her pocket. "You'll need this also." He gave her a spare house key. "This week isn't that bad, but starting next week, I start working evenings until the March 1 filing deadline. After that I have a week or two of breathing room, but then I'll be right in the mix until April 15. On those heavy weeks, I'd appreciate it if you can be at the house in the morning to get the kids to school, since I try to be at the office by 6:00 a.m. Then you'll need to stay with them until I get home. I'd need you to clean and cook for them, too."

Faith didn't look flustered at all. "Do you want me to stay at the house or bring them back to the farm?"

Jay exhaled sharply. "I'd prefer they stay at the house, just so they get their homework done. But I don't think regular visits with Dad and Bess are a problem. Do what's easiest, especially if you've got work here to do." He looked around the cottage.

Faith nodded. "Thanks, Whitfield. This is saving my life."

Jay didn't quite know what she meant by that, but he felt Becky's approval lift the fine hairs on the nape of his neck.

THAT EVENING at the dinner table, Faith watched a vein in Patty's forehead pulse at her news. Faith pointedly avoided making eye contact with Bruce, who seemed disappointed that she had maneuvered to sit next to her father rather than the place he'd reserved for her.

"I can't believe you're actually going to move out to the Whitfield farm," Dearie Weaver was saying.

Faith's father, Stan, helped himself to another slab of Patty's roast beef. "This is great, honey," he complimented Patty, then turned a bushy eyebrow toward Faith. "I thought this was going to be family time. If you move, you'll never be here."

"I'll visit with you both," Faith assured him hastily. She glanced over at her mother, who was dabbing her napkin at the corner of her mouth. "It's a long time until the party," Faith explained. "And I'll go nuts if I don't have a project."

"If you need a project," Patty suggested. "I have plenty of projects for you to work on. My charity committee brainstormed several events you can work on if you want."

"I promised I'd help Jay out with his children."

"And you promised you'd help with the planning of the anniversary party," Bruce reminded Faith, drawing a sharp intake of breath from Patty. He passed a bowl of vegetables to Faith.

"Which Patty told me she'd rather I not ruin," replied Faith, not bothering to hide her hurt, accepting the bowl, then realizing that Bruce had skipped his wife. She held out the bowl for Patty, who ignored it, so Faith passed it back to Bruce.

"With good reason," Patty retorted. "I can't believe you actually wanted a vegetarian barbecue."

"It was a joke."

"Parties don't get planned on jokes."

"Girls!" Dearie Weaver held up her hands. She directed her attention at Faith. "It seems that if you do

move, you'd be spending more time with the Whit-
fields than with us.'' Her eyes drifted to her husband.
''I still can't believe that Gil married Bess Hawkins.
No one can. I wonder what came over him.''

Faith was silent.

''Back in high school, Faith spent more time there
than here,'' her father commented.

''It was almost like you were Michelle's daughter
more than mine,'' Dearie complained. ''She always
knew more about you than I did.''

''You were busy with Patty, Mom.''

''Don't blame it on me,'' Patty said as she rose from
the table.

''Well, you were the costly daughter, Patty,'' Stan
said, defending Faith, his mouth full. ''Cheerleading,
Harvest Queen, all those pageants that your mother
spent her time sewing costumes for, singing lessons.
Faith was downright cheap.''

''Faith had a lot of natural beauty,'' Bruce commented as he offered Faith another roll. Two red spots
appeared on Patty's cheeks.

Faith felt her face burn as she waved the rolls away.

Dearie frowned. ''Now, let's not start with who's
the prettiest Weaver girl.''

All Faith wanted to do was slide to the center of
the earth. She tried to find a compassionate face in the
lot, but she supposed that her eighteen-year absence
had given them plenty of time to establish a family
dynamic that she just wasn't a part of. Her mother,
father, sister and brother-in-law had established their
interactions with one another more out of habit than
real interest, and that seemed to ensure the Weaver

family dinner table discussions never dug too deep or became too reflective.

This was so unlike the lemonade break she'd shared with the Whitfields before heading back to Patty's. Jay's whole clan had seemed to accept her presence as if she were a logical addition to the family. She'd met a very pregnant Phoebe and made a special point to thank her for Mitch's help with the cottage. Phoebe just shook her head and laughed, saying that these days, Mitch took advantage of any excuse to escape her hormonal mood swings. Faith enviously watched Phoebe discuss the twins, Eric and Hannah, age three, with Bess, and it was hard to believe that Phoebe was the woman's daughter-in-law and not her daughter. Faith would beg, borrow and steal for as close a connection with Dearie.

"We know who's the prettiest, don't we, Bruce?" Dearie's words ended that particular conversation as she rubbed Patty's hands.

And Faith—who truly thought she'd grown past the need to have her mother tell her she was pretty or intelligent or capable—realized, with horror, she hadn't.

CHAPTER FIVE

DESPITE HER FAMILY'S vigorous protest, Faith picked up Sam and Andy the following afternoon. She felt like a fraud driving around in Jay's practically brand-new station wagon and tried to ignore the speculative looks given to her as she picked up the boys from school. It was surprising how many people knew who she was, why she was in town, and what she was doing for Jay.

The first week, she'd taken the kids to Gil's, but soon realized that time with their grandparents meant all fun, no homework, especially if the twins were there. Also, Faith discovered that Jay had so little free time that she wanted the boys to be at the house in case he dropped by home for a quick bite during dinnertime. Sometimes the boys got to spend a precious hour with their father, other times she had to help them work through their disappointment when he called to say he had picked up some Chinese food and was eating take-out at his desk. It was hard not to feel abandoned and she wasn't even his wife. At first, the boys appeared indifferent to Jay's absence, but Faith realized after that first highly educational week that their bad behavior and overall disrespectfulness was probably more of a reflection on Jay's absence than a natural inclination toward evil.

It seemed as if Andy in particular wanted to put Faith through her paces. Twice when she went to pick him up in front of the school, there was no sign of him at all. After twenty minutes of frantic searching, she'd spotted him with some friends in the parking lot of the local market, one block down, leaning nonchalantly against the concrete steps of the post office.

No harm, no foul, Faith reasoned.

She'd come to the same conclusion about Sam. While he was generally a more pliable child than Andy, if he didn't get his way, he had a stubborn streak that seemed to manifest itself into what Jay referred to as a tricky stomach—which really meant Sam hyperventilated to the point of vomiting. After changing her clothes and washing her sneakers for the third time, she and Sam had a long talk. She told him she was more than willing to give him all the attention and all the hugs he wanted, if he would try as hard as he could not to throw up. He promised he would try.

That was the first week.

The second week, Andy's mutiny over any authority escalated until he refused to eat any dinner unless it was pizza. He'd push away the plate that Faith put before him and gag as if he was choking. With every defiant move, with every pressed-lipped mutiny, his blue eyes watched her carefully as if he was wondering how she would react, or whether he could scare her off, or if she'd break down and tell Jay. So far, she'd not said a word. This was between Andy and herself.

Tonight, come hell or high water, she would get that boy into the shower. When she had arrived early on the previous mornings, she'd seen him tumble out of bed with just enough time to pull on day-old clothes and plop sullenly at the kitchen table, his hair wet only on the top, as if he thought he could fool her into believing that he'd actually washed.

He couldn't.

In addition, she saw his teeth were coated with yellow gunk. How could Jay not see that his son rarely, if ever, brushed his teeth? Andy seemed to think that dousing his pearly whites with mouthwash was just as effective and less time-consuming than using a toothbrush and toothpaste.

He certainly managed to dupe Jay.

After the scant number of dinners Jay had at home, Faith knew why. Even when Jay was sitting with the boys, he wasn't present. He nodded attentively at Sam's unending chatter and Andy's interjections, but at the same time he scribbled notes on important-looking documents—tax codes or city council work, she couldn't tell—which overflowed from his briefcase. Faith realized her second week into the nanny stint that Jay really didn't need a nanny, he needed a wake-up call. Andy and Sam didn't want for shelter and food, but Jay was oblivious to what mattered most in his boys' lives. Yesterday, the day before Valentine's Day, on their way home from school, Faith had asked the boys if their classes were doing anything to celebrate.

She had been met by silence in the back seat of the

station wagon, not the general enthusiasm associated with a break from the usual routine.

"Valentine's Day is stupid," Andy had grumbled. Faith looked at him in the rearview mirror as he stared pensively out the window. "It's just for girls. It doesn't mean anything."

Faith had suppressed a smile. He was training early for the classic American adult male response to one of the most emotionally potent holidays of the year.

"But it must be fun to have snacks and exchange cards with your classmates. Do they do that still?"

Again, silence.

"Granny Doris made us cookies to take last year," Sam informed her.

Andy had shot Sam a dirty glare. "Granny Doris isn't here anymore."

"Would you like cookies to take tomorrow?" Faith asked as she slowed for a stoplight, her signal on for a right-hand turn. "We can just go straight to the store and find cookies to make."

Silence.

It had been hard to gauge what they wanted to do. Sam looked hopeful but wasn't saying anything. Andy just shrugged. So she made the decision and headed in the direction of the supermarket.

Once there, Andy unbent enough to offer his opinion on what kind of cookies he wanted, and Sam looked excitedly at his brother when Faith put two bottles of heart-shaped sprinkles in their cart. Then they lingered by the cards—Sam choosing a pack with dinosaurs on them, and Andy, a pack with jokes.

It was the first afternoon Andy didn't protest about

doing his homework right away or eating his dinner, since both he and Sam were so eager to make the cookies and fill out their cards. They each chose a special card for Jay while Faith supervised the class list, making sure that no child was forgotten, even though both boys were less than enthusiastic about sending the Valentines to the girls. By bedtime, the cards were packed in paper lunch bags and the cookies were put in tins for each class.

That had been yesterday.

Tonight, Faith sat listening to the events of the day. Both boys had the Valentine's Day cards they'd received spread out in front of them. But she couldn't ignore the fact that her grace period of cooperation from Andy had expired. He'd fiddled with his cards all afternoon, reading them over and over, but didn't do his homework. Then he'd complained, choked and poked at his dinner plate. What kid didn't like spaghetti? She'd even used heart-shaped pasta for fun.

"Is Dad coming home for dinner?" Andy asked sullenly as he flipped through his cards.

Faith shook her head. "Sorry, kid. He called earlier."

"He's never home. He didn't even get our cards."

"Yes, he did," Faith said.

Andy sent her a suspicious look. "How?"

Faith leaned toward him. "I'll tell you how. The Valentine fairy put them in his briefcase."

Sam smiled in delight. "You mean there's a Valentine fairy?"

"No, stupid. Faith put them in Dad's briefcase."

"You're stupid."

"No, you're stupid."

"You're stupider." Andy hit Sam in the arm.

Sam's face scrunched up as he tried not to cry at this latest assault. "You're the stupidest and you *smell*."

"I do not smell." Andy lashed out, peppering Sam's shoulders with pointed jabs. "Take it back."

"That's enough!" Faith caught Andy's upper arm and hauled him upright, then marched him down the hall. She pulled him into the boys' bedroom and shut the door firmly.

Andy stared at her in surprise, then growled as he tried to wriggle out of her grasp.

She let go and Andy backed up.

"What are you going to do?" he asked, his eyes narrowing. "Hit me?"

Faith was so surprised she laughed. He'd probably never been hit in his entire life. "Why in the world would I hit you? Although, I suppose you deserve it a lot more than Sam did."

"He said I smelled," Andy muttered.

"Only after you hit him," Faith said, her voice reasonable.

"He bugs me."

Faith shook her head. "No, buddy. You're just mad that your father's not here."

"No, I'm not." Andy crossed his arms, his eyes sweeping the ground, his foot shaking impatiently.

Faith nodded. "Okay. But you know what?" She gentled her voice. "It's okay to miss him."

Andy plopped onto Sam's lower bunk, grabbing a small rubber ball on the way down. He began to bounce the ball off the bottom of the top bunk. *Bo-boomp.* "I see him every day." Andy's voice was hard. *Boomp, boomp, bo-boomp.*

"I know. But you want him to be a regular dad."
Boomp, boomp, bo-boomp.

Faith pulled up a chair and sat across from the bed. "You want him to make cookies with you, show up for school events, but mostly just be an 'always-there' kind of dad. But your dad's not like that."

"I know, I know, he's got to be nice to everyone," Andy said bitterly.

Boomp, boomp, bo-boomp.

Faith shook her head. "That's not true. He's not nice to people because he has to be. He's nice because that's the kind of man he is. He's a good man who's trying to do the best he can."

Andy glared at her, squeezing the rubber ball in his clenched fist. "I wish he wasn't so nice."

Faith nodded sympathetically. "You think if he wasn't so nice, he wouldn't be so busy. I know it's rough for you, especially during tax time. But that's no excuse for how mean you've been lately, especially to Sam."

"I don't hurt him."

"Yes, you do. You hurt his feelings. He thinks you're better than Nintendo. And mark my words, he's going to be your best friend when you grow up."

Andy groaned.

"You want to know how I know that?" Faith leaned forward.

Andy was silent.

"I know because you and he are the only ones who will know what it was like to grow up with your dad."

Andy just stared at her.

"Well, enough of the lecture. Have you done your homework?"

"Not spelling," Andy said. "I hate spelling. It's stupid."

"Maybe because you're not doing so great on those tests on Fridays?"

"How do you know?"

"I talked with your teacher last week."

Andy avoided her gaze. "You're not my mom," he muttered.

Faith shook her head. "No, I'm not. But I would like you to be able to spell better. I'll help."

"Yeah, right."

"Don't trust me?"

Andy shook his head.

"Why not?"

"Because grown-ups always say stuff they don't mean. They make promises they don't keep."

"Tell you what. I'll always try to say what I mean, and I'll always try to keep my promises."

"And what do you want from me?" Andy asked warily.

"Not a thing. I want you to be happy. Come on. Let's get going on that homework." Faith ruffled his hair and found her fingers got caught in it. This boy needed a shower. Badly. "Once you finish that, then you can take your bath, and then bed."

"Only sissies take baths," Andy muttered.

Faith sighed, thankful that Sam was out of earshot.

He'd enjoyed a fun bath just that afternoon. "Then you can take a shower. Why don't you do that now and then we'll practice spelling?"

The small step they'd just made vanished. Andy's mouth turned down into a scowl and he shook with anger. "I don't have to," he snapped at her. "And you can't make me."

Faith was silent and then nodded. "You're right. I can't make you. But I'd think you'd want to." She didn't wait for him to answer but opened the door and started down the hall.

Footsteps came up behind her.

"Why?" Andy demanded.

"Because Sam was right. You smell."

Andy looked at her, horrified. "I do not," he denied.

Faith suppressed a smile. "You do, just like cabbage casserole. I can't imagine that it's too pleasant for the people who sit next to you in class. I'd think they'd complain the loudest. Anybody say anything to you lately?"

Andy's face turned ashen.

Faith nodded. "Ah, I thought so." She arrived at the table and started to clear it, taking their dinner dishes to the sink. "Splashing water on your hair doesn't take the place of shampoo. And it only makes bad smells smellier."

"I'm hungry now," Andy complained.

"Have some spaghetti."

"I'll make a sandwich."

"Sorry. I used the last of the bread to make your lunches tomorrow. No more peanut butter, either."

"Let's order a pizza," Andy suggested sullenly.

"I'm not hungry, and I've eaten dinner. Sam's had enough for two."

"I haven't yet."

"That's your choice."

"I'm going to call my dad."

Faith gestured toward the phone. "You know his number."

"He'd order pizza."

"Too bad he's not here."

The front door swung open and Sam squeaked, "Daddy's home!"

Faith heard Jay give an oomph. Sam was a hurler. The first time Faith had picked him up from school, he'd thrown himself at her, almost knocking her over in his enthusiasm.

Accusation burned in Andy's eyes. "I thought you said he wasn't coming home."

"Just came home for dinner," Jay called as he walked into the kitchen carrying Sam. He fished in his pockets and pulled out two small cards. "I found these."

"The Valentine fairy put them in your briefcase," Sam whispered.

Jay put Sam down. He sniffed appreciatively. "What smells so good?"

"Spaghetti." Faith tried to hide how pleased she was to see him.

"Dad, can we order pizza?" Andy asked, standing right next to Jay, looking up at him.

Jay looked puzzled. "I thought Faith made spaghetti."

"It's nasty."

Faith grinned. "Vegetables."

"I think you can eat spaghetti with the rest of us."

"We ate already."

Jay looked surprised.

"Except for Andy," Faith said smoothly. "Sam has some free television time before he gets ready for bed because he did his homework already." She looked significantly at the clock, then at the little boy. "Sam, you have half an hour before seven-thirty."

"Who goes to bed at seven-thirty?" Jay sounded appalled.

Faith looked at him sharply. "It takes about a half hour to get in the bed."

"I don't have that strict a bedtime for the boys," Jay said.

As Faith reached for a plate for him, she squelched the urge to tell him that Sam had been going to bed at eight o'clock for nine of the past ten nights. The one night he didn't go to bed at eight was Sunday, Faith's day off. She'd had a heck of a time rousing both boys Monday morning.

"And that's why your children are so hard to wake in the morning. Bedtimes are critical for normal mental and physical development. Children need plenty of sleep. Just because you can survive on four hours of sleep a night, doesn't mean your children can or should."

"Don't you think we should have talked about this?"

Faith gave him a crisp smile as she scooped out the pasta and smothered it in sauce. A zucchini floated up to the top. "I believe we did already. But you might have been in a work haze."

Jay flushed and said, his voice defensive, "It's a hectic time of the year."

Faith nodded. "I see. Well, as long as I'm the person responsible for getting them up in the morning, I'll be the person responsible for putting them to bed at a decent hour."

"Kyle stays up until eleven," Andy put in.

"You go to bed at nine," Faith said.

"Da-a-ad!" Andy appealed to a higher power.

Faith stopped and met Jay's eyes. She could see his indecision and prayed he'd back her up.

JAY FELT FAITH'S JUDGMENT. He'd never worried about bedtimes and the boys had seemed to do just fine putting themselves to bed when they got tired. Usually, they were asleep next to him on the couch by the time he looked up from his paperwork. It was an easy thing to just lift up Sam and put him to bed and then prod Andy to stumble down the hall and drowsily climb into the top bunk.

That had become a comforting routine for Jay after Becky died. Even after they moved to the new house, Jay hadn't liked going to bed alone. So he took to sleeping on the couch. When the boys had nightmares, they would join him and he hadn't seen a reason to change.

Since the boys protested when he sent them to bed and Jay liked the company, he never thought about setting a bedtime. He had just accepted that his sons were hard to wake up.

"As long as Faith is getting you to school in the morning, she's the one who determines when you go to bed," he said and was rewarded by a stunning smile from Faith.

Andy, however, was less pleased.

"Dad! That bites."

Jay winced and wondered when his son had become so disrespectful.

"It's shower time, Andy," Faith said quietly.

"I'm hungry."

"Then have some spaghetti with your father."

"I hate spaghetti."

"When did this happen?" Jay joked. "You love spaghetti."

"I hate her spaghetti. She ruined it."

Faith nodded cheerfully. "Nothing like a few veggies to send schoolboys running."

"Her spaghetti is worse than those casseroles."

"Hmmm," Faith said with a twinkle in her eye. "I guess I can defrost one of those for you."

Jay laughed at Andy's dismay.

"Can't he have a sandwich?" Jay offered, and then, by the flash of warning in her eyes, knew he'd stepped in it yet again.

"No bread left," Faith said quickly. "It's spaghetti or starve."

"I'll starve," Andy said.

"He has to eat something," Jay said.

Faith regarded him seriously. "There's spaghetti."

"We could order a pizza," Andy suggested.

"No," Faith said firmly.

"Well, I'm sure we could—" Jay started, as Andy fixed his eyes pleadingly onto his father.

"Whitfield, can I speak to you a moment?" Faith said with a pleasant smile. She eyed Andy, who was listening avidly. "Alone?"

FAITH WAS SO MAD she could feel the veins in her temple throbbing.

Once out of earshot of the children, she went nose-to-nose with Jay.

"Just what do you think you're doing?" she demanded.

"Well, Andy's got to eat something," Jay said shortly. "I don't think you're proving anything by starving him."

"He's not starving. He's spoiled."

Jay's face turned impassive. "Are you saying that I've spoiled him? That I'm a bad father?" The words shot out of his mouth.

Faith shook her head and took a deep breath to calm herself. "I wouldn't say you're a bad father. You're a busy father, an absent father...."

"Which?" His voice was clipped.

"Which means you compensate by giving them the wrong kind of attention."

"I have a lot of responsibility. And if I have to see them a little later so they go to bed a little later, then I think it works out for the best."

Faith said bluntly, "This isn't about you, council member Whitfield. This is about your children and their well-being. It's about parental boundaries that help children to feel safe even if they don't necessarily like the rules. You can't keep a nanny because Andy doesn't respect any rules except yours—which is pretty bad, because you have none!''

JAY FELT HIS FACE grow red with anger. She was a fine one to talk about rules, when she was the person who broke every single rule in high school. She was the one who played hooky, she was the one to ignore curfew, and she was the one who got him grounded for three weeks, when his father discovered them half-naked and entangled in the pickup.

''I'm not that person. That person is gone,'' Faith said, and he wondered how she was able to read his mind. She continued, ''This has nothing to do with who I was. This has to do with two little boys who desperately need someone to take care of them, even if taking care of them doesn't necessarily make them happy. I think you're so concerned with being their friend, you aren't willing to make the hard choices needed to be a parent.''

''And you have so much experience as a parent.''

Faith's face became more determined and Jay felt his resolve slipping.

''I have a lot of experience raising children,'' she replied quietly. ''And these children need a regular bedtime. They need fruits and vegetables in their diets. Andy, especially. He needs someone who makes sure his homework is done and that he takes showers and brushes his teeth. Personal hygiene is very important at this age. Do you know that the kids at school tease him?''

''Andy takes showers,'' Jay said defensively.

"Oh, really." Faith folded her arms across her chest. "How do you know that?"

"What do you mean how do I know? I just do. I hear him in the morning."

"And how is that possible? He gets up just a few minutes before I get here to take them to school and you're on the way out."

"His hair's wet in the morning."

"Does that mean he's actually put his body under water and scrubbed with soap?"

"Yes." Jay had the sensation he was floating into a dangerous zone.

"You're positive?"

To Jay it was like he was taking some sort of final exam for fatherhood. Of course his children washed. But something nagged in the back of his mind.

"Let's see." Faith strode toward the kitchen.

"Can we get pizza?" Andy asked when they arrived back in the kitchen. He looked at Faith with such intense dislike that Jay felt guilty, but Faith was unperturbed, draping a casual arm around Andy.

"What's this?" Faith asked, pointing to Andy's arm.

Jay inspected it closely.

Andy squirmed.

Jay's face grew hot with embarrassment. There was a layer of dirt on Andy's arm. Jay had mistaken it for an early tan.

"And back here." Faith put a gentle hand on the scruff of Andy's neck.

"Hey!" Andy protested, and ducked away.

Jay caught him, reeled him back in and saw an actual dirt line at his collar.

Faith stared at him expectantly.

"No pizza," Jay announced quietly. "Either you eat spaghetti or you go take a shower."

"I took a shower this morning."

Jay shook his head.

"Okay, okay," Andy said hastily, backing down from the hard expression Jay was trying to maintain. "I'm going."

FAITH CAUGHT THE GLINT in Andy's eye as he sent another withering look her way and retreated down the hall.

"You'd better go with him," she said, feeling no victory at her observation. Jay looked stricken.

"What?"

"Go with him. Make sure he actually gets into the shower and washes."

"If he says he's going to, he will," Jay said weakly, and sat down at the kitchen table.

"If you don't go check on him, I will." She started down the hall.

Mortified, Jay rose. "No. I'll go."

HE WAS SLIGHTLY RELIEVED when he heard the shower going. He knocked on the door.

"I'm in the shower." Andy's muffled voice rang out.

He turned and found Faith standing right behind him.

"You need to go in," she advised.

"He said—"

She stepped forward and rattled the doorknob. "Andy, I'm coming in, so you better be in the shower."

"Faith!" Jay was aghast.

"He's a little boy. He doesn't have anything I haven't seen already." She pushed at the door and found it locked. She reached above the molding, grabbed a small key and unlocked the door.

Steam poured out. When it cleared Jay saw Andy sitting on the counter, completely dressed and sweating, playing with his handheld video game. Guilt was written all over his face.

See? Faith raised her eyebrows.

"Okay, Andy. I think it's time you actually took off your clothes and got into the shower."

"I was waiting for it to warm up," he said as he wiped the steam off his monitor.

"I think we'd have to take you to the hospital for first-degree burns if you actually showered in that," Faith said dryly, working the handles to adjust the water temperature.

"I don't know what the big deal—"

"Personal hygiene is very important." Jay found Faith's words coming out of his mouth. He wrinkled his nose and wondered why he hadn't smelt how rank Andy was. "Faith, would you please—"

When he turned to address her, he discovered she had already left, closing the door behind her to give them privacy.

From then on each step was a fight. First, Andy wouldn't undress completely, and then he didn't want to step into the shower. Then Jay had to remind him to use soap and shampoo. Finally, Jay just stripped off his own shirt, pulled aside the shower curtain, poured shampoo in his hand and started to vigorously scrub Andy's head all to the tune of the boy's complaints. Rivulets of dirt ran down the drain.

When they emerged, Andy was several shades lighter, his hair nearly blond. Faith smiled at them when they entered the kitchen. ''Hungry?''

''Starving,'' Jay said.

Andy looked at the spaghetti. ''I guess I could eat that.''

''Look, I took out the zucchini,'' Faith said with a grin. ''Taste it. See what you think.'' She offered a spoon to Andy.

He tasted it. ''That's good.''

Jay moved next to Faith and looked at the spaghetti sauce suspiciously. ''What happened to the zucchini?''

''Pureed.'' She gave him a dazzling smile. ''My mistake.''

BY NINE, ANDY was finally in bed, with permission to read a comic book for half an hour, and Sam was long asleep. Jay glanced at his watch. He should have been back at the office two hours ago. He still had a good six hours of work to do if he didn't want to get buried tomorrow.

''You need to go back.'' Faith made it a statement, not a question.

''Do you mind? I've got to make up the hours sometime.''

''You should hire more people.''

"I can't keep them all in work for the full year."
He frowned. "I have a problem with offering them
work and then just laying them off when the tax season's over. They need to support their families, too."

Faith smiled, looking at him with admiration.

After the blasting she'd just given him, he basked
in her approval.

"You look exhausted," he ventured.

She nodded. "It's been a long day."

"I'll see if I can get back early."

"Take your time. And don't work too hard."

"Not something to tell an accountant in the middle
of February. Our work is just beginning," he said,
grinning. He leaned over and impulsively gave her a
quick peck on the lips.

Startled, Faith reflexively moistened her lips. He
stared at them, fascinated by the contours, the softness.
Suddenly, the peck didn't seem to be enough, so he
stepped closer, pulled her against him and then settled
his lips on hers, gently exploring the curves of her
mouth, surprisingly more familiar than unfamiliar.
This was an infinitely more satisfying experience. And
then Faith moved away and Jay felt distinctly disappointed.

Faith turned her head, her cheeks flushing, and then
asked gruffly, "What was that for?"

Jay didn't know what it was for. Maybe it was for
her setting a bedtime, or washing his children, or slipping their Valentines into his briefcase. "It's a thank-
you for caring about my sons."

Faith looked away, her embarrassment touching him
even more than her brassiness. "Go to work, Whit-

field,'' she ordered as she pushed him out the door
and closed it behind him.

WHEN FAITH DROVE BACK to Patty's house, it was
nearly two in the morning. She was deep down, bone
tired. Battling with Andy had been exhausting. Making
up with Jay had been stimulating. However, even
pleasant musings about his unexpected kiss couldn't
combat her fatigue. Jay's station wagon rode so
smoothly, she'd rolled the windows all the way down
and let the chilly air blow through the cab to help her
stay awake.

As she turned the final corner, her thoughts went to
the progress she was making on the little house. The
fumigation tent would come off tomorrow, and pale
yellow miniblinds would be hung on Friday—the
same day the beds would come. After that she could
move in. She couldn't wait. Even though the long
hours she spent caring for Jay's children had kept her
away from Patty and Bruce, while she was there the
atmosphere was stifling.

But as she parked in front of Patty's house, she had
to admit it looked awfully good. As she walked up the
steps, all she could think about was how much she
preferred a soft bed to Jay's lumpy couch.

"It's about time you got back," an unmistakable
voice commented lightly, and every ounce of fatigue
disappeared as the fine hairs on her arm rose. Her heart
pounded in her throat.

"Bruce, what are you doing up?" She tried to make
her voice sound as casual as possible. Lately, Bruce
seemed to be fond of lurking in dark corners. He'd be

waiting next to the bathroom, a towel slung over his shoulder, when she emerged from her morning shower, with a helpless grin, a shrug and a brief complaint about the time Patty spent in the master bathroom. Or she'd be fixing herself some cereal for breakfast and he'd appear in the doorway, surprising her.

Bruce smiled, his white teeth glowing. "You're sure keeping late nights with the councilman."

Faith deliberately walked inside and switched on a lamp, flooding Patty's impeccable living room with light. Even though she had no reason to think Bruce would hurt her in her sister's house, every nerve under her skin tensed, especially when she saw him sitting casually in one of Patty's white armchairs, his stocking feet propped up on the matching ottoman, a single red rose resting in his lap.

"Reading with the light off is bad for your eyes," Faith said in jest. She walked carefully toward the stairs. "I've got an early morning tomorrow. Good night, Bruce." She was pleased at how well she controlled her voice.

"Faith."

Against her better judgment, she stopped her ascent and turned, only to find Bruce a few steps away from her. He extended the rose to her.

"Happy Valentine's Day, Faith," Bruce said with a small smile.

"Valentine's Day was two hours ago," Faith replied. "And anyway, I think you should give it to Patty."

He shook his head. ''Patty got three dozen today at her office. This one I saved for you. You deserve it, Faith. I bet that Jay didn't even know that it was Valentine's Day.''

CHAPTER SIX

"TAKE THE ROSE, FAITH," Bruce pleaded gently. "It's for you."

Faith stared at Bruce. She didn't want to take the rose; she didn't want him staring at her with such intensity. In fact, all she wanted was to go to sleep. She glanced at her watch. She had to be back at Jay's in four short hours.

"By all means, Faith, take the rose." The bite in Patty's voice startled both of them. Bruce drifted away from Faith as Patty descended the stairs. With her face smeared with a pale white cream, her sister looked like a ghost.

Ahh. Jay was right.

We pay for every decision we make, one way or another.

And she was paying right now.

She'd been foolish to think she could live peacefully with her sister. There was no escaping their history together. Faith tried to shore up her frazzled nerves, made even more vulnerable by exhaustion.

Patty pushed her face into Faith's; Faith could smell the citrus tang of Patty's face cream. "You always did want to ruin things for me."

"Patty," Bruce tried to interject. "I just thought—"

Patty ignored her husband.

"Exactly how could I ruin things for you?" Faith asked bluntly. She started to move up the stairs, but her sister blocked her.

"You ruin things by being here," Patty spit out.

"How can I do that?" Faith was baffled, but hurt radiated through her body from her sister's harsh words. "I'm not here most of the time and I'm moving out this weekend."

"You don't get it, do you?" Patty asked, shaking her head.

"Get what?"

"That you're not welcome here."

The words hit harder than she'd thought they would. Bruce made a sympathetic noise behind her. Faith took little comfort from him. "Patty," she pleaded softly, extending an open palm. "I'm really wiped out. Can we have this conversation in the morning?"

"No. I don't think so." Patty folded her arms tightly across her chest.

"Patty." Bruce tried to placate his wife.

"Don't you have somewhere else you need to be?" Patty's head snapped toward him quickly. "I'd like to speak to my sister alone."

For the first time, Faith felt regret when Bruce left the room, but she noticed he didn't move far. She could hear him breathe.

When Patty thought he was out of earshot, she said furiously, "What are you doing with my husband?"

Faith's face flushed and she answered, her voice calm, "I am doing nothing with your husband. We were having a polite conversation."

''You always wanted what I had, didn't you? You were always jealous of me, of the pageants I won, the time Mom spent with me. That I had Bruce and you didn't. That's why you slept with him. You thought you could ruin things for us, but you didn't. You just ruined your own life.''

Faith felt her defensiveness make her face hot. ''I didn't voluntarily sleep with Bruce.'' But even though she knew that was the truth, even though she'd processed the incident during the sixty hours of therapy she was required to undergo for her master's degree, she did feel responsible. Her parents' and her sister's persistent disbelief only ate away at the edge of her denial. Maybe she had caused it, maybe she was jealous of Patty. Faith closed her eyes, stunned as realization smacked her right between her eyes.

She knew why she'd come home. She knew why she'd agreed to stay with Patty and Bruce. Her throat constricted. She'd come because she wanted her mother and father and her sister to believe her. She'd come home because she wanted Bruce to admit he raped her.

Faith pushed past her sister and started up the stairs.

Patty grabbed her arm. ''I'm not done.''

Faith tried to shrug off Patty's grip, but it was like steel.

Patty's eyes bored into her. ''You were better off when you stayed away. I don't know how I let Bruce talk me into this reconciliation thing. I don't know why you're here or what you want. But you can't have what's mine.''

"What are you talking about? What would I want that's yours?"

"My life." Patty's voice was flat. "You think Jay's your ticket into it. But you know, Faith, in this town you have to earn your respect, not sleep your way to it. I'd have thought you'd learned that lesson by now."

Faith felt as if she'd just been slapped.

Patty leaned in close and whispered. "Do us all a favor and just get the hell out of our lives. I'll talk with Mom and Dad. They'll believe you had an emergency."

Faith shook her head. "No, they won't. Besides, I promised Jay."

"He'll get over it. Just leave before you do any more damage."

The dislike in Patty's eyes, her pupils tiny, contracted pinpoints of black, chilled Faith.

For once she didn't argue. She ran to her room and shoved her few things into her duffel bags. Twenty minutes later, she descended the stairs. Patty was nowhere to be seen, but Bruce waited for her by the door, his glasses slipping down his narrow nose, his face a shade paler than normal.

"Don't, Faith," Bruce said, his voice placating, as he took possession of the handles of her duffel bags in an attempt to stop her. "She'll calm down in the morning. It's late. You're tired and upset. Get some sleep. You can work it out in the morning. There's got to be a way to fix this."

"There is," Faith said faintly, not trusting her voice. "Tell the truth, Bruce. Tell what really happened."

Bruce looked at her, puzzled. He cleared his throat, his eyes staring straight into hers. "I have told the truth, Faith. If you want to revise history, you're more than welcome to, but I've told the truth."

"Let *go*," Faith said as she tugged the bags from his hands and hurried out of the house. Somehow she managed to get herself and her bags into the beat-up car. Feeling emotion press behind her eyes, she turned the key. Nothing happened, just a click. She turned the key a second time, pumping on the gas. Again, a click.

Damn!

Bruce tapped on the windshield. "Faith, just come back into the house."

She got out of the car and grabbed her bags. The door slammed as she strode toward Jay's station wagon.

Bruce followed behind her. "It'll all be better in the morning. Patty does have these moods...."

Faith stuffed the bags in the back, closed the hatch and then got in the driver's seat.

Bruce held the door open. "She doesn't mean it. She's—"

Faith yanked the door shut, and Bruce jumped out of the way as Faith gunned the engine and reversed down the driveway. She blinked furiously, refusing to cry, even though there was unbearable pressure on the back of her throat and eyes. Faith's hands clenched the steering wheel, the urge to gun the engine and travel as far as she could in the dark of night powerful. The luminous dash seemed to want her to head for the interstate, and then south to Los Angeles.

It took every ounce of self-control to stop in Santa

Nella, a small freeway town about eight miles west of Los Banos, and sit in an all-night restaurant, nursing a cup of coffee she didn't need. Even though she was dog tired as dirt, the anonymity of the coffee shop was welcome. She studied the CHP officers taking a break in the corner booth, and spotted a young couple eating ravenously, their clothes and weary appearance attesting to hours of travel. Faith realized she had nowhere to go. It was so late, she couldn't arrive on her parents' doorstep or Gil's. The cottage was still tented. Faith's bottom lip trembled, but she tightened it as she stared out the window at the headlights of passing traffic on I-5. Big trucks rumbled by at regular intervals.

She could be in Los Angeles in four hours.

Faith shut her eyes, shaking her head, fighting the primal response to run. But by the time she'd drained her coffee, paid her bill and used the ladies' room, she'd made up her mind. In Jay's station wagon, Faith pulled onto the freeway, the windows rolled down, the stereo blasting. She'd make L.A. by rush hour. Running was good, and flight was an admirable quality. She really had nothing to stay for. Her parents would get over her absence. Jay would eventually get his car back. And Andy and Sam would—

Faith swallowed hard. What would Andy and Sam do? They'd already lost their mother and Granny Doris.

Grown-ups always say stuff they don't mean. They make promises they don't keep.

Unwashed Andy.

She's not a lady. She's a mom.

And what about Sam?

Faith bit her lip.

Her biggest crime wouldn't be stealing Jay's car; it was stealing the fragile trust of his children. Who would take them to school and pick them up? She'd also be stealing Jay's trust. He'd trusted her with his kids. Even though Patty expected no less from her, Faith couldn't, *wouldn't* let Jay down. He had a lot on his shoulders and she'd made him a promise. She could keep her promise for two more months. Just two months, then she'd leave.

Much later, she found herself parked in front of Jay's house.

She pulled her coat around herself and stared at the blinking glow of the station wagon's clock. It was only five, but it felt as if she had been gone a lifetime. She leaned the driver's seat back and stared out the moon roof at the tree above, dimly backlit by a streetlight. It was an odd place to feel safe. But she did.

FAITH WOKE TO A PERSISTENT tapping on the window. She blinked. Dawn was just breaking, and she groaned as the seat belt dug into her hip.

"Faith," a voice said loudly. "Open up."

Faith shifted uncomfortably, to identify the voice. She peered at her watch, attempting to bring the analog face into focus.

"Faith, open the door," the voice commanded again.

Faith looked at the face made blurry by the foggy window. She swiped her sleeve a few times at the window, then found Jay staring down at her, his brow furrowed with concern.

How did he manage to look fully rested with only five hours of sleep? She felt like throwing up. The caffeine withdrawal from her late-night cup caused the world to spin.

''Open the door,'' he repeated.

He didn't look angry.

She obediently opened the door and nearly fell out of the car as she felt her muscles creak with stiffness.

Jay caught her easily and helped her to stand up. The warmth of his grip on her upper arms gave her a clear impression of his strength, his steadiness. Even though she was propped up against the car, trying to smother a yawn that quickly overtook her, he didn't drop his hands.

''What are you doing here?'' he asked a little less urgently, his blue eyes skimming over her face, as if he were taking inventory.

Faith flushed, his proximity unsettling her. She could smell his shampoo and the just-washed scent of his skin. She shrugged herself out of his grip.

''I got here a little early and decided to take a snooze.'' It wasn't a lie. She *was* early. She glanced at the time—6:15 a.m.—and tossed him a smile. ''I guess I overslept.''

JAY STUDIED HER FACE.

Her eyes were bloodshot and she looked as if she'd had a hell of a night. Her face was shaded and drawn, and dark circles were etched beneath her eyes. She was wearing the same clothes she'd been wearing the day before. He decided not to believe the blithe tone of her voice.

"Try again," he said quietly.

Her face went pleasantly neutral, the brightness of her cheeks the only sign that something was out of the ordinary.

"What?"

"Try again. Tell me what's wrong."

She impatiently flicked her hand.

"Nothing's wrong," she denied. As she shook her head, the rattle of beads empathetically made her point. "I got here a little early and didn't want to wake you by ringing the doorbell."

"You have a key to the house," Jay pointed out.

Apparently, Faith had forgotten that because she avoided his gaze, dropping her head so her face was hidden by her hair.

"Uh, I didn't want to disturb you" was the muffled response.

"So instead you slept in the car in the same clothes you were wearing not six hours ago." Jay could feel himself becoming slightly annoyed.

"These work hours are brutal," she said matter-of-factly, and motioned him to get out of the way so she could walk around.

Ouch. Guilt swept over Jay as he stepped aside. Faith stretched dramatically before settling against the damp hood of the station wagon and putting a distinct three feet between them. He was so used to pushing himself beyond any reasonable limits that he barely noticed when he was doing it to other people. What was it that people called him? Driven? He realized they were absolutely right.

The hours he just assumed she would keep *were*

brutal. She'd been with the boys for more than ten hours yesterday, and he hadn't even thought about what being back here by six would mean. Frankly, having the boys in competent care was such a relief, he hadn't considered the toll it was taking on their caretaker. He mentally kicked himself; he needed Faith more than she needed him. The cottage, which she hadn't even moved into yet, was hardly compensation for all her hard work. He'd have to find a way to pay her since she'd refused all his offers of monetary remuneration.

"Oooh," Faith moaned as she rubbed her face with both of her hands. "I'm getting old. Sleeping in the car ain't what it used to be."

Jay chuckled until it occurred to him that she wasn't kidding. She probably had slept in the car. Had Faith been homeless? Jay found that concept disturbing.

She rolled her eyes at his expression. "You really have led a sheltered life, Whitfield. There's nothing like sleeping in the car, the windows wide open, salt spray drifting in, the surf so loud you'd think you were at a rock concert, and you're the only human being on a five-mile stretch of beach." She got a faraway look, and Jay could imagine Faith sleeping on the edge of the earth, the breeze tugging at her, no one else around.

"Sounds dangerous."

"Sometimes the most dangerous things are the ones that exist in your everyday life," she said under her breath.

Jay was silent, wondering about what lay behind those words. Had Faith encountered danger before? He didn't like to think about that. Even though his wife's illness was tragic, Becky hadn't been frightened when she died. In fact, she'd told Jay of the extreme peace she was experiencing even as she got weaker and weaker. Faith looked anything but peaceful. There was a rigid tension emanating from her.

"So," Jay asked quietly. "Are you going to tell me why you spent the night in front of the house?"

Faith looked at Jay for a long time, studying the intelligent planes of his face, appreciating how his eyes probed with true concern, even though it would be easier if he'd buy her story of sleeping in a car on the beach. How she wished she were that carefree. But she seemed to have left that person behind a long time ago. Finally it was time to turn and face, rather than run from, a demon that had kept her on the road for eighteen years.

Until last night, she'd believed the demon was Bruce. However, in her early-morning delirium, she'd realized the truth. It was her parents' persistent disbelief that haunted her. She could understand Patty's denial—Patty had a lot to lose if she admitted that Bruce was capable of rape. But her own mother and father? Faith squeezed her eyes tightly. Her mother had a lot to lose as well. If she had to choose between daughters, it was understandable she'd choose the one she'd invested the most in.

"No, I'm not," she said shortly to his question. "Are the boys up?"

"Sam spotted you out of the window." Jay opened his mouth, his eyes probing into her soul. Then he added, "He came and got me out of the shower."

"Then I should go in." Faith looked toward the window, where she saw two heads. She waved and Sam waved back, his face lit up with a smile. There was her reason for not running. She started to walk to the house, but Jay caught her forearm and gently pulled her close.

"Yes?" Faith asked warily. She didn't want his gentleness, his concern, because she took too much comfort from the arms that were sliding around her back, holding her tightly. She pressed her face against his smooth cotton shirt. She'd liked it when he'd kissed her last night. She liked his strength, the tightness of his hug. His touch could become addictive. *He* could become addictive. He could make her dream of roots and a home with children and a family.

"I think you should go back home and get some sleep," Jay said quietly.

"I'm fine," she insisted, listening to the pounding of his heart. Such a strong heart Jay had. "I'll catch a quick nap on your couch after I take the boys to school."

"Take that nap—" Jay's voice was blunt "—while I take the boys to school. We need to keep you in good health."

"Will it be another late night?"

"I'll try to finish up by ten."

Faith felt her lips quirk up. "The secret life of a CPA."

Jay grinned and she felt his smile all the way down to her toes. *Don't get used to it. It'll be that much more to miss later.* "Yes, we lead a double life. Numbers and IRS codes are our mistresses, hanging on to us late into the night. They just won't leave us alone. But come April 16 you'll see a completely different man.''

There was an awkward pause as his voice trailed off.

Faith realized that he hadn't loosened his hug and regret pulsed through her. Whether or not Jay was a different man after tax season wouldn't matter to her one way or another. By then, he'd have found a new nanny to take care of his children and her parents' anniversary party would be a past event. According to Patty, she'd already overstayed her welcome.

"Trust me, Faith," Jay whispered in her ear before he released her. "I will find out what chases you from one beach to the next."

After Jay and the boys left, Faith took a long shower in the boys' bathroom, used *Tyrannosaurus rex* shampoo and conditioner on her hair and washed her body with a green frog puffball and brontosaurus-shaped soap minus the neck and head. After her shower, she changed clothes and carefully repacked her duffel bags before stowing them in Jay's station wagon. Then with the weariness of a long-distance traveler, she stretched out on Jay's family room couch and dropped into a deep, restless sleep.

The shrill warbling of the telephone rang out again and again and again, finally penetrating Faith's deep slumber. She fought to open her eyes, her surroundings not immediately familiar. Then she shot off the couch when she realized the call could be about one of the boys. Oh, God! What time was it? Had she overslept? Were Sam and Andy waiting at school for her to pick them up?

"Yes?" Her voice croaked out, panic thumping under her ribs.

"Take it easy, Faith." Jay's voice was soothing.

"What time is it?"

"Noonish."

Faith took a deep breath of relief and cleared her throat. "I thought I'd missed the boys."

"No. Sorry to wake you up, but I needed to talk to you about tonight."

Tonight? Faith wiped the grains of sand out of the corner of her eyes and yawned now that her heart rate had slowed. "Since you're working late, we'll probably just do homework and have Andy take another shower just to get a two-day streak going. There's probably some extra grime he could scrub off tonight."

There was a silence on the other end of the phone.

"Is there a change of plans?" she asked.

"You don't know, do you?" Jay's voice was quiet.

"Know what?"

"That Patty's invited me and Amanda to a planning dinner for your parents' anniversary party."

Faith swallowed down the hurt, not knowing why it should surprise her, and asked casually, "When'd she do that?"

"This morning."

"And the dinner's tonight?"

"Yes."

"Oh. Well, I didn't know. But thanks for telling me, because I'll make an effort to be there. What time?"

"About six. Dinner first, then planning."

"Will do." She was proud of how light she'd made her tone.

"What about the boys?" Jay asked.

"Oh, I'm sure Patty will love to have them, too."

FAITH, ANDY AND SAM arrived at Patty's immaculate white home at quarter to six. Neither boy had been pleased by the prospect of spending the evening at a dinner with just grown-ups. But Andy had eventually bargained for a sleepover with their grandparents. After Faith agreed to talk to their dad and suggested that they could also stop for fast food on the way, both boys' attitudes changed dramatically. They stood on the doorstep with backpacks full of activities to keep them busy and their children's meals clutched in their hands.

"Let me ring the bell!" Sam insisted, his cheeks flushed red from the evening chill.

"Okay."

Andy beat him to it, and they heard the chimes echo through the house.

"Andy!" Faith reprimanded the older boy.

He just flashed her a mischievous smile.

"Ring the bell again, Sam," Faith prodded as she put a restraining hand on Andy's shoulder to keep him from pressing the bell once again.

Sam pushed the doorbell. Twice.

They heard high tittering laughter and the rapid clicking of high heels, then, "Just a minute, Jay. Hold your horses. Impatient, isn't he?"

Faith smoothed down her beige shirtdress, one of

the more conventional items of clothing that she owned.

The door swung open.

"Faith!" Patty's eyes narrowed at the sight of her, and Faith stiffened, although she worked hard at sustaining a pleasant smile. Her sister looked stunning as usual, her outfit a white cashmere sweater set with matching wool pants. Faith hid a tiny twinge. Obviously, Patty expected that she would be long gone and she'd called together Jay and Amanda to celebrate. Faith could see that the dining room table was elegantly, and intimately, set for four.

"This is the anniversary-planning dinner, right?" Faith asked cheerfully, a hand on each of the boys' shoulders. Andy squirmed away. Sam leaned closer and pressed his face against her stomach. Faith took a great deal of comfort from that. She stepped into the house, her voice casual. "Jay called and told me about the planning dinner and I thought I should be here."

She met Patty's eyes and found that her sister actually flinched in surprise.

Patty recovered quickly as the boys took off their backpacks, undid their jackets and chucked the lot into a pile in a corner. "Uh, Faith. This is a private dinner," Patty hissed emphatically, then added, her voice superficially light, "Besides, I thought you'd be basking on a beach in Tijuana by now."

"Nope." Faith gathered up the backpacks and the jackets, trying to think of a place in Patty's white house to set the boys up for the evening. She nodded to Amanda Perkins—groomed as impeccably as Patty in a pale olive-green outfit—who gave her a stiff, small smile before exchanging meaningful glances with Patty.

Patty eyed the boys. "I really wasn't expecting children." *Or you* remained unspoken. Andy stared down at his shoes, his arms crossed defensively.

"They've brought homework to do," Faith said, her movements efficient. "They can sit anywhere. Maybe in the kitchen? I thought it was important that I be part of the planning. Don't you?"

"Kitchen." Patty nodded with relief. She walked very quickly in that direction. "Yes. Let's put them at the kitchen table."

The boys passed the table with big eyes. It was laid with elegant dishes, no doubt ready for one of Patty's five-star dinners.

"I'm hungry," whispered Sam.

"You'll be eating in under ten minutes," Faith assured them.

"And what do you intend to feed them?" Patty asked, distinctly annoyed.

"We have our own stuff," Andy said loudly, making sure that Faith understood that dinner was in his hand, not some grown-up casserole.

"You couldn't smell these fries?" Faith asked Patty as she helped Sam unpack his chicken strips and fries. She fished around the bottom of the bag for a few strays and popped them in her mouth.

Patty's nose wrinkled. "Is that what it was? And what are you going to have?"

Faith smiled. "I thought I'd join you. You always make enough for an army."

"Oh, Patty. I'll just eat less," Amanda offered, appearing in the kitchen. She patted her perfectly flat stomach. "I don't need the extra weight." She tossed Faith another smile. "It's a pleasure to see you again, Faith. It's been such a long time. I've heard a lot about you."

Faith just nodded. "I'm sure you have."

Amanda bent over to greet Sam and Andy. "And how are you two young men?" Her voice was inappropriately high, and Faith winced as Andy shot Faith a malevolent glare. Faith indicated that he should answer back.

"Fine."

"Fine," Sam echoed. He bravely withstood the pinching of his cheek, followed by a little shake for emphasis.

"You boys have grown so much." The coo in Amanda's voice made Andy grimace.

"You just saw us the other day," he said, his voice barely this side of rudeness.

Amanda flushed and straightened, patting her hair as if it had been ruffled by Andy's bad manners. "I hear you're their nanny."

Faith refused to feel put in her place. She smiled easily at Amanda, suddenly noticing the fine lines around her eyes, despite the expert coverage by makeup. She replied, "Temporarily. Until Jay finishes with tax season."

The doorbell rang and both Patty and Amanda turned simultaneously. "Amanda, why don't you get that?" Patty suggested as Faith restrained Sam, so bits of chicken and fries only landed in his lap and not on Patty's hardwood.

"Jay!" Patty called with a broad smile as Amanda ushered him in, and then flashed a quick warning to Faith as she walked out of the kitchen to greet Jay in the living room.

"Sorry I'm late."

Faith could hear his apology before she could see him. But the pleasant timbre of his voice leant a whole different atmosphere to the house. Even when she saw Amanda latched on to his arm, Faith felt significantly better just by having him there.

"Just in time," Amanda said, her hands fluttering up by her hair. "You know dinner doesn't start until you get here."

Faith suppressed the urge to gag.

"Dad!" Andy looked at him with newly appreciative eyes, eyes that mostly said, *Take us home. Please.*

Jay crossed to the kitchen in several easy strides and Faith dampened the silly feeling of well-being that had settled over her.

"You two look like you're eating well." Faith's heart contracted as Jay picked a piece of French fry out of Sam's hair.

"Planning on taking this home for lunch?" he teased.

Sam giggled.

Then Jay looked at her and said simply, "Hi, there."

Faith smiled back, feeling a small shiver of pleasure trickle down her back. "Hey, yourself. We beat you."

"I know. Had two tax emergencies come up. I'll have to get back to them this evening."

''I just don't understand how you can put in all those hours,'' Amanda said sympathetically.

Jay shrugged. ''It's difficult *not* to work hard when a good chunk of your clients knew you when you were eight and a brat.''

Amanda laughed, her hand shimmying down his arm. ''Come on, Jay, you won't believe what Patty's made for our dinner.'' She led him away from the kitchen.

''She's worse than gum stuck in your hair,'' Andy muttered.

Faith stared at him and then tried not to smile. ''What makes you say that?''

''She's always like that around Dad,'' Andy said with a shrug. ''She's so fake.''

''She touches him all the time, too,'' Sam added as he tried to get another piece of chicken into his mouth and missed. They all watched it fall into his lap.

''I hadn't noticed,'' Faith said, automatically, picking up the piece of errant chicken and popping it into his mouth, her eyes suddenly acutely aware of Amanda's hand resting lightly on Jay's forearm or plucking at the material of his jacket by his elbow. Jealousy nicked at Faith.

''Even though he's real nice to her,'' Andy whispered. ''He doesn't love her or anything.''

Faith focused on cleaning up Sam, but she couldn't keep her gaze from straying into the dining room where Jay listened attentively to Amanda as she talked.

''I think he's clean,'' Andy said dryly.

''What?'' Faith looked up and discovered that she

had scrubbed Sam's face pink. "Are you done?" She eyed his near-empty bag of fries.

Sam nodded. "Uh-huh."

Amanda laughed lightly and Jay chuckled. Faith tried not to look at them.

"He doesn't *love* her," Andy said meaningfully.

That caught Faith's attention. She studied the ten-year-old and he stared back just as frankly.

Finally, she replied, "I don't know why it matters whether he loves her or not."

"Because you want him to love you," Andy said simply. "It's obvious. I saw you by the car this morning."

Faith opened her mouth to deny it, but then closed it, remembering that she'd promised Andy she would always try to tell him the truth.

CHAPTER SEVEN

As soon as he could, Jay shook off Amanda and rejoined his family in the kitchen. He arrived in time to watch Faith efficiently clear the table, sweeping Sam's debris into a brown paper bag, then crumpling it into a ball. Andy followed suit with his.

"How was school?" Jay asked as he sat down, feeling stiff and formal.

"Fine."

Jay sighed.

"How 'bout you?" he addressed his youngest son.

"Fine."

They all sat silently, well aware that they were in someone else's house.

"Is this work, too?" Andy blurted suddenly.

Jay shook his head. "No. This is for fun. We're going to help Patty and Faith plan a party for their parents."

"What's it for?"

"They've been married for a long time," Faith replied. She prodded Sam. "Both of you go wash your hands so you can start your homework."

Jay hid his surprise when both boys rose from the table and went to the kitchen sink, Sam standing on his very tiptoes.

"Don't forget to talk to Dad about the sleepover,"
Andy said loudly over the rushing water. The lather
grew on his hands, until Faith took the soap away.

"I won't."

"What sleepover?" Jay asked curiously.

"The boys want to sleep over at your dad's when
I move into the cottage this weekend. We wanted to
talk to you before mentioning it to Gil."

"I appreciate that." And he really did. If the boys
had even breathed a word of a sleepover to his father,
Jay wouldn't have any say in the matter.

"Can we, Dad?" Andy looked at him hopefully.

"Yeah, can we, Daddy?" Sam's higher voice
echoed.

"We'll see."

Both boys' faces fell with disappointment.

Faith tried to ease their discouragement. "Come on,
let's do your homework and show your dad how re-
sponsibly you're behaving."

"Why?" Andy asked. "We're not going this weekend."

"How do you know that?" Faith asked logically.
"He said he'd think about it. It seems likely that you
will, since it means he'll have more time to work if
you're with your grandpa Saturday night."

"No," Sam said, his eyes downcast. "When Daddy
says 'we'll see,' he *always* means 'no.'"

"But if he's going to work…" Andy had an encouraging look on his face. "He'd be glad to get rid
of us."

Jay shifted uncomfortably. They were talking about
him as if he wasn't even sitting there.

"It's tax time, Andy," he said quietly. "I know I'm busy, but come April 16, I'll have a lot more time. And I want to spend every moment I can with you."

"Doesn't matter," Andy said. "After the sixteenth, you'll still be working for the city."

"That's my job, too."

"Isn't being a dad your job?" Sam asked.

The question stunned Jay and he didn't know how to reply.

"How are you all doing?" Amanda came up and sat down next to Sam, who scooted away. Jay couldn't help but feel intruded upon. "We're just about ready to eat. We're waiting for Bruce, but Patty's on his cell phone with him and he shouldn't be long. Did you boys have a good dinner?"

The boys refused to answer.

Amanda leaned close to Sam. "Did you like the food? I noticed you're saving some for later."

Sam looked at her, puzzled.

A beat later, Andy said with an impatient sigh, "You've got gunk on your shirt, bird turd."

"Andy!" Amanda said, appalled. "Don't be a brat. I'm sure your brother doesn't appreciate your insulting him. Do you, Sam?"

Jay winced at her tone. Amanda tried too hard with them.

"Whatever." That was Andy. "When can we go home, Dad?"

"In a little while."

"And you're going back with us, right?"

Sam's eyes were hopeful.

Jay shook his head regretfully. "Sorry, guys. I've

got to go back to the office. You remember this from last year.''

Both sets of brows furrowed. They didn't remember. Their beloved Granny Doris had stayed with them almost constantly, so Jay had never been missed. Suddenly it became very important to Jay that at least Andy remember how seasonal his work was. He wondered if Doris had ever told Andy where he was and what kept him away from them.

''Remember last year when I worked this hard? We barely saw each other but you were with Granny Doris.''

Andy still looked perplexed.

''Do you know what I do for a living?'' Jay asked finally, very curious what his children thought.

A long pause later, Sam said proudly, ''Taxes!''

Jay nodded enthusiastically. ''You're right, I do taxes. Do you know what that means?''

''It means you're never home,'' Andy replied.

Ow.

Amanda filled in the silence that followed with a small laugh. She moved so close to Jay he could smell her perfume, the gel in her hair.

''No rest for the wicked, is that it?'' Amanda said, and then wagged a finger at his sons. ''Your father is a very important man. He plays a very important role in our community.''

''I wish he'd play with us,'' Sam said wistfully.

''He will, Sammy,'' Faith announced as she put two generous scoops of ice cream in front of the boys. Jay felt her eyes flicker over him and Amanda and then away as she circled the table. Jay tried to subtly shift away, but Amanda pressed closer as Faith continued, ''I figured Bruce wouldn't mind if we raided his stash. Maybe when tax time is over, you guys can go camping or something. Your dad used to be a great camper.''

Camping. Jay remembered camping. With Becky. Becky had loved camping, making things easy on him by assembling all the equipment, planning the meals, repairing the fishing rods. When she died, camping became another activity that was too painful to contemplate, even though his sons were now the perfect ages to camp. Jay had limited their outings to day trips. Yosemite. The Santa Cruz beach boardwalk. The Monterey Bay Aquarium. But even those kinds of trips were few and far between.

''I remember camping with my mom.'' Andy spoke suddenly.

''You do?'' Amanda asked, her voice pitched an octave higher. ''Weren't you too little?''

Jay frowned because he'd been down this road with Andy before. He said patiently, ''You were awfully young. You couldn't have been more than three the last time we went.''

''I remember,'' he said, his thin voice stubborn. ''I remember we were in these big trees.''

''There's always trees when you camp, silly,'' Amanda said lightly.

Andy ignored her. ''Mom told me about the fire ants.''

''Two years ago, we went to Yosemite with Granny Doris and she told you about the fire ants,'' Jay said. ''There were lots of trees there.''

"No. This was with Mom. I remember lots of things about Mom. *Lots!*" Andy showed clear distress and Faith placed a hand on his shoulder to calm him. Jay immediately noticed that Andy, recalcitrant Andy, actually leaned back against her.

"There've been studies of children who retain memories in the womb," Faith commented.

Amanda snorted. "You can't believe that. Remembering in the womb. What would they remember?"

"Well," Faith said reasonably. "I imagine they'd hear loving conversations between their mother and their father. They'd hear laughter and feel the endorphins released by it. Fluid acts as an amplifier. In fact, when scientists put a small microphone in a womb, they could actually hear not just the mother's voice but also a television down the hall! I wouldn't dream of thinking that Andy couldn't remember going camping with his mother."

Jay watched as Faith gently smoothed back Andy's hair and his son visibly relaxed.

"Do you think Andy remembers, Daddy?" Sam asked. "Or do you think he's making it up?"

FAITH STARED HARD at Jay, willing him to say the right thing while not quite managing to ignore the fact that Amanda was almost in his lap. All he had to say was that he believed Andy. It was such a small thing.

"Well," Jay hedged, and their eyes met. "I suppose Andy could remember—"

Faith held her breath.

"But, I don't know, sport. I remember Granny Doris explaining fire ants to you."

"Mom did." Andy cross his arms, his whole body stiff. "She told me not just about the ants, but, but—" He was searching, grasping at straws. He put a big spoonful of ice cream in his mouth and swallowed before his next words burst out. "She told me all about her diary that was a secret, too!"

"Andrew." Jay's voice held a warning. "Your mother didn't keep a diary."

"Yes, she did. She showed me." Andy shoved some more ice cream in his mouth.

"Andy, you were only five when she died. She didn't—"

"Why don't you believe me?" The tone of Andy's voice was a red flag to Faith. She was sure this was more than casual dinner conversation to him. He stopped eating in mid-bite, and chocolate ice cream dribbled down his chin. Faith tightened her hand reassuringly on his arm as her heart went out to both son and father. Andy desperately wanted to hang on to Becky, and for some reason, Jay just couldn't allow him to.

"I believe you," she said quietly.

"Faith!" Jay spoke to her sharply. "I would have known if Becky kept a diary."

"You were probably busy," Faith reminded him. "She could have kept one during those long, lonely tax seasons."

Jay flushed slightly.

"I've been keeping a journal since I was fourteen," Amanda said suddenly. "It'd be a hard thing to keep from my husband. That is, when we were married."

She directed a quick glance at Jay and then added, "Which we're not. Not anymore."

JAY WAS ANNOYED. He looked impatiently at his watch and wondered where Bruce was. It was getting on to seven. He was annoyed his sons couldn't talk to him, annoyed he was seen as the property of a woman he didn't think of in that way, annoyed that Faith was encouraging his eldest son to believe he remembered conversations with Becky. As the silence lengthened, Amanda excused herself discreetly, and Jay followed Faith to the sink. "Just what do you think you're doing?"

"Me?" she asked with an arched brow. "What do you think you're doing? It is a very small thing to support your son in the belief that he remembers conversations he had with his mother—"

"He was only five when she died!"

"So what?"

So what? Jay stopped in his tracks.

"Jay, we don't always have proof for what we know in our minds." She shrugged and began to wash the few dishes the boys had used. Her voice was low, and she appeared to be merely chatting with him, but her tone was earnest. "Maybe Andy doesn't remember. But maybe he does. Maybe he remembers a collage of conversations. What's the harm in that?"

"It makes him believe in something that doesn't exist." Jay shook his head. He took the dish towel that she put in his hand and started to dry the spoons the boys had used, irritated that he was fascinated by the efficient movements of her hands. "Faith, it's hard enough without Becky, but to have him believe in a relationship that barely existed for him—"

Faith gave him a look of disbelief as she handed him a bowl and took the spoons from him. She walked across the kitchen to slide the spoons into a drawer. "You can't mean that."

"He doesn't have a mother," Jay said flatly.

And I don't have a wife.

She returned to the sink and carefully stacked the plates before she looked at him, her face softening with compassion.

"Of course he has a mother," she said. "He will always have a mother. Sam will always have a mother."

"You know what I mean. He doesn't—"

"Okay, Andy *had* a mother," Faith interrupted, her voice still laced with empathy. "But he had that mother for five years of his life. And in that five years, Becky probably had a million conversations with him that you weren't a part of. She talked to him every day when she bathed him, dressed him, fed him his cereal. I bet they played games and sang songs and took naps together. He probably still has some residual memories of her heartbeat safely stored in the back of his mind."

Jay heard what she was saying but he couldn't let those memories out. If he did, all the pain he'd been storing for the past twenty years would rain down on him.

"It doesn't matter." He couldn't keep the flatness from his voice.

Faith turned the water back on and scrubbed Patty's

perfectly spotless sink, her hair hiding her face. Then she asked, "Why would you deny your child memories, real or imagined, of his mother? You'd think you'd embrace Andy's memories of his mother, since you're always absent." She gasped, her hand flung to her mouth too late to keep those last words in.

JAY'S FACE CLOSED UP, his eyes pointedly avoiding hers, his head cocked as if listening for any sign of Bruce. Faith was overcome with remorse.

"Jay, I'm sorry."

His eyes flickered back to her, as if he was assessing her for the first time, but he didn't say anything.

Faith rested her hand on his arm. "I'm really sorry."

"It's easy for you, Faith, isn't it?" He carefully removed her hand from his arm.

"What?" She looked at him warily, wringing her rejected hand.

"It's easy for you to come in, see what's wrong and then just fix it."

Faith shook her head. "No, it's not. It's the hardest thing in the world to do. And I didn't mean for it to sound—"

She stopped before she said the wrong thing.

"Sound?" Jay prompted her.

"To sound as if you wanted to be as busy as you are. You don't have a lot of choice these days." She cleared her throat and said in a low voice, "I also know how hard it's been for you. First your mother and then Becky."

"Jay? Faith?" Amanda came back into the kitchen.

"We're going to start without Bruce. He'll be here as soon as he can. You accountants and your paperwork!"

Faith felt terrible, but Jay had to know the price he would pay if he couldn't allow his children to have memories. It was almost as if he wanted Andy and Sam to exist without feelings the way he did. But she realized that she shouldn't have said anything, especially in a semipublic space. That was wrong, but she couldn't apologize further, because Jay had already moved toward the dinner table.

After making sure that Andy and Sam were working on their homework, she slowly made her way to the table, where Patty had set her up in a corner with a folding chair. When Faith sat, she felt as if she was a child being allowed to sit with the grown-ups, since the table came to the middle of her chest. Patty passed around the food, and the three of them, Patty, Amanda and Jay, discussed the latest issues concerning the city. Usually, Faith would be indifferent to such a discussion, but now she found herself listening avidly, as she discovered the full scope of Jay's duties as a council member.

While she ate the baby-green salad with sesame vinaigrette she learned that Jay was on a committee to study a joint venture to supply water down the creek from the Detention Dam. Both Patty and Amanda were well versed in the implications of his work. During the salmon and asparagus, Faith got a feel for how resilient Los Banos had been during its recession and the new challenges it faced due to its rapid growth. Patty, as a Realtor, was all for growth. Her commissions had tripled in the past two years. But Amanda disagreed, arguing that if growth came without jobs, the town could suffer an out-of-control unemployment rate.

A new respect for Jay's work developed within Faith.

He and his fellow council members were trying to increase jobs, while being extremely sensitive to the fact that Los Banos was traditionally and culturally an agricultural town. More population meant a larger tax base, but it also meant crowded schools and a more congested infrastructure. How to embrace, even anticipate, the inevitable so that the town wouldn't be steamrollered into changes it couldn't control by the state government was a very real problem.

And then there were the much smaller, but still important issues of the average citizen. As the others talked, Faith, who had never stayed in one town long enough to even vote for a city council member, slowly began to see the lure of being involved at the civic level.

"Faith, will you help me clear the table before we serve dessert?" Patty asked.

Faith looked at her sister in surprise, but there was no animosity in Patty's aquamarine eyes. Jay and Amanda were engaged in a heated argument, and Faith tried not to feel bad that Jay hadn't directly spoken to her the entire meal. She pushed away that thought and replied, rising, "Certainly."

Patty was already rinsing the dishes and arranging them neatly in the dishwasher when Faith brought a stack of china into the kitchen.

"Thank you, Faith," Patty said as Faith put the dishes carefully in the sink.

"For what?"

"For leaving Jay and Amanda alone."

Faith remained silent.

"I guess it'll be okay," Patty continued, her watchful eyes making sure Faith didn't bang her china or scratch her sterling.

"What's okay?"

"Your staying in town until the party. I noticed you took your bags—"

"Do you blame me?" Faith asked.

Patty flushed. "It's very difficult with you here. Bruce—"

"What happened to Bruce tonight?" Faith interjected, surprised when Patty's face tightened.

"Work. He couldn't get away," Patty said briskly and then changed the subject. "Anyway, I'll expect you home tonight, because I understand that the cottage won't be ready until Saturday."

It wasn't much of an invitation, but Faith took it as a small peace offering. "Thank you, Pat—"

"I can see Jay really is over you and you really are just a nanny to him. So you don't pose much of a threat to Amanda."

"I never thought I was one."

"So it will be easy for you to leave once you fulfill your promise to Jay. You'll stay just until tax season is over, right?"

Faith didn't know about that. Listening to the dinner conversation had been curiously stimulating. Even though she had nothing to do with Jay's council work, she felt a great deal of pride at his commitment and his value as a member of this community. She glanced at the boys, their heads bent over their work. Even in the short time she'd been caring for them, they'd attained special places in her heart, much different from the other children she'd cared for. Perhaps it was because her other charges had had both parents. Sometimes it appeared as if Andy and Sam had none. Even if Jay managed to find a suitable replacement for her, Faith wasn't so sure it *would* be that easy to leave.

"Well," Patty said, her voice brisk. "It's not like you'd be happy here."

"Why would you say that?" Faith was curious.

"Surely you don't imagine yourself living in that cottage on the Whitfield farm permanently?" Patty looked at her in horror.

"Nothing is permanent," Faith said evasively. "But one home is as good as another, isn't it?"

Patty leaned forward, her face so close to Faith she could smell the coffee on Patty's breath. "There's one difference."

"And that is?"

"That this town is *my* town. It's Jay's town, and Amanda's town. I'm not sure there's room for you."

"I don't take up all that much space." Faith tried to joke.

Patty gave her coiffed head an impatient shake, their small truce over. "Be careful. Don't get too comfortable."

As Amanda and Patty discussed the plans for the party, it became evident that neither Faith nor Jay had needed to be present. The dinner had been merely a ruse to throw Amanda and Jay together. Faith tried to join in, but every time she offered an idea, Patty or Amanda shot it down. Finally, she just sat back and waited for the ''meeting'' to end. Jay remained friendly and poised, contributing ideas when directly asked, which Patty and Amanda invariably scribbled down, but he wouldn't look at Faith.

After thirty minutes, Patty had assigned several duties, none of which were given to Faith.

''I'll be happy to address the invitations,'' Faith offered.

Amanda and Patty exchanged looks. ''Actually,'' Patty said, ''we've decided to get a calligrapher.''

Faith nodded.

''Maybe there'll be more for you to do when it gets closer to the event,'' Amanda said sympathetically. ''This stuff is boring, anyway. You have your hands full with Jay's boys.''

Finally, the evening was officially over and she told the boys to pack up their homework. Andy didn't need to be asked twice. With haste that left her cringing, he crammed his papers into his backpack. Sam, on the other hand, was more tidy. He put his homework in his folder and carefully smoothed down the pages before closing the folder and putting it in the backpack. Andy looked at him impatiently.

''Can we play a game of Monopoly or something when we get home?'' Andy asked as he stuffed his arms into the jacket Faith brought him.

''No. It'll be bedtime when we get home. It's already a little late for Sam, and you have school to-morrow.''

''Da-a-ad!'' Andy looked to Jay for help.

JAY FELT SIX EYES ON HIM, two pairs looking at him as if he were a higher power, one telling him to do the right thing and back her up. He cleared his throat. He didn't appreciate what Faith had said to him ear-lier, but he was in her debt because of the children. He glanced at his watch. He'd be late again. He shouldn't have even come tonight, but if truth be told, he'd wanted to be with Faith.

He had worked steadily through his lunch hour so he could be at this dinner. And while he'd known he'd be monopolized by Amanda, he hadn't expected to argue with Faith.

He was surprised by how much she'd shrunk into herself. Even now as she watched him, she showed neither the brashness nor the bravado he'd come to associate with her. Apparently, she liked fighting just about as much as he did.

His ears and conscience still stung from her earlier observation. *You'd think you'd embrace Andy's mem-ories of his mother, since you're always absent.*

''Hello?'' Faith waved her open hand in front of his face.

''No.''

''No, what?'' Faith asked.

''No, we're not going to play Monopoly. You're going to bed when you get home.''

Faith gave him a relieved smile.

The corners of Andy's mouth turned down in disappointment, and his voice became sulky. "So I guess that means you're not coming back with us?"

Jay shook his head regretfully. "I'll be back later tonight."

"When we're asleep," Andy added.

Faith put her hand on Andy's shoulder, but Andy shrugged it off.

"Come on, champ. Let's go home."

They were on their way out, their goodbyes already said, when the door swung open and Bruce rushed in.

"Faith! Thank God!" Bruce said immediately.

Jay watched Faith recoil ever so slightly, noticing that she pulled Andy and Sam against her almost as a shield.

"Hi, Bruce. Sorry to have missed you at dinner."

"I'd have been here," Bruce assured her, not even glancing at Jay, "if I'd known you were still in town."

Jay looked sharply at Faith, who dropped her head to hide her face.

FAITH FELT JAY'S STARE penetrate her defenses.

"Gosh, I'm glad you decided to stay. I didn't want you to leave under those conditions," Bruce said earnestly. "But I thought with the way things were left last night, you'd have gone back to Los Angeles."

Faith shook her head. "I don't know what gave you that idea."

"Los Angeles?" Jay inquired silkily, although his voice sounded sharp to Faith. He looked between her and Bruce.

"Yes. Faith and Patty had quite a fight last night."

"Bruce is mistaken," Faith said, her tone light. "It

wasn't a fight. Just a misunderstanding.'' She looked directly at Jay, hoping he'd ignore what Bruce was saying. "I never intended to leave you and the boys. I promised to stay through tax season and I will."

She met Bruce's eyes stonily, daring him to deny what she was saying.

Bruce rubbed his chin, not reading her signal well at all. "You were distraught. I was worried about you driving all night."

Faith shifted uncomfortably.

"Last night? You were driving around last night?" Jay's sharp eyes missed nothing.

"I had some things to think about," Faith said tersely.

"Thank God you're safe," Bruce added. "I felt better that you at least took the station wagon rather than your own car."

"You were going somewhere?" Jay's voice was tight.

Faith couldn't look at him. She didn't want to read the expression on his face. Jay didn't need to know any of this. Then she muttered, "Don't even think what you're thinking."

Jay searched her face. "You couldn't possibly know what I'm thinking," he said shortly. "Anyway, it's time we leave. Bruce, sorry you missed a fabulous dinner." Then Jay caught Faith's arm and physically propelled her and the boys out the door.

"I'm so glad you decided to stay," Bruce called again, and Faith felt as if she were two feet tall, because Jay had yet to relinquish his grip on her arm. It seemed like a protective gesture, but Faith wasn't quite sure why.

She pulled her arm out of Jay's grasp. "You don't need to treat me like I'm a two-year-old," she muttered as she took the keys out of her pocket and gave them to Andy. With a worried glance backward, Andy and Sam ran down the block to where the car was parked.

"Then don't act like you're two," Jay said, his eyes hard and glittering. His voice was low and cutting, and it took everything Faith had to stop herself from flinching.

But even that wasn't enough when she heard his next words.

"For God's sake, Faith. I saw you this morning. You looked like hell. Tell me what happened."

CHAPTER EIGHT

"I D-DON'T KNOW WHAT you're talking about."
Faith's face burned with embarrassment. She wasn't
used to her life being on public display, especially in
front of Jay and the boys, who'd only heard that Bruce
thought she'd be gone.

"You didn't say anything about a fight with your
sister." His voice had softened considerably.

"It wasn't a fight," Faith denied. She could feel her
heart hammering in her rib cage, and she slowed her
pace so the boys wouldn't hear. Andy was just putting
the key in the car door.

She knew what Jay thought. She'd had a fight, sim-
ilar to the one she and Patty had had before, and that
meant she was packing up and going. Taking off without a look backward or a word of explanation. But this
time was different. Yes, she'd thought about leaving,
but she'd come back.

"I came back." She stopped in the middle of the
sidewalk, suddenly feeling the chill on her neck, and
she stared down at the cement, noticing a jagged, di-
agonal crack. That's how her heart felt now. She was
afraid to meet Jay's eyes, knowing she'd see the same
look of angry disbelief he'd had when she told him
she'd had a fight with her parents and her sister and

that she was leaving. He'd been caring for Stinky then, visibly relieved to see her, shocked when she had announced her departure.

Faith felt her throat tighten. She hadn't abandoned Jay back then. Not really. Stinky wasn't her son. Besides, her own family had just chosen Bruce over her. She couldn't see any choices then. She could see several now. So she'd come back. Could Jay understand that?

Finally, with a deep breath, she met his gaze, expecting the worst. But the blue eyes, darkened by wide pupils, weren't angry, weren't accusing. In fact, they appeared remarkably compassionate. Faith held back the urge to cry.

"Just tell me, Faith," he said softly, urgently. "Tell me why you were sleeping in the car in front of my house this morning. Tell me why Bruce thought you'd be in L.A. Tell me what the fight was about."

Trust me, his eyes begged. *Trust me.*

Faith opened her mouth and then snapped it shut. Maybe in the future she could trust him. But not now. Even though tears pressed up against the back of her eyes, even though the pressure building up after all these years might be relieved, she couldn't confide in Jay. Not now.

JAY STEPPED BACK at her silence. He glanced up the well-lit street to where the boys were grappling with each other, both trying to get in the front passenger seat. Then he looked back at Faith. The glitter in her eyes told him that she was on the verge of telling him something very significant.

"Let's go." Her voice was brisk and she started to walk rapidly toward the car.

"Faith," he said, catching her arm again. "You can't just run away."

"I'm not running away," she replied matter-of-factly. "I'm right here."

Jay knew exactly what she was doing—the same thing she'd done in high school. Back then, he'd tried to find some explanation to Faith's abrupt departure, some clue to why she'd left with only that hasty goodbye. For the longest time, he'd believed it was his proposal that had sent her packing, but now he suspected that it had had nothing to do with him at all.

His heart began to pound. He'd been so distraught by her rejection, piled as it was on top of grief for his mother and the pressure of helping to raise Stink, that he hadn't realized something had happened to Faith, something she couldn't or wouldn't talk about. He'd never been privy to what the fight had been about. Eighteen years later, he apparently was still in the dark.

She pulled herself out of his grip.

He finally found his voice. "Why don't you tell me what happened?"

"Why do I need to tell you anything?" she said, irritation in her tone. She'd caught up with the boys, and made sure that Sam was securely buckled into the back seat before making Andy move from riding shotgun to the back where it was safer. Both boys looked at her with large eyes and she lowered her voice. "Is it any of your business?"

Jay stopped.

Was it any of his business?

Of course it was his business.

Jay shifted uncomfortably. Well, not really. It was only his business if Faith confided in him. And she didn't look like she was in any mood for that.

Faith shut the passenger door and moved quickly around to the driver's side of the car.

Jay followed close behind her.

"This isn't over," Jay said abruptly, hanging on to the door so she couldn't close it.

She jammed the keys into the ignition and the station wagon started right up.

"It's none of your business, Whitfield."

Andy interrupted before he could reply. "Do you have to go back to the office tonight?"

Jay leaned in the back window, which Faith had rolled down. "I won't be gone too long. But you'll be fast asleep when I get home."

"I'm not tired. Besides, we didn't get to have any fun tonight," Andy complained.

"Well," Jay said with a grin, suddenly remembering Faith's earlier request. "You'll just have to make up for it Saturday night when you sleep over with your grandpa and Uncle Lee."

Andy looked surprised, and Jay once again felt like a good father. He ventured a glance at Faith, who suppressed a small smile. His heart expanded with her approval.

"There you go, Sam," Jay said to his youngest son, who didn't appear cheered by the news. "'We'll see' doesn't always mean 'no.'"

Sam looked up at Jay, his eyes worried. "Is Faith leaving?"

Ahh. *That* was the problem.

"Faith, are you leaving?" Jay asked.

Faith shook her head. "Nope. Not going anywhere. So, Andy, you still have to take a shower tonight."

Andy groaned, revealing his own apprehension when he said, "I don't like it when you fight."

Jay stood up. "We weren't fighting, sport. Just having a discussion."

AT THAT MOMENT, FAITH SNUCK a quick peek at Jay's face as he joked with the boys, making both giggle. She felt a tenderness start to swell inside her. And with it came an awareness of the lines around his eyes. He was pushing himself to a bone-tired exhaustion. A five-year nonstop push that had taken its toll on his whole family.

"Look, Jay," she said quickly. "I'm sorry for whatever happened tonight."

He stared at her for a long time. "That's okay, Faith. We've got plenty of time to work it out." He gave her a small smile. "I guess things aren't as buried as I thought they were."

Faith nodded, knowing exactly what he was talking about.

"It still hurts, Faith." He laughed to show he'd recover. "I was surprised at how much it hurt."

"What hurt?"

"Realizing how much I really don't know you." His finger lightly brushed her cheek, lingering on her jawline. "I should be home by midnight." Before she could answer, he shut the door and, with a last wave to the boys, walked quickly away.

Faith pulled away from Patty's house feeling they had much unfinished business.

WHEN JAY PUT THE KEY in the front door, it was nearly one in the morning. Faith had left the porch light on for him. She'd still looked tired, so he hoped she'd managed to get a few hours of sleep. On the other hand, he wanted her to be awake, so they could talk. It seemed as if they had much to talk about. He'd spent most of his time at the office thinking about Faith, wondering what could be serious enough to make Bruce think she'd leave town. He'd known something was wrong when she'd jumped at the chance to take the cottage. In his experience, Faith was as straightforward as they come, but apparently that was only when she was dealing with others.

As he quietly pushed open the door, he was greeted by the glow of a lamp in the hall, but the rest of the house was dark. There was no sound of the television. No signs of movement.

"Faith," he called in a quiet voice, as he walked past the kitchen. The family room couch was vacant, but her backpack was propped against the armrest. He found her coat draped over a kitchen chair and her keys on the counter.

He walked down the hall to the boys' room, letting his eyes adjust to the light. Both beds were empty. His heart beat rapidly and his eyes scanned the room after he flipped on the light. Andy's backpack was hanging from the bedpost. Sam's was leaning against the closet door. True, the room looked like a tornado had hit it, but there didn't seem to be any sign of a struggle.

Jay went back to the kitchen, checking the bathroom on his way past. Surely, if Faith had taken the boys anywhere, she would have left a note. He looked in the garage and went into the backyard. Everything was quiet and still. His father wouldn't have come and picked them up in the middle of the night without calling him first. But then it was hard to say what Faith and his father had cooked up.

"Where are you?" he asked out loud, not quite ready to panic yet. Only one room left.

His.

He pushed open the door and exhaled in relief. All three were on the king-size bed, the near-silent television casting a blue glow on them. Faith was curled on her right side with Andy, sprawled behind her and Sam securely tucked under her left arm.

They were all fast asleep.

After his heart rate returned to normal, he studied the trio. Faith looked like she belonged in his bed, her hair spread over the pillows. He glanced at his clock, grimacing because it was nearly one-thirty in the morning. It was a brutal schedule he had her on. She'd said so just that morning. It seemed cruel to wake her up to send her home when she'd have to return only a few hours later. He knew now why nannies lived in.

He left the bedroom. As he took off his shoes in the boys' room, then draped his tie over the back of Andy's chair, he wondered at the crazy relationship he had with Faith. Whether he wanted her or not, she had become a part of his life. He probed the feeling, surprised to find he didn't mind that at all.

With a deep sigh, he stretched out on Sam's bed, only to have to raise himself to remove a very hard plastic dinosaur from under his back. His feet stuck over the edge of the mattress, and he made a note to consider larger beds for when the boys became teenagers.

A BLARING ALARM and a talk radio news bulletin fought their way through Faith's consciousness. She was annoyed by the sound and by the fact she was very hot. She tried to lift herself up to stop the sound, but her arm was asleep and something that felt like a foot was wedged between her shoulder blades. She shifted her head to see an unfamiliar clock radio with glowing red numbers—5:32 a.m. It wasn't even light yet. She tried to move but the deadweight on her arm kept her firmly pinned. The heel in her back didn't help, either.

She nudged backward, and the deadweight in front of her stirred, yawning loudly, sending a generous puff of morning breath in her face. Sam. She peered over her shoulder, hoping the foot in her back didn't belong to Jay, and breathed a sigh of relief that it was Andy, who was sleeping perpendicular to her, his head nearly lolling off the side of the bed. She carefully eased her arm from under Sam and repositioned Andy so his head was back on the pillow, then crawled out of Jay's bed.

She wondered if Jay was still at the office. Surely he would have called. She padded in her stocking feet to the front door. It was still dark, but she could see his car parked next to the station wagon. She went to the kitchen and peered into the family room.

He wasn't there.

Finally she tried the boys' room and sure enough, he was there, lying fully dressed on the bottom bunk, his feet hanging over the edge. As her eyes adjusted to the dim light, she thought she could see the shadow of stubble across his jaw.

"I don't know how Sam sleeps in this bed," Jay said dryly.

Faith jumped, surprised he was awake.

"He's about two feet shorter than you are," Faith replied, and leaned against the door frame. "If you want to catch a few more minutes in your own bed, you can just scoot the boys over. I'll go make some coffee and get things together for the boys' breakfast."

Jay shook his head and tried to get up, groaning as he hit his head on the top bunk. He sat back down on the bed and looked helplessly at Faith.

"Ouch. Be careful." She rubbed her own head in sympathy.

"I knew it was there." His voice rumbled in his chest.

"Are you okay?" Faith resisted the impulse to cross the room and see. If she did, she'd be tempted to plant a kiss on the tender spot. He looked awfully appealing in his rumpled clothes.

"I have a hard head."

"It's not the same distance from one bunk to the next if you're seven," Faith said kindly. After a short pause, she continued, her voice matter-of-fact, "I'm sorry about taking your bed. But Sam had a bad dream and that woke Andy, and neither of them would go back to sleep, so I suggested we all lie down on your bed. I was going to move them back before you got home, but I guess I was a little tired myself.''

She felt herself rambling and realized she could barely look at him. All she wanted to do was fling her arms around him and feel what it was like to be pressed to the heart of a man who was that appealing after a night spent in his son's bunk bed. When Jay just eyed her quizzically, she added, ''You should have woken me up. There's no reason for you to have to sleep in here.''

JAY STUDIED FAITH. One tube sock was halfway up her slender calf, the other was scrunched down at her ankle. She was wearing an old pair of gray jersey running shorts with an oversize college sweatshirt. He didn't remember that from the dinner at Patty's. In fact, Faith had not been wearing her usual gypsy garb, either, but a nicely tailored shirtdress, which clung, rather alluringly, to her hips.

It took a moment before he realized that she was wearing *his* tube socks and *his* shorts and *his* university sweatshirt. And she looked adorable, her hair sticking up in every direction. At his stare, she self-consciously smoothed down the back of her hair, then plucked at the hem of her, uh, *his* sweatshirt. It was an oddly intimate movement, and his physical response was more powerful than anything he'd felt since he was fourteen. He was suddenly grateful he was sitting. He averted his eyes, hoping that without the visual stimulation, his nether parts would realize they were responding to the wrong thing.

It was Faith, for heaven's sake—and she was wearing his running clothes.

"I hope you don't mind. That dress was just too uncomfortable to lie down in."

"No, not at all," he said. The softness of her voice made the situation that much worse. If he stayed, he'd embarrass himself right here, right now. That was unacceptable. His mind made up, he lurched past her on the way to the bathroom, ever grateful that his back was toward her as he made his way down the hall.

"They look better on you than they do on me," he called. How was it that first thing in the morning she still managed to smell like soap? He shut the door to the bathroom and stared at his reflection. After several deep breaths, his heart rate began to slow and the swelling started to subside.

It was just Faith.

But that didn't seem to make a difference to his long-dormant sex drive. Didn't his libido know that Faith was off-limits? He rubbed his face. If he thought that he was immune to her, he was very mistaken. His body had given him a very stiff message, so to speak, to the contrary.

She won't share her secrets. She doesn't trust you.

That didn't seem to matter.

When he emerged from the bathroom, she was nowhere to be seen. He peeked inside the bedroom, but then heard clanging in the kitchen. He slipped past the still-sleeping boys, and once in the safety of his own bathroom, he stripped off his clothes.

He stepped into the shower, the bone-chilling cold aiding his particularly uncomfortable condition. A few minutes later he was out and was scraping yesterday's stubble from his face. He entered his bedroom, careful not to waken his sleeping sons, and chose a new shirt and tie. As he dressed, he wondered what he had gotten himself into—during tax time, no less! Why was his heart beating with such anticipation just because Faith was in the house, wearing his clothes?

Against everything he knew to be sane and reasonable, he'd actually managed to redevelop a crush on his high school sweetheart. He pulled on his trousers, chosen specifically for their generous pleat, tucked in his shirt and quickly tied his tie. With sure fingers, he put on his watch and then stared at the wedding band on his finger. He twisted the band around. No. He wasn't ready to take it off. Not yet. But the fact that he thought about it was unsettling.

He leaned over Andy and gave him a nudge. "Hey, sport. Wake up. It's time to get ready for school."

Andy moaned and rolled over.

"Come on, champ." Jay patted Sam on the head. "It's time to get up."

Andy yawned. "Hey, Dad."

"Hey, yourself."

He looked around. "What are we doing in your bed?"

"I think you all fell asleep here."

"Is Faith here?"

"She's in the kitchen." Jay smiled down at Sam, whose eyes were wide open.

Sam smiled back and sat up.

"She spent the night?" Andy looked pleased. "We had a sleepover with Faith."

Jay grinned, his imagination embracing a sleepover with her. "At least you and Sam did."

"You can sleep with Faith next time," Sam promised.

Out of the mouths of babes.

WITH DILIGENT SUPERVISION, Jay hustled the boys into the bathroom. He stood and watched Andy wash his hair and soap his body. As Andy brushed his teeth, Jay rolled up his sleeves and washed Sam's face. He should have showered Sam before getting dressed. He gave his youngest son a strong sniff. Sam was right at the edge of ripeness.

"I took a bath two days ago," Sam said. "I don't stink yet."

"Just checking. But it's bath time for you this afternoon. Maybe even one on Saturday before you go to Grandpa's."

Sam's face lit up. "I forgot about the sleepover. Saturday?"

"Saturday. But we have to talk to Grandpa and Grandma Bess just to make sure."

"Oh, Grandpa likes us. He'll say yes," Sam said confidently. "Is Faith still here?"

"Yes. I heard her in the kitchen."

Sam and Andy exchanged glances. "Maybe she made us waffles."

They hurried to their room. Sam started digging through his drawers to find something to wear. Andy, much to Jay's chagrin, was poking around in the dirty clothes pile for a shirt, having located a pair of jeans on the bottom.

"I wouldn't count on it," Jay said. "It's probably a cold cereal morning. Andy, isn't there something in the drawer you could wear? Something clean?"

"These are clean," insisted Andy, sniffing the air. "I smell something good. She promised us waffles this morning."

"It's probably just the freezer kind."

But the boys weren't listening. Andy was already down the hall, pulling his shirt over his head.

"Wait for me!" Sam squealed, hopping down the hall with his shoes and one sock in his hand. The other sock dangled off the end of his foot.

"She *did* make waffles!" Andy yipped with glee.

"I promised." Faith smiled.

"And you don't break your promises," Andy finished for her. He sat down and took a big swallow from the glass of orange juice set at his place. Jay watched thoughtfully. Andy was actually drinking something without sniffing, inspecting or prodding it. He glanced at Faith, who didn't seem to notice that his son had just done something miraculous.

Jay surveyed the table and it looked like the kind of Sunday breakfast Becky used to serve. Heart-shaped waffles were stacked and steaming in the middle of the table. He saw the butter on a small plate and the syrup in the plastic bottle. He looked at the time. Six-thirty. She had assembled it so quickly that there would actually be time for a real breakfast before the boys had to be at school.

Andy was already reaching for the waffles, pulling

off half the stack with his fingers and putting it on his plate.

"Da-a-ad! Look how much he's taking," Sam whined as he tried to wrestle his shoes over socks that were hastily pulled up. They were caught on his heels and wrinkled along the soles. "Tell Andy he can't have it all."

"Andy, put a few of those back," Faith interceded.

"I can eat them all," Andy assured her, stuffing two large bites in his mouth.

"It doesn't matter if you can," Faith replied as she came around the kitchen counter to put another batch on the table.

"You brought more," Andy pointed out.

"I know I did, but you can't just take half of what's there. You have to be polite and let everyone have some. If there's any left over, then you can ask to have more." Faith rounded the corner behind Andy and sniffed his hair. "You smell clean."

She paused and her nose wrinkled. Then she went back, pulled up the back of Andy's shirt and inhaled deeply. "You wore this already."

"I only wore it once."

"But you sweated in it. It smells. You'll have to change before you go to school."

She sat down and scooted her chair toward Sam. "Give me your foot," she said to Sam, and then continued to address Andy. "You'll change those jeans, too. I just put away a bunch of clean stuff for you."

Sam lifted his foot to her. "I'm wearing clean clothes."

"Yes, you are, sweetie," she said.

She unlaced one shoe and took it off.

"What are you doing?" Jay asked curiously.

"Sam's sock is scrunched." Faith smiled at Jay as she straightened the sock, making sure it was smooth on Sam's foot.

"Eat while it's hot," she ordered Jay.

"Other foot," she said to Sam.

Jay sat down and watched another miracle occur when Andy flung a couple of the waffles onto Sam's plate. Sam tried to butter them while his leg was extended at an awkward angle, being ministered to by Faith. Jay felt his heart slam against his ribs.

He hadn't just redeveloped a crush on his high school sweetheart. He'd fallen in love with her.

If a stranger had been watching, he would have thought Faith was Sam's mother. Her forehead was furrowed in concentration, the tip of her tongue lodged in the corner of her mouth. She acted like a mother, telling Andy to change his clothes, something Jay couldn't accomplish successfully even though he'd witnessed his son donning the offensive shirt.

"I think you're going to need a new pair of shoes, Sammy," she said with a final shove. "Your feet seem to be growing faster than the weeds out back."

Faith gave the shoe a pat and looked around the table to make sure everything was in the right place, before she relaxed and helped herself to a waffle.

"Pass the syrup, please," she requested.

Andy stopped eating long enough to give it to her. Three miracles in one morning.

"So what's going to happen today at school?" she asked.

"We're going to learn," Sam said.

Faith laughed. "And what are you going to learn?"

"Stuff."

"I have a test." Andy frowned.

"Spelling on Fridays," Faith said with a nod.

"I hate spelling," Andy complained. "Why do we have to spell if the computer knows how to do it for us?"

Jay ate in silence, like a useless appendage. Why was it that he had no idea Andy had spelling tests on Fridays? Or that he didn't know Andy hated spelling? Had he just figured that, since Andy's grades were always good, his son must love all his subjects?

"Spelling's a lot harder this year than it was last year," Faith said sympathetically. "Good thing we went over them last night before bed. You should have no problem acing the test."

Jay felt a flush of guilt rise up his neck. He'd never helped Andy with spelling. He read to them occasionally, but Granny Doris helped them with their homework. But now there wasn't a Granny Doris. Now there was Faith and she was only temporary.

Or was she?

Jay frowned, shaking his head, trying to rid himself of the hope born at the thought of Faith as a permanent member of the household. He cut off that thought, before he could remember the way Sam looked curled up in her arms or the fact that Andy drank orange juice without complaining.

Faith was, at best, a visitor.

She'd proved long ago she had absolutely no staying power. He'd wanted her to stay before and she wouldn't. He saw how attached Sam and even Andy were becoming to Faith. The deadline for all good U.S. citizens to file their tax returns was fast approaching, and he had to prepare the boys for Faith's departure.

The ring of the doorbell was a welcome relief to his disturbing thoughts.

Exchanging a quick glance with Faith, Jay got up in mid chew to open the door.

"Patty!" he said with surprise.

"Hi, Jay." Without being invited, Patty walked straight into the house, her face animated and excited. "I know it's early, but I got this brainstorm after the party last night. I've decided to roast my parents, and I came over to see if you'd be willing to be the master of ceremonies—"

She stopped short, noticing that he was just swallowing.

"I'm sorry. I'm interrupting your breakfast."

"No problem. I'm flattered you'd want me. I'd love to do that for your folks. Do you know who'd have stories to tell?"

"Well, Amanda and I started a list. She's going to call people and see if they'd be willing to participate. It would be great fun for my mother and father. We don't want it to be too long because we do have the band, but I thought it'd be a nice touch." Patty talked as if she'd ingested far more than her usual dose of caffeine.

"It sounds like a great idea," he said, trying to steer her back toward the door.

"Then you'll do it?"

"Sure." Jay glanced over his shoulder to see Faith standing in the hallway, one hand on the wall. In dismay, he felt the early tremor of tension, much like a dog before an earthquake.

CHAPTER NINE

MAYBE, IF HE MOVED around, he could get Patty out the front door before she saw her. He glanced quickly at Faith, who had now firmly planted herself on the wall, her body angled almost defiantly, her arms crossed. Using his body to block Patty's view, Jay began to herd her toward the door.

Patty looked up at him and said teasingly, ''If I didn't know any better, I'd think you were trying to get rid of me.''

''Hi, Patty,'' Faith called deliberately, pulling herself off the wall to walk a few steps toward her sister, a smile hovering on her lips. ''I couldn't help overhearing about the roast. It sounds like a terrific idea. Dad will love it.''

''Faith!'' Patty whirled, trying to see around Jay, who felt the tremor turn into a full-blown quake. The almost childish excitement in Patty's face changed to cool and detached speculation. If he didn't know better, he'd swear he'd just witnessed small icicles form on the tip of Patty's nose.

Jay closed his eyes and groaned.

Patty evaluated Faith—taking in the sweatshirt, the baggy shorts, the sweat socks—and her shoulders stiffened with an animosity Jay knew Faith didn't deserve.

Apparently, what they'd fought about earlier hadn't been resolved. Patty really hadn't expected Faith to be around when she'd invited him to dinner.

"You've made yourself, uh, comfortable." Patty's words dripped with sarcasm.

Jay winced at her tone and saw Faith flinch.

"Things aren't always what they seem," she responded, her voice even.

"That seems to be the case with you, doesn't it?" The insinuation was unmistakable. "I thought you said you were coming home last night. I see you've found yourself better, er, accommodations."

"Patty, don't start." Faith sounded weary and defenseless. "I just wanted to tell you your idea for a roast sounded good. That's all."

Before Patty could reply, Jay wedged himself between the two sisters and repeated graciously, "Patty, I would be more than happy to be the emcee for the anniversary dinner."

It was as if he could feel the darts Patty was aiming at Faith zing right through him. Didn't some well-meaning buddy once tell him that the worst place to be was between two women during a fight, sisters at that?

Patty recovered herself, bestowing on him a generous smile, obviously meant to exclude Faith.

"Amanda doesn't have a date yet for the anniversary party," Patty announced, her thin line of an eyebrow arching. "If you aren't, er, tied up, you might think about asking her."

"You know I always go stag to these events," Jay reminded her, keeping his voice as light as possible.

"Besides, it's two months away. Plenty of time for Amanda to find a date."

"You've got to date sometime." She glanced over her shoulder, not bothering to lower her voice. "When Faith's gone in April, Amanda will still be here for you. Amanda's always been around for you."

Jay felt his own smile tighten. "I guess that's my business, isn't it?"

Patty nodded and started toward the door. "Take it from me, Jay. Faith will only break your heart." Without even a glance back at Faith, Patty was gone.

Jay exhaled sharply.

As much as he respected Patty, he knew, just knew, that her first phone call would be to Amanda. And together, they would speculate and synthesize.

And he hated that.

FAITH WAS MORTIFIED. The boys had stopped eating and were staring at her.

"What did she mean Faith is going to break Dad's heart?" Sam asked.

"Nothing, stupid," Andy said roughly, and took one last swallow of milk. "She just wants Dad to like Mrs. Perkins."

"I don't like Mrs. Perkins." Sam looked dismayed. "Does that mean Mrs. Perkins is going to be our new mom?"

"Stupid." Andy smacked at Sam, who automatically ducked. "Dad's got to marry her first."

"Why can't he marry Faith?"

"Dad's not going to marry anyone. He works too much."

"I like Faith."

"We don't get a choice. Dad's doing the marrying."

"Dad?" Sam's voice held uncertainty, as if he expected Jay to confirm that there really was no Santa Claus.

Before Jay could answer, Faith got her own voice back and ordered brusquely, "Both of you, go brush your teeth and get your stuff ready for school. Sam, remember you left your homework on the couch in the living room. Your lunches are in the fridge."

As the boys ran down the hall, Faith called, "Andy, put on clean clothes—that means a new shirt and new pants *from the drawer*—and I'm going to be looking at your teeth. If there's gunk caught in them, back you go."

Andy didn't bother with a reply, but when she heard the drawers in his room being pulled open and then slammed shut, she knew he'd heard her. Uncharacteristically, Faith felt a little prick of disappointment when she realized that Andy hadn't agreed when Sam said he liked her.

Perhaps that was because her psyche had taken a pounding from Patty.

Apparently, her psyche didn't seem to realize that she didn't care what Patty thought about her. It also shouldn't care that Jay was obviously going out of his way to hide her from Patty. After all, she couldn't expect him of all people…

"I'm sorry," Jay said, as he walked past her into the kitchen. He took his and the boys' plates to the sink and started rinsing them off.

What was he sorry for? The fact that he didn't want to marry her or the fact he had tried to hide her?

"We didn't do anything wrong," Faith said faintly.

She watched him load the dishwasher. Neatly, orderly. And he even managed to keep his tie from getting wet.

"I know that and you know that," Jay said with a disgusted shake of his head. "But sometimes it doesn't matter whether or not you are guilty. The mere appearance is enough to get the rumor mill churning."

"So you're saying this will affect you?"

Jay shrugged. "It would have been better if Patty hadn't seen you. She's an important influence in this town." The orange juice glasses clinked as he lined them up along one side. He gave her an inquiring look. "Usually she's not so frosty."

Faith replied bitterly, "I guess it's best not to offend Patty's overactive, judgmental senses."

"Faith, you know it's not like that." Forks and knives clattered into their holder. "But the history between you and Patty is, at best, difficult. It's obvious you've never resolved it. Does this have anything to do with what Bruce was talking about last night?"

Faith clamped her mouth shut.

"Faith, stop it!" Jay said abruptly, the exasperation in his voice apparent. The door to the dishwasher banged shut, the inhabitants rattling. The tone of his voice was startling, and Faith was unable to control the trembling of her shoulders. Jay hadn't touched her, but she felt as if he'd given her a good hard shake.

"Stop what?" she finally asked, her voice a croak.

"This martyr routine."

"What martyr routine?" she asked. She couldn't help how defensive she sounded. Besides, being defensive was better than crying.

She wouldn't cry.

Not in front of Jay.

Not in front of Patty.

"The everybody's-against-me routine. Faith, the only person causing you problems is you."

"Well, that's helpful." The sarcasm leaked out. "Thanks for telling me."

JAY STARED AT THIS WOMAN who fascinated and frustrated him at the same time. She was extremely open and generous with his children, but incredibly closed with him. She was annoying as hell.

"Faith, I'm on your side." Jay felt the words had been wrenched from his gut.

"My side?" Faith looked at him with disbelief.

Jay just stared at her face, realizing that Faith's features were frozen. They should have changed during an argument, the way the desert changed during an unexpected storm. When he and Becky had fought she always burst into tears, fluid leaking from every orifice.

It wasn't pretty, but at least Becky had had a way of releasing her hurt.

Faith didn't. The only evidence that she was even disturbed was the tension that held her shoulders so straight and tight, she looked as if she might shatter. Faith kept her face bland, neutral, and it reminded him of when she'd talked to him just before she'd left. She had held her jaw with tight control, too much control for an eighteen-year-old, he realized now.

Jay heard himself utter out of the blue, "Do you have a date for your parents' anniversary dinner?"

It was an odd question to ask in the kitchen right before work. He glanced at Becky's pictures and felt a small sting of disloyalty, a tiny shimmer of her disapproval. But his mouth had a mind of its own this morning.

Faith gave him a stricken look as if he had just made a bad joke.

When he added faintly, "If you don't, uh, have a date, I'd like to take you," he knew he had lost his mind.

A long pause extended between them.

Finally, Faith asked, "Why?"

Jay didn't know why. Second thoughts crowded him like ants to a crushed garden snail. Not fifteen minutes ago, he'd told Patty that he was going stag, that two months was plenty of time for Amanda to find a date. So why was he asking Faith, right now? Would taking Faith be like making some kind of declaration?

But when he saw her jaw relax, he knew exactly why he'd done it. To make up for the fact that she thought he was ashamed of her. "Because I'd be honored to escort you." On one hand, he'd just be feeding the rumor mill, especially with such an early invitation giving people plenty of time to speculate. But on the other, there was something inside of him, something infinitely lonely that really needed Faith to say yes.

Faith cocked her head, considering his words.

Either a minute or a month passed, he couldn't tell.

"Sorry, Whitfield," Faith said eventually. "Can't do that."

Probably for the best, his head agreed.

"Why not?" his mouth asked.

"It's a pity date."

Jay resisted the urge to give a swift boot to her well-rounded bottom.

"And I don't do pity dates," Faith said. "You know I'm not a great candidate for you. If you need a date, take Amanda. It'll make your life a lot easier. Remember, I'll only break your heart." Faith repeated Patty's words bitterly.

"There are two things you need to know about me," Jay said, making his voice as bland as possible, even though all he wanted to do was place his hands around her slender neck and shake. Hard. "One, I never let people make plans for me. That includes you. I haven't asked Amanda. I wasn't intending to ask Amanda. And I won't ask Amanda.

"Two, since when did I say I needed an easier life? If I wanted easy, I wouldn't have dated you in high school. I wouldn't have had you as a nanny. Nothing, not one damn thing, has ever been easy around you. So do you want to go with me to your parents' anniversary party or not?"

It wasn't the most romantic of invitations.

And it occurred to Jay that he was making one of the worst mistakes of his life. Despite the fact that Faith was contrary, closed and sometimes downright ornery, there was something about her that sparked a

tiny flame in the pit of his stomach. It was troubling.
No, *Faith* was troubling.

But worth every bit of it.

FAITH FELT AS IF SHE was being crowded on all sides.
But Jay hadn't moved an inch. In fact, he had retreated
two paces, but his eyes, nearly blue-black with emotion, stared intently at her, making her feel dizzy, her
legs tremble. It was a terrifying sensation that Faith
had never experienced before.

This is love.

She stiffened. *It can't be love. It's too soon.*

He's waited eighteen years for you.

No, no, her rational mind denied, *it's a pity date.*

But the blaze of intensity in his eyes, the tight
clench of his fists—as if he had to physically keep
himself from touching her—belied the concept of a
pity date.

He repeated deliberately. "Will you go with me?"

Faith shrugged offhandedly and took the only route
she knew when it came to Jay Whitfield. "Give me
one good reason." Her low voice had a tough, husky
edge that sparked desire in his blue eyes, and she felt
a burst of heat warm her whole soul.

He didn't have to say a word.

Faith actually backed up a step from the force of
his intent. But just as he closed the distance between
them, Andy and Sam tumbled into the room, worry
written all over their faces.

"You're fighting again," Andy accused them, disappointment in his voice.

"Don't fight," Sam pleaded, shaking his head. He
sounded close to tears.

"Does this look like fighting?" Jay asked his sons, a slow smile on his face. Instead of backing away at the arrival of the two boys, Jay put his hand behind her neck, causing all sorts of nerves to tingle along her hairline. Then he gave her a slow, deliberate kiss on her forehead, a kiss she felt all the way to her fingernails.

After what seemed to be an eternity, Jay pulled away, his voice husky. "That's one good reason to go with me. Would you like me to give you another?"

Wordlessly, Faith shook her head.

"Good," Jay said with a satisfied nod. "So why don't you think about my invitation and let me know." He looked at his sons. "So, was that fighting?"

"Okay, Dad. You weren't fighting," Andy conceded hastily. Then he ran to open the front door and flew down the driveway, making gagging sounds. "Yuck! C'mon, Dad. Let's go!"

With relief, Faith watched Jay bundle the boys into the back seat of his sedan. She wasn't particularly comfortable with the newly unearthed emotions that burned through her. Twisting to look out the back window, Sam waved goodbye vigorously as they drove down the street.

With an equally enthusiastic wave back, Faith shut the door and leaned back against it for a brief moment before finishing the cleanup Jay had started. Even though he knew well and good it would give Patty fits for days, Jay had asked her to her parents' anniversary party. Her sister's reaction was almost enough reason to say yes. Faith put away the butter and grabbed the syrup bottle. Ugh. It was sticky. She frowned. Going with Jay would make circumstances very uncomfortable for him. Very uncomfortable. It seemed as if he and Patty shared a solid friendship. Why would Faith put that in jeopardy?

As she walked down the hall, she reluctantly took off Jay's shorts, sweatshirt and socks, folding them carefully, even the socks. She'd been so tired last night, it had been easier to put on his clothes than try to find her own.

How long had it been since she felt tingles for a date? Never. Not since their prom night. She hugged his clothes and closed her eyes tightly.

What should she do? Two months was a long time away. A lot could happen in two months. Look at what had happened in the past two weeks.

As she dressed, Faith thought about the invitation. If Jay didn't live in Los Banos, if he wasn't a city council member and didn't have to interact with Patty and Bruce on a regular basis, she would say yes in a heartbeat. But he did live in Los Banos, he was a city council member, and he was entrenched in the same circles as Patty and Bruce. Three solid reasons for Faith to say no.

She rubbed the spot on her forehead where he'd kissed her, as if she could still feel the warmth of his lips.

That was the only reason to say yes.

She wandered out to the hall and stared at Becky, who smiled back at her.

"What do you think?" she asked the photo.

Take good care of them was all she heard.

Faith took a deep breath and was sad.

It wasn't the answer she wanted, but she nodded. To take care of them, to truly take care of Jay, she would need to refuse his invitation. No matter how much she liked him, no matter how much the intensity in his eyes produced feelings Faith had believed were permanently buried, Jay belonged to a different universe. He belonged with Patty and Bruce, and even Amanda and her casseroles. He belonged to the town. He was a fourth-generation native son. She was, for the most part, a transient. Jay was as rooted as they came, committed not just to his job and family, but to the community.

She'd grown up in Los Banos, but she was still an alien, even though she'd attended the same schools, hung out at the same places, laughed at the same jokes. In their teens, Patty had always made note of Faith's differences, though she'd been infuriated when her attempts to inculcate Faith into the world of teenage peer pressure failed. It had always bothered Patty that Faith hadn't wanted to be part of the ''in'' crowd.

Instead, Faith had dreamed of a world beyond the brown hills of Los Banos. When she and Jay had sat in the bleachers for football games, she'd wondered what it would be like to sit in the bleachers for a professional one. After the game, while they'd eaten more pizza than was good for either of them, she'd wondered what pizza was like in Mexico, whether they even had pizza in Mexico. When he'd driven her to the farthest end of his father's property and they'd lain in the back of his father's truck, covered with a rough wool blanket, staring up at the stars, talking and kissing and talking some more, she'd wondered if the stars would look the same from a deserted beach, if she'd feel the same with him on that beach.

Jay had just laughed at those wonderings. She'd always known that Los Banos was enough for him. Then his mother had died, and Jay had become more entrenched as he shared the responsibility of caring for Lee with Gil. Except for college, Jay had every intention of settling in Los Banos forever.

Faith shook her head, not wanting to be reminded of how Jay had looked at her earlier, but her brain sent out tiny searches for those memories, anyway. Had she seen that look before? She couldn't recall ever seeing the lonely need in his eyes. It would be so easy to pursue that trail, to experience Jay's love again, but no matter how tempting, something inside told her to take responsibility. She couldn't pine for Jay. In two months, she would leave him again. After her parents' anniversary party, after April 15, after he found himself a new nanny, Jay would still have his community and she would have her freedom.

That was her answer.

LATE SUNDAY AFTERNOON, Faith watched Andy and Sam on their hands and knees, knocking on the hardwood slats of the floor of the cottage's big bedroom. On the tail end of their sleepover with Gil and Bess, the boys had insisted on playing at the cottage until their late Sunday supper at Gil's.

"What are we listening for?" Sam asked in a loud whisper.

"Shh."

''What are we looking for?'' Sam repeated in a voice just slightly lowered.

Faith held back a smile. For some reason, both boys thought she couldn't see or hear what they were doing. In fact, she had a perfect view right into Jay and Becky's old room. However, their behavior seemed harmless, so she continued to attack the grout between the antique tiles with a toothbrush. She'd felt an incredible sense of freedom since she'd moved in Friday night.

The Whitfields all helped. Bess called Phoebe for some extra twin-size sheets so Faith didn't have to buy new ones. Stink and Mitch assembled the newly cleaned beds and the mattresses that'd been delivered to the main house. The chubby twins, Eric and Hannah, presented her with a plastic water bottle filled with colorful weeds for her bedroom. So while the boys played with the twins all Saturday and slept over Saturday night, Faith spent her time cleaning, bit by bit, section by section. The more she cleaned, the more attached she became to the little cottage.

She'd gotten permission from Gil, as well as a modest amount of money, to further renovate as she thought fit. The baby-chick-yellow miniblinds had already been installed and the amount of light they let in made the cottage appear to be much bigger. But Faith also liked how snug it was. She could see why Becky had fought to keep Jay in the small space.

She scrubbed around the sink, erasing years of neglect, still listening for the methodical knocking of the boys.

''Don't you think we can stop now?'' Sam was tired

already, Faith could tell by his voice. "Faith said she'd play one of those games with us. I like Memory."

"No," Andy answered shortly. "I know it's here."

"What's here?"

Faith cocked her head to hear Andy's answer. She'd asked Andy what he was looking for, but he hadn't replied.

"I remember," Andy said stubbornly.

"What'cha talking about?" Sam heaved a sigh. "How come I never know what you're talking about?"

"The secret door."

"Secret door?"

"Where Mom's diary is, stupid."

Diary. Now Faith understood. The other evening at Patty's house. Andy was on a mission to prove to Jay that Becky had kept a diary.

More knocking.

"I think this is it," Andy said with excitement.

"What is?"

"A secret door. Mom told me about it."

"On the floor?"

Faith sighed. If there *was* a secret door, she would have found it when she and Mitch had pulled up the carpet, some of which had been almost welded to the floor. There was nothing on the floor, but, well, floor.

She rinsed the grout around the sink and peered at her work.

Thunk! Ka-thunk, ka-thunk!

Faith raised her head sharply.

That wasn't a harmless noise.

"So, what are you up to?" Faith asked as casually

as she could manage. She tried not to cringe as she saw what Andy was doing. Apparently, he'd decided to pull up the floorboards.

Two faces shot up and instantly looked guilty.

"Nothing."

"Nothing, huh?" Faith squatted next to them and looked at the fresh, deep nicks in the hardwood. Maybe they could be sanded out. She'd planned on calling for an estimate on refinishing the floors. She picked up a flat-head screwdriver and turned it over in her hand, studying the object. Andy must have found it in Gil's toolbox. Then she looked at both boys and said frankly, "This doesn't look like nothing. Are you looking for your mom's diary?"

"She told me. I know she did," Andy said defensively, his young face flushed. Obviously, he was still smarting from Jay's not-so-gentle rebuke.

"Your dad didn't mean it that way." She attempted to make her voice a cross between matter-of-fact reality and gentle mothering.

Andy couldn't hear her tone but continued stubbornly, using a different tool to poke at the hardwood. "I know it's hidden under here. She told me. She told me about a secret door."

Faith lay a firm hand over his, stopping the destruction. "I believe you."

"No, you don't." Indignation seemed to choke him, and he tried to free his hand from her grip. "Dad doesn't believe me, why should you? If Mom was here, she could prove I was telling the truth."

"I'm not your father. I believe you."

Andy stopped stock still, his face a heart-rending mix of stoic masculinity and hurt child.

Finally, he asked, his voice faint, ''You believe I remember my mom?''

Faith nodded and swallowed hard.

She believed him, because she saw so much of herself in his eyes. God, it was so hard when the ones closest to your heart didn't believe you. She admired Andy for his candor. At least he said what he knew and was willing to defend it to an extreme measure. He didn't bury it deep inside himself, so that even when it was safe to confide, when it was better to confide, he couldn't.

She put a gentle thumb under his chin and said instead, ''You look like your dad.''

''I don't look like him.'' He flushed and his eyes darted away, but he didn't jerk his chin away.

Ahh, these children were so deprived of touch, the kind of touching that only mothers gave their small boys. Later, when the boys were men, they'd receive that tenderness from their lovers. But Andy had no mother, and although he was fast approaching that in-between stage—where touch was off-limits—Faith made a mental note to hug, squeeze and touch him as much as possible.

Faith nodded. ''Yes, you do. But you have something very different from what your father has.''

''I do?''

''Yes.''

Faith saw that he wasn't going to ask, but was waiting for her to tell him. She continued. ''You have the ability to accept what you know. You trust yourself.

And that's something you should try to hang on to for as long as you can.''

''What's that mean?'' Sam demanded. ''How can he 'except' what he knows?''

''Accept. People think Andy shouldn't be able to remember conversations he had with his mom because he was too little. But Andy knows he can. And now he's looking for proof. Isn't that right?''

Sam nodded vigorously. ''Proof.''

''But let me give you a hint.''

Andy stared at her wide-eyed.

''If you have to chip away at the wood, I don't think that's going to be the secret panel. It should open easily, with the lightest touch of a spring.''

She stood up and placed the tools on Becky's antique dresser.

''Maybe the spring is rusty,'' Sam noted.

Faith laughed. ''Maybe it is. But if you want to find that secret place, you have to tap softly, not try to get to it using a sledgehammer.''

''Or a sledge screwdriver,'' Sam chortled, laughing at his own joke. He looked up at Faith. ''Can we still play a game?''

''Sure, Sam.'' Faith agreed. It was one of their easier requests to grant. ''Go pick one for us.''

A quiet rap on the door startled them all. Faith looked at the sky. It couldn't be Jay. He'd considered coming to supper, but then decided that since the boys were taken care of, he'd work late into the night.

Faith strode to the door, feeling a small tingle of anticipation. Jay did arrive unexpectedly sometimes. She yanked the door open with a smile.

"Faith."

Her smile faded and she glanced at Andy and Sam, who stood in the bedroom doorway, balancing in their stocking feet on the short step.

"Bruce. What are you doing here?" Faith couldn't keep the sharp edge of tension out of her voice and she looked around for Patty. Usually, where Bruce was Patty wasn't far away.

"We were invited for Sunday dinner, but Patty's at home with a headache," Bruce said, his smile not quite making it to his eyes. He seemed haunted. "Can I come in? I see you're not alone." He sounded slightly relieved.

Faith glanced over her shoulder at the boys, who had come up behind her. She felt Sam grab on to the back of her blouse.

Bruce waited quietly, leaning over to greet Jay's sons. "Hi, guys."

"Hi, Mr. Young," both Andy and Sam replied.

Finally, she stepped aside and gestured for him to enter. "Sure. Come on in."

He carefully stepped into the cottage. It seemed to have suddenly gotten smaller, and the pipes in the cottage groaned eerily. He glanced around. "I thought I'd come to visit. Make sure you've settled in all right. I understand why you decided to move, but it's not the same without you at the house."

"The atmosphere is probably a lot more cheery," Faith joked.

Bruce didn't laugh, just pushed his glasses up the bridge of his nose, his brown eyes serious. "It's never cheery. It's expensive. It's white. But it's not cheery."

He wandered around, his hand clasped behind his back respectfully as he studied Becky's antiques. "Cozy." He smiled slightly. "I can see what attracted you to the place."

"Faith!" Sam tugged on her shirt.

"What is it, Sam?"

"My tummy feels funny."

Faith stared down at Sam in alarm. He hadn't had any "funny" tummy incidents for at least a week. "It's okay, Sammy. We'll play the game soon."

Sam eyed Bruce suspiciously.

"Would you like to sit down? Andy, why don't you take Sam into the big bedroom and play a game with him."

"No-o-o," Sam whined. "I want to play with you."

"Well, I'm going to talk to Mr. Young now, so you'll have to wait or play with Andy in the bedroom."

Bruce had moved to one side so Faith could resolve Sam's issue.

Sam wasn't happy but he agreed to play with Andy.

Faith sat perched on the edge of one of Becky's straight-back dining room chairs. "Have a seat, Bruce," she offered. She could be friendly. She was in her own little space and the children were right in the next room.

Bruce hesitated and then sat on the couch.

They stared at each other for a long time. Andy and Sam started arguing and even that was a welcome relief from the silence.

"I hear you spent the night with Jay," Bruce finally blurted out.

Faith tried not to be surprised. She'd hoped for an exchange running along the lines of the lovely weather they'd been having for mid-February or a new banana-nut bread recipe he'd had that he really wanted to share with her. Becky's cottage somehow engendered such conversations. Just yesterday, Bess had dropped by with the sheets and they'd chatted for a few minutes, leaving Faith with a lovely sense of community.

Faith shrugged. "That's one version."

"Patty wasn't happy," Bruce said almost abstract-edly, his eyes flitting around the room. He looked nervous, wiping the palms of his hands on his tan pants.

"Why doesn't that surprise me?" Faith asked.

"She's got a lot invested in Jay and Amanda getting together."

"And what do you think?" Faith was curious about her brother-in-law's take on the whole situation.

"I think the two of you are adults." Bruce paused. "So does this mean you're planning on staying?"

"Faith, my tummy feels real bad," Sam said from the doorway. He shuffled over to her, then leaned against her, his neck craned back so she wouldn't miss his pitiful look.

She felt his forehead. It was sweaty.

Faith bent over. "Sweetie, how come? There's nothing happening to make your tummy feel bad."

But Sam didn't answer. He shook his head and gulped air.

CHAPTER TEN

FAITH CROUCHED NEXT to Sam and asked bluntly, "This isn't because Mr. Young is visiting and you want to play a game?"

"He's fine," Andy said, coming up behind him. "Aren't you, puke chunk?"

He gave Sam a light shove as if to prove it.

Sam gulped for air and hit back at the same time. That told Faith everything she wanted to know.

"Don't call your brother a puke chunk," Faith said automatically, as she pushed Sam's hair from his forehead. He still felt damp, but not feverish. She put her hands on Sam's shoulders and started to steer him toward the kitchen. "Let's get you fizzy water for your stomach." She looked apologetically at Bruce, who stood up as if that were his cue. "Sorry, Bruce. Duty calls."

"Is he okay?" Bruce asked.

"Yes," Faith said quietly to Bruce, although she knew that big ears were listening. "I think he's going to be fine."

Faith walked the four strides to the kitchen and opened the small refrigerator. It was brand-new, compliments of Gil and Lee. She fished around for some sparkling water and some apple juice concentrate.

"Can I have some, too?" Andy asked from behind her.

"Do you want some, Bruce?" Faith called.

Bruce shook his head, looking distinctly out of sorts, as if he were caught in a movie that held no interest for him.

She filled two of Becky's crystal goblets with ice and mixed an apple juice cocktail for the boys. Miraculously Sam's stomach felt better and both he and Andy gently took the goblets she handed to them. "Use two hands, Sam. And be very careful. Those were your mom's. And use a coaster."

"Let's play this game," Sam said hopefully, putting the goblet on a leather coaster. He then quickly held up the Memory box, nearly knocking over the goblet. He looked at Bruce.

"Not now." Faith shook her head. "We still have company."

"No, no. I was just leaving," Bruce replied hurriedly. "I'll see you at Gil's."

"You're welcome to stay."

"No. I can see that you've got your hands full." Bruce kept talking as he left. "Play your game, Faith."

"What did Mr. Young want?" Andy asked as he sipped his drink.

Faith smiled inwardly, noticing that Andy was extremely gentle with the glass. Jay would have never believed he could trust his boys with something so precious as their mother's crystal.

"I don't know, Andy. I think he just wanted to see what the cottage looks like." Faith really didn't know, but she planned to avoid future conversations with him.

"Let's play Memory," Sam tried again, now that company was officially gone.

"That's for babies," Andy commented, but Faith noticed he had taken the box from Sam and was now laying the old cardboard cards with their blue backs faceup on the small coffee table.

"Is Dad taking you to that party for your mom and dad?" Andy asked when she sat on the floor with them.

"I don't know."

"How can you not know?" Sam flipped two cards over and quickly flipped them back.

"Sam, you've got to show us what's on the cards or it's cheating," Andy protested.

Sam stuck out his tongue at Andy but showed the cards as he was supposed to. "It's a shoe and a tiger."

Satisfied, Andy went next. "A girl and a rotten apple."

"That's not a rotten apple," Faith observed. "It's cubist art. Wait, Sam, it's my turn." She kept him from turning over more cards and flipped two cards. "A horse's head and a fish."

"That fish looks like the rotten apple," Sam commented.

"So how come you're not going with my dad?" That was from Andy.

"Don't you like us?" That was from Sam.

Faith stared at the two boys, emotions churning inside her. "Of course I like you."

"Enough to be our mom?" Sam asked.

Andy smacked at Sam. "She can't be our mom unless she and Dad get married."

"Why don't they?"

"Why don't you, Faith?" Andy asked.

"Because he hasn't asked me." Faith tried to make her voice light.

"Would'ja marry him if he asked?"

Faith didn't know how to answer.

"You prob'ly won't marry our dad because of us," Andy commented skeptically.

Faith furrowed her brow. "If I wasn't going to marry your dad, it would be because I didn't love him. You would be two very good reasons to marry him."

"Really?"

"Really."

"Do you love him?" Sam's nose was just inches from her. He balanced himself by resting a small hand on her shoulder.

"I don't think that's any of your business, buster," Faith joked, then grabbed him around the waist and pulled him into her lap. Sam giggled and snuggled in closer to her.

"I'd be nice to Sam," Andy said suddenly.

"What?" Faith asked, giving Sam a tight hug, until he squirmed out of her lap. "You'd do that for me?"

"If you stayed, I'd be nice to Sam more often."

Faith shook her head regretfully. "Thanks so much for the offer, but I can't let you make that promise. I think it goes against the very grain of your being."

Andy frowned.

Faith didn't like the frown, so she added gently, "I'll stay with you guys as long as I can and I'll make sure that your father hires a good replacement for me.''

Andy was silent for a long time. Then he looked up, the dark lashes fringing his blue, blue eyes, his father's eyes. ''You promise?''

Faith nodded.

''Would you promise something else?'' Andy asked, his voice very serious.

Faith looked at him warily. ''Depends on what it is.''

''Do you promise that if you do love him, you'll stay with us?''

''That's a good promise,'' Sam agreed. ''Make that promise.''

THE NEXT WEEKS FLEW BY for Faith, faster than she really wanted. While she was living with Patty, three months had seemed like an eternity, but now between the renovation of the cottage and caring for Andy and Sam, Faith found herself slipping into a very stable routine, one filled with more pleasure than she had experienced for a long time.

She was eagerly welcomed into the Whitfield family, having been issued a permanent invitation to dinner. And sometimes in the evenings if Jay came home early to be with the boys, Bess and Phoebe would meet Faith at the cottage, where they'd sit around studying decorating and antique books, sharing ideas and comparing paint strips. Faith even noticed herself becoming envious of Phoebe's growing belly and her profound connection to her husband, Mitch. For the first time in her adult life, Faith deeply regretted that she would never have children of her own.

She hadn't had much opportunity to talk privately to Jay, though. He worked in frenzied spurts, and the times that he had free, Faith left him alone with the boys so he could focus on them. She still hadn't given him an answer to his generous offer to escort her to her parents' bash. At first, she simply needed time to think. Later, he was busy and there never seemed to be an appropriate time to mention it. There were more pressing concerns to talk about. Like Sam's need for new shoes or Andy's dental appointment or what Jay wanted in a nanny, because whether Faith wanted to face it or not, her time with the Whitfields was quickly running out. She and Jay traded information in quick little snatches, because she'd also taken on the duty of "message lady" for his council duties.

It was difficult for Faith to say to him, "Sam got really car sick, so I had to have the back seat of the station wagon professionally cleaned, and Phil Mendes wants you to call him back about the project development 100-209a, and, oh, by the way, I'd love for you to take me to my parents' anniversary party." What she needed was some private time with him so they could discuss all the ramifications of his offer. But talking about it also meant discussing what was going to happen after the party, after Jay had filed his last tax return, after the new nanny was hired. The last thing Faith wanted to hear was "goodbye."

JAY LOOKED UP FROM the documents he was studying and wondered if he was ever going to get an answer from Faith. It'd been well over a month, in fact, nearly six weeks, since he had asked to escort her to her parents' anniversary party. April 10 was approaching fast and the tax deadline followed right behind that. Then Faith would be gone.

She'd already placed an ad in the local paper advertising for a full-time nanny-housekeeper and was sending out feelers for names she could follow up on. What a good employee. She was helping to find a replacement for herself. But since he hadn't heard *anything* from her about the party, not a yes, not a no, he wondered what lay beneath her silence.

Granted, he hardly ever saw her because he and his staff had been busy with the March 1 deadline for farmers. In the month after that, he'd handled a few tax emergencies, spent a few quality days with his sons, only to start again on the long hours. The next thing he'd known, he'd received his official invite to the anniversary party, which listed him as the master of ceremonies. Debbie, his office manager, had ordered his tux, but he still wasn't sure if he had a date.

It was partly his fault. He hadn't reissued his invitation, but he hadn't retracted it, either. He didn't think she would have forgotten, but it was almost as if she'd put a damper on any small embers that could be smoldering between them. Not that he necessary wanted embers. He just wanted to explore the possibility of embers. Trouble was, ember-exploring was time-consuming, and he and Faith had developed a delicate routine in which they passed the boys and information concerning the boys back and forth between them like hot potatoes. After she'd briefed him, she'd shrug into her jacket, her shift finished.

By now, Patty and Faith seemed to have come to some unspoken truce, as everyone got on with their lives. Even Patty couldn't sustain an active hostility for so many weeks. Besides, Faith was no longer a novelty. She was regularly seen with Sam and Andy, attending many of their school activities, helping out in their classroom. Jay had also discovered that she was volunteering two mornings a week at the public library.

Did he care if she said yes or no? It wasn't like he was going to find another date. He would do what he had done for all the other events he'd gone to over the past five years.

Go stag.

He wasn't even sure what had come over him in the first place. He grunted. He supposed he did have some primal urge to protect Faith, but mostly he wanted to knock her over the head with a club and drag her into his cave, so they'd have a chance to figure out how deep their feelings ran. *A pity date.* Her words still burned. Far from it. If anyone could take care of herself, Faith could.

"Your father's on line one." Debbie poked her head in his office door.

Jay nodded and picked up the phone. "Dad."

"I just wanted to let you know that Stink'll take the kids next Saturday night."

"What are you talking about?"

"The Weavers' party. Of course, Bess and I are going to be there, so I can't sit, but Stink doesn't want to go. He'll take the boys, so you and Faith can have a nice evening together. If Phoebe hasn't dropped the kid yet, he might take the twins as well and let Mitch and Phoebe have a romantic evening out.''

Jay felt his color rise. ''Me and Faith?''

''Yes. I heard you were taking her to the anniversary party.''

''Where'd you hear that?''

''Oh, around.'' Gil chuckled. ''It'll be just like old times.''

Damn, Jay felt himself flush. He mentally flogged Faith.

Why was it Gil knew something he didn't? Had she told his father she was going but hadn't bothered to tell him?

As Jay listened, Amanda Perkins appeared in his doorway. Jay waved her in. ''Dad, I've got someone here, so I can't talk.''

''So you'll mark it down on the calendar?''

''Sure, yes, I guess so.''

''The boys want to make sure that you and Faith get to have your 'alone' time together. They wanted to spend the night, okay?'' His father wasn't subtle.

''Yeah, sure,'' he responded cautiously. Why did he feel as if he was being set up? Was Faith trying to make their evening something it wasn't? Yes, he would like to escort her. No, he wasn't planning to sleep with her. Is that what she was planning? How the hell would he know what she was planning? She hadn't said ''boo'' to him.

''Have them bring their sleeping bags. They can camp out in the yard, if it's not too cold.''

"We'll see," Jay hedged, schooling his tone to be patient, rolling his eyes to Amanda, who suppressed a giggle. "I've got someone waiting, Dad. Talk to you soon." Jay hung up and smiled at Amanda. "My father."

"Gil taking the boys this weekend?"

"Uh, no. Stink, er, Lee is for next Saturday. Dad's going to the Weavers' party." Jay smiled at her politely, but gave a vague wave of his hand because merely mentioning the party to Amanda made him uncomfortable.

"I know," Amanda said with a smile, her eyes expectant. "We received their RSVP last week."

"So what can I do for you?" He turned his full attention on Amanda, whose face broke into a million-dollar smile.

Jay couldn't help liking Amanda Perkins. He knew she wanted something more than a platonic relationship, but even if she made casseroles his kids would eat, or if she could make Andy and Sam laugh the way Faith did, or if Faith hadn't reappeared in his life, he still wouldn't be able to generate anything more than a friendly affection for Amanda.

In fact, that affection was so bland that however physically attractive Amanda was, however much she flattered him with her not-too-subtle advances, all he felt was the gut response of a younger brother when asked if he liked his older sister.

Some men might think about Amanda in more than sisterly terms, Jay realized. Her light green spring shift fit her slender shape well and was very complimentary to her eyes. Her lips were full and probably kissable.

But Jay still tossed up a quick prayer to the goddess of hope that Amanda's visit concerned a leaky recreation facility, an ill-timed stoplight or a donation for a charity event. Not the Weavers' party.

"Speaking of the Weavers' anniversary party," Amanda replied briskly. "I was just wondering if you're hard up for a date. After all, since you're going to be the emcee, it's hardly appropriate that you go alone."

She was sitting on the edge of her seat, leaning forward, both hands on the smooth wood of his desk. "I thought it was time we took our relationship to the next level. Since it seems like you're never going to ask me out, I'll ask you." She gave him a bright smile, the curve of her lips dancing, as her eyes regarded him seriously.

Apparently, the hope goddess had switched sides. Jay groaned to himself. How could he tell Amanda that if he had wanted to go with her, he would have asked her?

Jay smiled cautiously back and said, "Um, Amanda…"

Amanda looked away, as if to ward off his rejection. Then, cheeks flushed, she turned back and asked boldly, "So what do you say, Jay? It'll be a lot of fun."

What could he say?

He'd already invited someone else. If he was in a better mood, he might be amused by the irony. He'd invited someone who hadn't yet accepted the invitation. And now Amanda had issued another invitation.

"Earth to Jay."

Jay shifted his focus back to Amanda, who watched him with such hope he thought he could actually see the bodice of her dress move with the quick beating of her heart.

"I'm sorry, Amanda," he said regretfully, hating the fact that her face fell and her smile had turned into a forced twist of her lips.

"So it's true?" Amanda asked as she stoically absorbed his quiet rejection.

"What's true?"

"That you're taking Faith."

Jay regarded Amanda for a long moment.

"How did you hear that?" he asked quietly, feeling a small coal of annoyance at Faith spark to life. He hadn't told anyone, but if his father knew and Amanda knew, then the whole town knew, including Patty. He wondered why this irritated him so much. He hadn't thought to swear Faith to secrecy, but it'd been a long time since he'd had to guard against such private inquiries. In the past five years, despite being a public figure, he'd become a master at keeping his private life private. Of course, since Becky died, he hadn't had much of a private life, but that didn't make him feel any better.

He was used to and even mostly enjoyed standing in the grocery store, taking notes while people questioned why the lights on Pacheco Boulevard weren't synchronized correctly, fielding complaints about the condition of the swimming pool locker rooms or the cracked cement in front of the city museum. But this new sensation of people knowing more about his personal life than he did was disconcerting, almost alarming.

"It's a small town, Jay." She gave a forced laugh. "Don't you think people know when your old girlfriend comes into town and spends nights with you?"

Jay stared down at his appointment book. "I don't think that's any of your business."

"Really?" Amanda asked in surprise. Obviously, she hadn't expected such an answer.

"Really," Jay replied.

The tension in his office prickled and Jay hated that because he truly had considered Amanda a friend. She'd been there, helping and supportive, during Becky's illness. After, she had been a friendly visitor even before her separation. When she was officially divorced, she wasn't shy about what she wanted.

She wanted him.

But it had been too soon for him to date anyone then. Five years later still felt "too soon." But apparently it wasn't too soon to blurt out invitations he regretted later. This was highly ironic, given that in all this time, he had carefully chosen his words lest Amanda or any other interested woman misinterpret his friendliness.

"I didn't know you very well back then," Amanda said, trying another tack. "But I do know what it was like after Faith left."

"What what was like?" He could hear his voice cool.

Amanda shifted in discomfort, but answered hotly, "What your life was like."

"And how do you know that?" He leaned back in

his chair and propped his elbows on the armrests, carefully bringing the tips of his fingers together. He looked at her over the tent his fingers made.

She sat back as well.

"Patty told me," Amanda admitted. "You were absolutely miserable. Because you'd proposed, and she rejected you by sleeping with Bruce."

"Is that so?" Jay feigned neutrality, praying that Amanda believed his casual attitude. He felt his ears burn. After Faith left he'd heard rumors that Faith had slept with Bruce, but pride had never allowed him to fully believe it—though it did eat at him. Was that why she'd left? Suddenly, all sorts of conversations made sense to him. Patty had always talked to him as if he'd accepted the rumors as fact. Faith and Bruce? Impossible. Faith would never choose Bruce over him. She'd told him as much that first day at the cottage.

"So what makes you think she's any different now?"

Have you changed? His words and Faith's expression closing on him came back with a slap. As soon as he'd asked that, their conversation had come to a screeching halt.

"She's only going to hurt you again," Amanda whispered. "She wasn't here when Becky died, she wasn't here when you were campaigning for office, she wasn't here for your victory party. She wasn't here for any of it. She wasn't here for you...."

I was.

The small words hung unspoken between them.

The silence lasted a full minute before Amanda finally rose. She had the look of someone who knew she had gone too far but was glad she had.

"You may still love her, Jay, but there's no guarantee she's going to stick around much past finding you a new nanny."

"I'm sorry, Amanda." Jay stood, too.

Amanda wouldn't look at him but managed to plaster a strained smile on her face. "I just said it because I care about you."

"I know you do and I appreciate that you were so honest with me," Jay said soothingly. He rounded the desk and put out a hand to give her a clumsy pat on her shoulder.

"I guess I'll see you at the party."

Jay nodded. "I'm sure you will."

They stared at each other awkwardly.

"Well, I better be going."

"Amanda, I really am sorry."

"Me, too," Amanda said with a shrug, and moved swiftly out of the room.

Jay sunk back into his chair, unable to sort through the emotions churning through him. *Nothing, not one damn thing, has ever been easy around you.* His words haunted him. He hadn't lied. Faith was nothing but trouble. His impulse to ask her out had just been the trick of the morning light. He looked at the phone. He could just call her and tell her that due to unforeseen circumstances, he wouldn't be able to take her. Then he'd call Amanda and ask her. That would be the right thing to do.

For whom?

Jay shook his head and grabbed the phone receiver.

He punched in the numbers for the cottage, annoyed that he'd already memorized Faith's phone number, and then stopped. He hung up the phone. Some things were better said in person. He ignored the huge pile of documents on his desk, though he did shove three files into his briefcase.

"I'm going for lunch now," he told Debbie as he walked out the front door. "I don't know when I'll be back."

CARRYING A SMALL BAG of groceries, Faith slowed her pace when she spotted Jay's sedan parked in the driveway. She'd had a busy morning. She'd met with Sam's teacher about chaperoning a field trip to the Hershey's chocolate factory in Oakdale and gone to get a prescription for Andy's allergies, which were starting to act up. But busy as she had been, Jay hadn't been far from her thoughts.

She'd received her invitation to her parents' party on Friday and had spent the entire weekend pacing through the cottage, her hand on the phone to call Jay and give him her answer. Finally she'd decided it would be best to refuse him face-to-face. She'd figured on tonight, if he came home for dinner.

She had rehearsed her words many times. *Jay, we're just friends, so let's go separately to the dinner.* She liked to think she'd come to this decision on her own. But it was heavily influenced by Sam and Andy, who still actively nurtured the idea that she and Jay would get together. Having a date with their father right before she was going to leave would be just plain cruel. It was better for both of them if they went separately.

When she reached Jay's car, she was surprised to see Jay sitting in the driver's seat, tie loosened, briefcase open, papers spread all around him. He looked very harried and not at all comfortable. He was also wearing reading glasses, giving him an intellectual demeanor that was unfamiliar. In the past two months, she'd never seen him at work. She rapped on the roof and he looked up, startled.

"Hey, there," she greeted him, bending over to poke her head through the passenger window.

"Faith, we need to talk." Jay appeared irritated, caught off guard, his voice clipped and harsh.

She regarded him warily. Surely there was nothing she'd done wrong. Not when her morning chores had consisted of volunteering for a field trip, picking up a prescription and buying veggies for dinner.

"Sure. You want to talk here or do you want to come in?" She glanced up at the house.

Jay pushed aside his papers and took his glasses off, laying them on the passenger seat. "I'll come in."

"Can I ask why you're in the car and not in the house?"

"I was waiting for you." He sounded distinctly irritated, especially when he added, "I thought you were at the cottage."

"And you couldn't wait in the house? You do live there, after all."

"Too hard to move it all. My car's set up for work."

She'd noticed that. No front-seat passengers for him. That space was reserved for the IRS and the city council.

Faith smiled over her shoulder and pushed the key in the door, to let him into his own house. It didn't feel strange. The truth was she spent more time there than he did. She went directly to the kitchen to put the groceries away. He silently followed her and she became very self-conscious. It was the first time they'd been truly alone in six weeks.

"Would you like some apple juice, lemonade or iced tea?"

He looked surprised, as if he didn't know his refrigerator contained such things. After a moment, he replied, "Iced tea, please."

Faith took two tall glasses and filled Jay's with generous amounts of ice and equally generous amounts of sugar. If she remembered rightly, he liked his drinks really sweet. She poured herself some lemonade. Taking a deep breath, she resolved to stay calm, to smile no matter what he said. She felt better when he looked up and smiled, easing the grim lines around his eyes.

"Do you want to talk in the family room?"

He nodded, and she went ahead of him, settling in the rocking chair. "So how can I help you?" Faith asked faintly.

JAY WATCHED HER NERVOUSLY fiddle with her glass of lemonade. He didn't feel like drinking the iced tea, so he carefully set it in front of him.

"I hear you're going with me to your parents' party," he said, his voice betraying a little of his irritation.

Faith raised an eyebrow. "Oh, really. Where'd you hear that?"

"My father." A moment later. "Amanda."

Faith looked at him in surprise. "Your father?" Faith paused as if digesting the information, then asked, "Amanda said I was going with you?"

"My father called to say that Stink'll take the kids so we can have some 'privacy,' and Amanda wanted to confirm whether or not the rumors I was taking you were true. You wouldn't have an explanation for this, would you?" His tone was accusing. "Seems everyone knows. I wonder how that happened?"

She paled slightly and then shook her head. "I have no idea."

Jay wasn't sure he believed her.

"So, are the rumors true?" Faith asked.

"I don't know. Are they?" He couldn't help feel a tad impatient. "The party's next weekend."

Faith bit her lip. "I was going to let you know soon."

"When?"

"Today or tomorrow."

"Or never."

Faith gave him a considering stare. "I would have answered you. It just never seemed to be the right time."

Jay acknowledged that with a nod of his head. She had a point. "So now it's the right time. Are you or are you not going with me?" The question just slipped out.

Jay tensed as Faith looked at him helplessly, like she didn't know what to answer. He tried to read her face, but it was bleak. She moved uneasily in the rocker, using her toes to push the chair back and forth, back and forth.

"There's a small problem," Faith finally said, as if stalling for time.

"Problem?" Jay felt several small fingers of dread creep up the back of his neck. "What do you mean, a small problem?"

Faith leaned forward. "Actually, two small problems. Andy and Sam."

"What do Andy and Sam have to do with this?"

"They want us to get married."

Jay swallowed hard. Of course, the boys were getting very attached to Faith, but—

"I just don't think we should get their hopes up," Faith said, her voice faint. "I'm leaving right after the party, so if they see us go out on a date, they might get the wrong impression. In fact, many people might get the wrong impression. It would be easier—"

Jay made an impatient noise. "This isn't about what is easiest."

"It's not?" Faith asked curiously.

"No." Jay took a deep breath, his mind racing. She was right. It was easier to go stag. It would be easier for the boys to accept Faith's departure if they didn't go out on a date. But Jay knew he spoke the truth. This evening was too important to allow what was "easiest" to make their decision for them. He shook his head. "It's not."

She gave him a wistful half smile. "Then what is it about?"

"It's about whether you want to go with me," he said simply.

"Do you still want me to go?"

Of course, I do almost slipped out before he caught himself. She was looking at him intently, her expression uncertain. A wave of respect for her washed over him. Faith was giving him an out, a way to gracefully uninvite her. Suddenly, he didn't want to back out. He was tired of going stag. He was tired of going home alone, feeling the emptiness of the house engulf him. He wanted to take Faith. He wanted her whether she was trouble or not, because just like the boys, he'd become attached to her, and deep down he wanted to trust her and, more important, wanted her to trust him.

"You know, I understand if it's too hard to take me," she said more specifically. She swallowed a big gulp of lemonade and then fiddled with her nails.

"Too hard?"

"On you. We know we're just friends, but if the town thinks something has been rekindled and that's going to put you in an awkward position..." Her voice trailed off. Then she gave him a bright grin, frank and reassuring. "If you don't want to take me, I'm not going to get my feelings hurt. In fact, I've just been trying to think of a way to tell you I don't want to go with you."

THOSE WERE THE MOST painful words that had ever come out of Faith's mouth—especially since she knew they were lies. Her feelings would be dreadfully hurt because she *did* want to go with him. But she wouldn't disrupt Jay's very ordered life. She didn't want Andy and Sam to believe that she and Jay would fall in love. She didn't want to get *her* hopes up. What they shared was more a leftover attraction from their high school days than anything else.

In two weeks, she would be packing up her car, moving on to another job, another city, and she didn't want to think about the fact that she would never be the room mother for Sam's class or teach Andy to drive. She would never wake up to feel Jay next to her, his warm body close, his long legs entwined with hers. She swallowed hard as the implications of her decision struck her with the force of a fist to the chest.

She got up abruptly. "Excuse me a minute," she said, and went to the kitchen, angling her back to Jay, trying to compose herself.

A sob erupted out of nowhere, dry heaves at first, then the tears of the past eighteen years, more tears than she'd ever allowed herself to cry. The tears she should have cried when she realized there was never any going back. All those times when she'd slept in deserted bus stations and then later in her car, anxiously waiting for the next town to bring her a sense of peace. She cried for the pressing loneliness she felt even when surrounded by her sister and her family and worst of all, for her complete distrust in human nature, which ran so deep that even when love looked her in the eye, she couldn't reach out to take it.

CHAPTER ELEVEN

JAY SAT IN THE FAMILY ROOM, listened to Faith weep, bawl really, in the kitchen and wondered what he should do. If it were Becky, he'd immediately seek her out, then pull her into his arms even though she almost always resisted, until she finally relaxed and her sobs turned to adorable little sniffles broken by the occasional hiccup. Then he'd raise Becky's face and kiss her on both eyes, then her red nose, before settling on her lips, which would cling as if his mouth was a lifeline. If he'd been the one to make her cry, he'd apologize, hugging her closely. If he wasn't, he'd just rock her, gently pressing her to his heart. That's what he'd do if it was Becky in the kitchen sounding as if her heart was permanently broken. But that wasn't Becky and he had no right to comfort Faith with kisses or tenderness.

Even if he did, he wasn't sure he could. Doing so was sure to make him feel unfaithful to Becky—justifiably or not. Even though, death did them part, even though he could take new vows, and he and Becky had talked about his meeting someone else, he'd never been able to imagine anyone filling her space.

Until now.

So he sat and waited. Thankfully, the sobbing soon

subsided and he heard the water running. He waited some more until Faith emerged.

"I guess I needed that," she said cheerfully, trying to make light of her distress, although her red and puffy eyes told a different story.

"You okay?" he asked as he stole another glance at her face. Suddenly, despite her paleness, Faith looked much the same as she always did, not at all inclined to give him the briefest glimpse of her soul.

"You know, we can both go, but not go together," she suggested.

"What?"

"You go alone, I go alone and then we meet up at the party."

"We probably wouldn't sit together." Jay wasn't too sure he liked this idea.

"Well, we'd be apart, anyway. You're the master of ceremonies."

"No."

"No, what?"

"If you're going to be there and I'm going to be there, I want us to be there together."

FAITH WAS INCREASINGLY SAD. *We pay for every decision we make, one way or another.* Jay's words rang in her ears. It was true. She couldn't do this to Jay even if she loved him, loved his children. No kindhearted person could intentionally build hope where there was none. Her longing for a family, for *Jay,* came from the fact she was flattered by the way he couldn't stop looking at her. He'd given her relief by offering her the job, treated her like a member of the family, showing the people around him that she wasn't trouble with a capital *T*. Jay *trusted* her and that meant something.

She would like nothing better than to go to her parents' party on Jay's arm, bask in his acceptance, no matter how many eyebrows it raised. But the last thing in the world she wanted to do was hurt him or his children. And one way or another Jay would be hurt by his decision to take her, if he expected the date to build into something more tangible, more real. She took a deep breath.

"I'm leaving as soon as tax season's over. I've told the boys as much," Faith said carefully.

"Will you be here next Saturday for your parents' anniversary party?" Jay asked.

Faith looked away. "Of course I will. I promised them."

"Then there's not a problem."

Faith felt her resolve slip. It was so real, so tangible, the connection between them. It was as if they'd been doing this forever, not just the past few weeks. What was wrong with acknowledging that connection?

"Patty'd really hate it if I went with you," Faith ventured. "She thinks I'm going to ruin your life."

"Really." Jay's voice was flat, his blue eyes calculating. "This has nothing to do with Patty or Amanda or my father. This has to do with you and me. I'm managing my life just fine, thank you, so I think you shouldn't worry about that."

"But I do worry. I worry that when I leave, you'll be hurt. Your children will be hurt."

And if I can't stay, I'll be hurt.

Jay was silent for a long time, his face inscrutable. Faith held her breath. Maybe she had gone too far.

Finally, he said, his voice gruff, "Faith, I don't think we could be more hurt than when I lost my wife and my children lost their mother. If we survived Becky's death, we certainly can survive any fallout, real or imagined, from taking you to a party."

"You might be sacrificing your casseroles."

"Andy, especially, would kiss your feet." There was a familiar twinkle in his eyes.

She searched his face looking for guidance, surprised to find the handsome angles of it held perfectly still, giving him an almost impassive quality. This was part of the new Jay that she continued to have trouble getting used to. He was now a confident, inscrutable man, not the teenager who'd worn his heart on his sleeve when he'd eagerly pulled out the ring with the diamond chip so small, she could barely see it.

"Let's just do it," Jay had said.

"Do what?" She hadn't been able to stop staring at the ring.

"Get married. We both got scholarships. We can live in married-student housing."

"No."

"No?" Jay had laughed. "What do you mean no?"

"I mean no." Faith had felt her voice rise an octave in emotional panic. "I'm not going to college, I'm not going to marry you—"

"You can't mean—"

"Yes, I can—"

"But what about us?"

"There won't be an us," Faith had said emphati-

cally, feeling tears clog her eyes. She was being smothered by her parents, by Jay and his responsibilities, by Patty's judgmental edicts. "I don't want to be an us. I don't want to go to college. I don't want to be Patty. I want to be me. I want to see the world."

"It's all the same."

"How do you know that?"

"Because it's all about love."

It wasn't anymore. Faith returned her gaze to Jay. If it *was* about love, Jay wouldn't be so detached. Trouble was, she couldn't tell what it *was* about.

But maybe, just maybe, it could be about love, a small voice murmured.

Faith held her breath, willing an answer to come to her.

Do you promise that if you love him, you'll stay with us?

"Sure," she said, barely able to make the word audible.

Jay blinked. "Sure, what?"

She looked up and smiled. "Sure, Whitfield. I'll go with you."

JAY WAS STUNNED at the brightness of her smile. It radiated out from her and warmed him, filling him with something akin to homemade soup on a cold day or socks straight from the dryer. It was a feeling he hadn't experienced in a long time—since Becky, and he had forgotten how good it was.

"Good. I'll pick you up at six next Saturday."

Faith nodded, then glanced quickly at the kitchen clock. "You should be getting back."

He stood reluctantly as Faith whisked his glass away.

"Uh, Jay?" she said over the running water.

"Yes?"

"How far from formal do you think I can be before Patty blows a gasket?"

Jay experienced just a twinge of indecision. "Well," he said lightly. "I'll be in a tux. Wear something to match it."

JAY ADJUSTED THE COLLAR of his starched white shirt and waited on the front porch of the small cottage. He'd already rung the bell twice. He knew she was home because he heard shuffling. He turned his gaze to his father's dairy and tried not to feel stupid waiting on the doorstep of a cottage he'd conceived two children in.

After she'd accepted his invitation, he and Faith had spent the next two weeks not referring to that day. It was almost as if they both thought that if they did talk, they'd jinx themselves. As Faith had predicted, Sam and Andy were ecstatic, assuring him in no uncertain terms that they wouldn't object if he decided to ask Faith to become their new mother.

All the while he'd worked nonstop on taxes and tried not to dwell on the tiny bit of misgiving that disappeared every time he saw or talked with Faith. It was the oddest sensation. When he was away from Faith he couldn't remember why he had asked her out in the first place. She was really nothing more than an old sweetheart turned nanny, who reminded him to buy milk or informed him that his sons didn't wash.

But when he was with her, he couldn't seem to resist her. There was something special about her that he didn't believe had anything to do with their past history.

At some point, he'd realized the high school Faith was long gone. And it was the new Faith that intrigued him. She was like a familiar hiking trail grown over, mysterious, tantalizing, unknown, with secrets that she would trust to no one. Then the evening arrived. With the boys clucking their approval at the way he looked, he loaded them into the car for their sleepover with Lee. When he'd dropped off the boys, Sam had whispered loudly, "Be sure that you're *nice*."

With a wink, Stinky flipped him the keys to the old Cadillac, the same one he'd taken Faith to the prom in. "Dad says maybe you'll have better luck tonight than you had eighteen years ago."

Jay had actually flushed. Contrary to popular opinion, he had no intention, no intention at all of asking Faith to marry him.

After the third ring, Faith answered the door, out of breath.

Jay felt his heart sink.

She was wearing a pair of old sweats and she looked as if she'd just finished a cleaning marathon. Without a smidgen of makeup on her face, Faith stood before him, her hair hanging in wet curls.

"Hi," he said.

"Hi. I'll be just a minute," Faith said, her face beet red. "I didn't realize it had gotten so late."

"Do your parents have a ride?"

"Patty picked them up an hour ago. I guess she

wanted to make sure they got there on time." She pulled the door open wider. "Come on in. Have a seat. I won't be long." Then she disappeared into the bedroom.

"Take your time," Jay said to the small living room. Even though every piece of furniture was Becky's, it didn't feel like the old cottage. He spied their old Monopoly and Memory games. They'd played those with Andy for hours. He waited for the pain of the memories. But there was nothing, nothing but a pleasant feeling of nostalgia.

Faith had done a ton of work on the cottage. She had hung miniblinds and taken out the old-fashioned draperies Becky had preferred, rearranged the furniture, so the larger pieces were flush along the wall. Gone was the ridiculous shag carpet Becky liked so much, but then waged bitter war with when it swallowed up her earrings, contact lenses and bits of small crayons. In its place was the beautiful hardwood floor burnished to warm brown.

Aside from the hard work she'd obviously put into restoring the cottage, Faith displayed no knickknacks, no hint that she'd like to stay beyond the remaining week. It'd been a long time since he'd nursed that heart she'd broken. He'd moved on from it, loved and married Becky. So why was he sitting there nervously, as if he was on the brink of something, well, wonderful? He mentally kicked himself. Okay, potentially wonderful.

Andy and Sam were rubbing off on him.

Faith was a good companion, was great with his children, had a frank, observant way of talking, but that wasn't enough for him. He wanted all of Faith, not just the parts she was willing to share. That decided, he sat and waited.

And waited.

And waited.

He glanced at his watch and fiddled with the corsage box.

And waited some more.

Nearly forty-five minutes later Faith called out. "Jay?"

"Yes?" He rose, his back creaking. Finally.

"I think you should just go without me."

Sensation flooded through Jay. Relief? Disappointment? He couldn't tell, but he was sure he didn't like it.

"Why? Faith, this is your parents' anniversary dinner."

"This isn't working," she said vaguely.

"What's not working?"

"This. This whole thing. This evening. I don't think it's a good idea if I go."

"Oh." Jay looked at his watch. Patty's head was probably starting to swell under the pressure. He'd promised to be early to greet the guests, who would be arriving in barely twenty minutes. Good thing he'd padded his timing with Faith.

"So you should just go." Her voice sounded strained and hopeful at the same time.

"Uh. Sure."

SURE?

Faith leaned up against the back of the bedroom

door, hiding from Jay, wrestling with the overwhelming anxiety sweeping through her.

He'd been so handsome in his tuxedo, nervously holding a gold foil corsage box, waiting at the door to be let into his own home. The flashback to their prom night was swift, sudden. True, his tuxedo wasn't powder blue as it had been eighteen years earlier, but then again, the eyes that smoldered with some undefined emotion weren't eighteen-year-old eyes, either.

She looked down at her sparkly shoes and the fitted dress and felt like a fraud. Patty had warned her. As long as she was relegated to the role of Jay's hired help, she could pretend she was just helping out a friend, she could pretend the tiny pinpricks of jealousy that poked her when she saw him smile at Amanda meant nothing. But having him *here,* dressed in a tux and patiently waiting for her, changed everything.

They weren't just going to the movies. They were going to her parents' anniversary party, a three-hundred-plus-person event. She should have never accepted his invitation, no matter how much she wanted to. Nothing good could come from dating him, kissing him, raising his children. Only hurt and heartache.

When she was far away from Los Banos, she didn't have to believe that what had happened to the eighteen-year-old Faith was real. She could disassociate herself from the young girl, left on the side of the road on prom night, picked up by her sister's boyfriend, taken to the reservoir, placated, then raped. She tightened her mouth to control her tears. Back then, she'd tried so hard to be angry with Jay. If he had just taken her home, she would have been fine. Or if he had just understood why she didn't want to marry him. But now she realized her nomadic life wasn't Jay's fault.

It wasn't Patty's fault.

It was hers.

She had come home under the guise of pleasing her parents, but really she'd come seeking support. Little did she know that she'd find it in Jay and his extended family, not in her own. Maybe she had come for just what Patty had accused her of—for the promise of Jay, for the appreciation in his blue eyes when his children laughed, for his trust that she'd take care of his boys. She hadn't known that then, but did now. She loved him, had never stopped loving him, loved him even more now that he had grown up, had children. She slid slowly down the wall. According to Andy, that meant she had to stay. She bit her lip.

A long silence persisted. She waited to hear Jay leave, but no sound of a door closing came. All she heard was his even breathing, as if he was standing just on the other side of the bedroom wall.

Finally, she called weakly, "Jay?"

"Yes?"

He *was* standing on the other side of the wall. His voice was so close, deep and comforting, she felt the vibration against her spine.

"You still there?"

"Yes." He didn't sound impatient.

Faith gave a half sob, half laugh. What in the world was he doing?

"I thought you were going," she stated.

"I am."

"So why haven't you gone?"

"I'm waiting for you."

"I just told you—"

"—that this was a mistake." His voice had an odd quality to it. Something tender, but also harsh and annoyed, almost as though he spoke against his will. In fact, he sounded slightly resentful—and that heaped on her yet another layer of confusion, of guilt. He was such a contradiction.

"So do you always back out of something you've already committed to? Or is it just me?" Now he sounded tired and disappointed.

"Believe me," Faith said, barely able to project her voice to him. "You'll thank me for this. It's much better for you to arrive alone than to take me."

"Alone?" Jay gave a raspy laugh. "Alone is never better. I've been alone, Faith. I've been alone for five years. Why in the world would I have asked you to go with me if I'd wanted to go alone?" His voice softened as he added, "If I wanted to *be* alone?"

"It's for the best," she said, willing herself not to cry.

"Since when do you know what's best for me?" The words were snapped out at her.

"Since I realized I'm in love with you," Faith said, and with a deep breath, left the security of the room.

FAITH'S CONFESSION RENDERED all of Jay's irritation, along with his doubt, impotent. And her appearance created a very different response within his body. At least that information he could process.

Faith was gorgeous.

Gone was the gypsy garb, the beads dangling from

her hair, the sandaled feet. He didn't know what he expected Faith to wear, maybe a slightly more formal version of her usual mode of dress. He certainly didn't expect a shimmering and tightly fitting pale pink gown. Her hair, which had been stringy and damp just an hour ago, was coiled on the top of her head, soft strands falling in loose rings about her face.

"God, Faith" was all he could say.

"I guess I didn't tell you about my six-month stint as a Sunday afternoon tea model for an exclusive L.A. department store," she said sheepishly. "Got a discount on the dress." She tried to smile, but it didn't quite make it to her eyes. She sat down on the small step between the bedroom and living room and stared up at him, her eyes filling with tears.

"I really wanted to go with you," she whispered.

He sat next to her, his mind still spinning from the stimuli Faith had just given him. Had he heard her right?

"I want you to go with me." His voice didn't sound like his own, being gruff and warm at the same time. He could feel the crinkle of the pink fabric as it brushed up against his slacks.

"Next time?" she asked, her voice wistful.

"No." He shook his head and said with certain conviction, "Now."

Faith shivered and looked away. "You'd better get going."

He stayed seated. Close was good. He could smell her shampoo. Her soap. No perfume at all. Most of all, he could feel her love.

"They're expecting you," Faith said in a small voice.

Jay laughed, still giddy. "Faith, they don't give a hoot about me. It's you they're waiting for. They're waiting to see if you'll show up. Or if you'll do exactly what they expect and not go at all."

"Can't disappoint them," she said tersely.

"But you can disappoint me." Jay realized he was speaking the truth. He was disappointed. He wanted this night with Faith all to himself. "Forget about all the people. Just think about me. I want to go with you. It's like prom night all over again."

She looked stricken and Jay wondered what he'd said.

"How can you want it to be like prom night? It was the worst night of my life."

"It wasn't all terrible."

She faced him, her eyes shadowed. "How can you say that?"

Jay searched her eyes, looking for some clue as to what was so carefully hidden.

"We had a great time..." he started, and then paused. Finally, Jay said carefully what they had avoided saying to each other since she'd gotten back. "Until I left you on the side of the road."

It sounded awful articulated like that. How could he have done that to her? He reminded himself that it had been a different time. Back then Los Banos had had about ten thousand fewer people. She'd only had to walk a couple of miles home. True, she'd been in her prom dress and high heels. But he'd half expected her to catch a ride home with someone she knew.

Apparently, that was what she had done, because when he went looking for her twenty minutes later, rather than sitting where he'd left her, she was gone. He'd driven to her house, but her mother had said she'd just called to say she'd gone out with other friends. *She rejected you by sleeping with Bruce.* Is *that* what had really happened? Or was there something more?

"When I turned down your proposal."

"You were right," he dismissed, his mind whirling. What had happened with Bruce? What would split Faith from her family? "We were too young."

Jay felt his heart thud in confusion as Faith bent over and clutched her knees, rocking slightly. Jay moved closer but was careful not to touch her. Funny, how demons unveiled themselves in many different ways. His came when he wasn't working, which was why he avoided down times even at the expense of his children. But Faith's demon wasn't like his. His would eventually fade with time; hers seemed to grow more powerful. So much so that silence was a better alternative than speaking.

"Faith, what's wrong?" He tried to keep his tone low and friendly. She had never told him what had caused her to leave so quickly, why she'd changed after prom night, what it was she fought with her family about. Maybe now, eighteen years later, she could put that night to rest.

"Faith. Tell me," he whispered. "Just tell me what happened. What was so terrible that you and Patty still fight about it today?" Something that was a mixture of a laugh and a sob came out of her. When she looked up, Jay exhaled sharply, not even realizing he'd been holding his breath.

FAITH STARED INTO Jay's eyes, feeling the secret she had held in for eighteen years being slowly pulled out of her. It would be so easy to tell him. He'd already opened the door.

How hard could it be to say, *Bruce raped me. But even worse was the fact that my sister, mother and father chose Bruce over me. They said they'd forgive me. I didn't want to be forgiven. I wanted to be believed.*

She should just open her mouth and tell him.

No doubt, Jay's acceptance and belief would heal her. Except, she wasn't eighteen anymore and Bruce wasn't her sister's boyfriend. He was her husband. He had become part of the family. The consequences of telling Jay now would be the equivalent of an avalanche. The rush of snow would wipe out Bruce, Patty, her parents, Jay, his father. In order for her to heal, she would need to ruin too many lives. The roots she'd severed from her life eighteen years earlier had grown more entwined, ever twisted, so tangled that the truth was better left unsaid. With a deep breath and a new understanding, Faith knew what she had to do.

As soon as Jay hired a new nanny, she would leave. It didn't matter that she was in love with him. It didn't matter that when he sat close to her, she could almost feel the blood that ran through his veins.

"Jay?"

"Yes." His tone was unhurried, accepting.

She looked away, finding his solid body pressing so

near disconcerting. Heat emanated from him. *Just tell him. Trust him.* Faith bit her lip and then blurted, "I'm ready to go," as she stood up quickly, not wanting to see the hurt in his eyes.

"Faith," Jay protested. "We need to talk about what—"

She shook her head and gave him the most ebullient smile she could manage, as she walked over to pluck her evening purse off the coffee table. "There's nothing to talk about."

She opened a compact, staring into the small mirror to readjust her makeup, dabbing her fingers around the corners of her eyes.

"But the—"

Faith could hear the frustration in his voice.

This was for the best. Eventually, the boys would forget about her. Eventually, Jay would remarry, probably Amanda. And Faith would find a place for herself, somewhere. Just not here.

She shook her head and offered him a hand to pull himself up with. He caught it, and as the warmth of his palm worked up her arm, she felt a twist of profound regret.

"Sometimes things are much better left unsaid," she murmured quietly, then relocated her smile. "Let's go and have a good time."

JAY COULDN'T HELP FEELING cut off from the conversation. But Faith was already out the door, sliding into the leather seats of the Cadillac. She made no comment on the relic from their past and actually was very silent on the drive to the fairgrounds. She had been so close to revealing the secret that haunted her. He wanted to understand the tension that crackled between the sisters, know what had happened and maybe help her heal. Later, as she entered the hall, her earlier uneasiness seemed to evaporate. She looked like a Sunday afternoon tea model, smiling, nodding, shaking people's hands.

Jay followed behind her, giving a low whistle when he got his first view of the expansive hall. Patty had outdone herself.

The hall was splendidly decorated with pastel streamers and balloons. The acoustic band that Patty had hired was playing fifties hits, but not too loud. Generous floral arrangements graced each round table, with a spectacular standing arrangement next to the front table where Faith's mother and father were already seated. Next to them sat the original members of their wedding party, all of whom were present and accounted for.

"It's about time you got here," Patty said quickly, coming up behind him. She looked around him. "Where's Faith?"

Jay just indicated her whereabouts with his eyes.

Patty blinked twice. "That's not Faith."

Jay watched as Faith finished the conversation she was having with a guest. She saw Patty and smiled before walking toward their parents at the other end of the room.

"It is indeed Faith."

Patty's gaze followed her sister down the aisle. "Well, at least she didn't embarrass us."

"She looks spectacular."

Patty shrugged and then held out a stack of index cards.

"What's this?" Jay asked, taking them from her while using his peripheral vision to follow Faith's progress around the hall.

"Notes about each person who wants to roast my parents," Patty replied as Jay flipped through them.

He nodded, quickly scanning the cards. They seemed endless. "I thought we were going to limit this to ten people." Faith, he saw, hadn't quite made it to her parents. She'd stopped to talk to a table full of well-wishers.

Patty gave him a helpless smile. "I didn't have the heart to say no. So many people wanted to contribute, I couldn't turn them down. We'll give people about twenty minutes after dinner is served—then we'll start the roast."

"There's no way that this is going to stay under an hour." He flipped through the stack. Faith was now standing next to the guests of honor. "No way."

"Do your best," Patty offered, her voice distracted as her eyes tracked a waiter apparently not dispensing appetizers with the speed and courtesy she expected. She started toward him and called over her shoulder. "You might have to cut them off if they talk too long. But I can't imagine they have all that much to say."

Jay watched Faith hug her mother and give a slightly more robust one to her father. Even as far away as he was, Jay could sense the distance between Faith and her parents.

"One way or another, Faith," he promised under his breath. "You *will* tell me what happened."

CHAPTER TWELVE

PATTY'S PLANNING may have been beyond reproach, but Jay discovered that her sense of timing was way off. When he got to the last introduction, the roast was running close to three hours. Apparently people had a lot to say after forty years. Dessert had long since been served but the audience remained politely seated, though over the past half hour, even Faith's parents were starting to nod off. Twice the band had started up, indicating they were ready to play. Patty, however, didn't seem to notice the loss in momentum. She hovered on the sidelines beaming at all.

A collective sigh of relief, his own included, ran audibly through the hall when he gave a final toast to the guests of honor, had the audience stand up and stretch, and signaled the band to start playing. While the hired servers pulled the dining tables away from the center of the hall to make space for the dancing, the lights were dimmed as a mirrored ball sent flashes of light across the floor. Feeling as if he'd been away from Faith for far too long, Jay searched the hall for her. He found her sitting alone at a deserted table in the back corner.

He slid into the folding chair next to her, as she watched her parents dance to a jazz rendition of ''Unforgettable.'' Her father had pulled her mother close, and with their heads bent, they swayed together as if they had been married for forty minutes rather than forty years.

''That's unusual these days,'' Jay said casually.

Faith started, then flashed him an appreciative smile. ''You're back.''

Jay was inordinately pleased by the way her eyes lit up when she looked at him.

She sighed and agreed with him. ''It is. Seems good if a couple makes it to twenty years, much less forty.''

''I'd say this party was a success. Something to remember.'' He winced. He must have used up all his clever sayings as emcee. Now all he could do was talk in platitudes. It was a shame, really, because Faith deserved so much more.

Faith's attention turned to her sister, who authoritatively directed the photographer to take pictures of the couples dancing. ''I don't think Patty even ate anything.''

''I saw her nibble on a couple of the courses,'' Jay said. ''But I think she was too nervous. How about you? Did you get something to eat?''

Faith nodded, with a twitch to her lips. ''All five courses.'' She patted her belly. ''And two desserts.'' Her eyes twinkled.

In her brown eyes was an expression he'd never seen before. It was as if for this one moment, she was letting down her guard to show herself to him. Perhaps it had something to do with her quiet confession that she was in love with him. Jay didn't know if he fully believed her, but he knew he wanted to explore whatever was between them. So he didn't resist the temptation to trace a curve of silky hair, which led to a gentle finger stroke of her soft cheek.

"I think I've got to kiss you," he whispered.

She looked away shyly but didn't move. She stayed right where she was, almost as if she was holding her breath. Taking that as an affirmative, he leaned forward and lightly brushed his lips across her cheek.

Faith made a small noise of disappointment.

She turned and raised her lashes to gaze straight into his eyes. He swallowed hard. Then her lips parted and she pushed back a strand of hair from his face, the tips of her fingers grazing his temple, her lips just a fraction of an inch from his. With the slightest movement, he closed the space between them, feeling the smooth texture of her bottom lip, the warmth of her mouth, the barest trace of her tongue.

"Mint," he said suddenly.

She pulled back and smiled, a flush spreading up her cheeks. "I told you I ate two desserts. Mint-chip ice cream. I ate the second one during the last hour."

"The roast was that boring?" he asked, his voice rueful.

Faith's eyes twinkled.

Jay groaned. "Bad?"

"Well, the stories started sounding the same by the ninety-minute mark. At two hours, people stopped listening." She looked around the table and laughed out loud. "The benefit of sitting way in the back," she said, "is that it's close to the door." Then she added, "But you were great." Her voice lowered with the compliment.

That said, they fell into silence, shy and impatient at the same time; the spell of the kiss was broken. Jay stared at the couples on the dance floor, the band having just started "When I Fall in Love."

"Would you like to dance?" He offered her a hand, relieved that it was steadier than he felt.

Faith regarded him for a long time.

"Yes," she said finally, putting her hand in his. "I would love to dance."

Jay's arm circled her waist and she was drawn up close, very close, to him. He guided her easily onto the dance floor, but as he started to lead, she stumbled.

Jay tightened his hold around her waist. "Relax," he whispered, his lips brushing against the tender line of her neck. "It's just you and me."

She glanced around nervously. But to her surprise, no one was watching her. No one was giving them poisoned stares. The hall had become so dim that it was almost impossible to make out people. Finally, she took a deep breath and relaxed. Jay's cheek rested on her forehead, and she allowed herself to be lulled by the music, by the muted lights, by Jay's body movements. She felt safe. Secure. As if it were just the two of them.

Jay didn't let her go when the music ended. He merely eased the tension of his arm around her waist, but she could still feel the muscular length of his legs, his solid chest, the strong beat of his heart. Then the music started up again, and as Jay swept her away, warmth spread through her. This was nice. This was more than nice. She curled her head in the crook between his collarbone and his neck. He smelled heavenly, a subtle citrus cologne that didn't overpower her, but rather teased her senses. She was so glad she'd come with him. She closed her eyes as his body rhythmically moved, guided, led hers through the music.

"May I cut in?"

Bruce's polite voice caused Faith to stiffen, and Jay responded by holding her tighter.

Jay swung her away from Bruce, who looked almost debonair in his tux. He played second to Patty's first magnificently.

"I think I'd like to keep her just a little longer," Jay said easily. "Like the rest of the night."

But Bruce was persistent, actually following them and tapping Jay on the shoulder again.

"Come on, Jay," Bruce said, his tone pleasant. "You need to share the prettiest lady at the ball."

Faith hid her face in Jay's jacket, clinging to him. "Say no," she whispered in his ear.

"Just one dance," Bruce cajoled.

Faith's heart plummeted when Jay pulled ever so slightly away. She closed her eyes when his arm left her waist, allowing cool air to rush in. She had to suppress a shudder when Bruce touched her wrist.

"I get her back," Jay said lightly.

"Of course."

When Bruce's arm came around her waist, she could feel him tremble. Faith pulled back. Rather than melding her body to his as she had done with Jay, Faith rested her free hand on Bruce's shoulder, locking her elbow.

"So are you having a good time?" Bruce asked with a smile.

Panic began to choke Faith. She tried to shake it off. This was Bruce. It was a crowded room. One dance couldn't be so bad. She looked around for Jay, reassured to find him watching from the edge of the dance floor near the bar.

"It's been a very nice party." Faith was glad her voice came out even.

"I guess Amanda's out of the running," Bruce commented.

"Why do you say that?"

Bruce laughed. It was a sad sound.

"Patty sat you all the way in the back and put Amanda at the front, right in Jay's line of vision, but he spent most of the night straining his eyes to see you." Bruce gently spun her. "See? He can't keep his eyes off you now."

Faith took a deep breath and relaxed. Jay was watching. But her relief was short-lived. Faith could just make out Amanda, who was hustling toward Jay like a bridesmaid with her eye on the bouquet. Faith's throat tightened, as Jay gave a glass of wine to Amanda and then ordered another.

She turned away, her face flushing. She'd told him that she was in love with him, he'd kissed her and held her tight, but none of that mattered because in a week, she would be gone. Tonight was just tonight. It didn't promise tomorrow or the next day. But it didn't seem to matter how much she repeated that, her heart wouldn't believe it.

"Relax, Faith." Bruce's voice rumbled softly in her ear. She could feel the heat of his breath. It smelled like wine, and he actually pulled her closer with one

smooth movement, rendering her elbow lock useless.
How different his chest felt from Jay's, thin and wiry.
How different the same request to relax sounded. Faith
tried to move away, but Bruce's grip was unyielding,
and she had to control a small leap of fear at his
strength.

"Please let me go," she stated simply.

He held her even tighter, his face buried in her hair.

"Bruce," she said. "Stop."

"Stop what?" He looked at her, truly puzzled.

"Stop holding me so closely."

Where'd she felt only security and warmth in Jay's
arms, now she experienced only revulsion. She tried
to reassure herself. Bruce wouldn't do anything to her.
The last time had been a mistake, a terrible, terrible
mistake. She had gone with him, she had gotten drunk,
she had helped him undress. Obviously, she hadn't
said no clearly enough for Bruce to understand.

Bruce didn't relax his hold.

"Bruce, what do you think you're doing?"

"Dancing with my sister-in-law."

Faith took a deep breath and decided not to struggle.
The song would be over soon.

She craned her neck to see where Jay was, but he
was in deep conversation with Amanda, their heads
bent together. As the dance continued, she felt another
part of Bruce pressing against her leg. A stiff part.

"No!" Faith gasped, lurching out of Bruce's hold.

He caught her wrist and tried to pull her back, genuine confusion in his brown eyes. "Faith, what's
wrong?"

Faith didn't answer. She simply shook off his grip
and blindly walked out of the hall. In moments she

was outside, the chill of the April night hitting her face.

"Faith, wait!" Bruce called, though he stopped at the edge of the double doors.

Faith walked faster and soon broke into a run, heading across the damp grass, down a pathway, through to the empty corrals. She knew the fairgrounds well from years of attending the annual May Day fair. She pulled her tight dress up to her knees, so she could run faster, feeling the dampness mingle with dirt and bits of gravel in her shoes, listening in case Bruce followed her, but he didn't.

She ran until she was out of breath and her ankles hurt. She stopped, sucking in air and spinning around, trying to get her bearings. It suddenly occurred to Faith that it was dark, very dark, and she began to search for the glow of the streetlights in the suburban housing development that bordered the fairgrounds. She couldn't see the hall from where she was but could hear the music.

Then she realized how cold she was, how wet her feet were.

She shook her head in self-disgust.

Here she was again. In the middle of nowhere in a formal gown. At least this time, she wasn't on a deserted country road. She was on the very familiar fairgrounds, a few hundred feet from her parents' anniversary party. Respectable ranch-style homes surrounded the area. It was small comfort.

ONE MOMENT JAY HAD BEEN having a fun conversation with Amanda, the next thing he knew his father was tapping him on the shoulder.

"Can I talk to you a minute, son?" Gil requested.

Jay glanced up with a smile, and noticed that Bess sat at a table not too far away, looking concerned. He nodded his apology to Amanda, who didn't mask her small pout.

"What's up, Dad?" Jay asked once they'd moved to a private corner. It had been nice to see him and Bess dance, and surprisingly, Jay didn't feel a stab of regret that Bess was not his mother. Bess looked very natural on Gil's arm, as if she'd been there a lot longer than a year.

"I'm wondering how things are going between you and Faith." Gil didn't practice subtlety.

Jay gave an impatient click of his tongue. Even though his father thought it was his concern, it really wasn't. He knew his father had great hopes, some of them in support of what Andy and Sam wanted, but Jay wasn't ready to talk about his relationship with Faith. First he wanted to see how it felt to be with Faith. Discussion would be premature. *She did say she loved you.* But that, too, was a secret.

"I think that's between Faith and me," he said quietly. "No offense. It's really none of your business, Dad."

Gil was silent as he glanced quickly at his wife. Jay saw Bess nod slightly, then look away.

"What is it that you wanted to tell me?" Jay asked, suddenly thinking that he'd been away from Faith for too long. He scanned the dance floor for Faith and Bruce.

"I certainly don't want to get into your business, but..."

"But what?"

Gil said gruffly, "Bess saw Faith break away from Bruce and walk out. Bess just thought you should know."

Jay continued to search the dance floor. His father's wife must have been mistaken. He'd just taken his eyes off Faith for a minute, when Amanda came over. He'd have seen her leave. "Maybe she just went out to get a breath of fresh air," Jay reasoned, already striding toward the door. "It *is* a little stuffy now."

Gil walked with him. "Bess couldn't really see her face but thought something wasn't right, just by the way Faith was walking."

What could have happened? What could Bruce have said to her that would make her upset enough to walk out?

"Jay Whitfield?" A hand stopped him, midway to the door.

Jay looked down, way down, at the unfamiliar, well-meaning face dusted lightly with wrinkles and topped with a curly mound of gray hair. He automatically smiled, although he looked over the woman's head to the door. "Yes?"

"I just wanted to let you know what a fine job you're doing as a member of the council. You were excellent tonight."

Jay nodded absently. "Thank you."

"And I was wondering if you had a minute to listen to an idea I had for our Arts Council."

Jay didn't have a minute, but he nodded, anyway. Then exactly one minute later, he said politely, with a big smile to ease his interruption, "Excuse me. I think you have some great ideas. Have you thought about becoming a member of the Arts Council?"

"Oh, no. I don't have time to get involved. I have my grandchildren, you see. Six of them. Sometimes, my daughters come visit. I couldn't possibly—"

"Well, then, I'll see what I can do to pass on the information." Jay bowed, then strode out into the night.

FAITH WAS TOO COLD for words, though her heart rate seemed to have slowed to a normal pace. She shivered and moved from her perch, ready to trudge back to the party. Earlier, she'd made the decision to leave. Staying would topple some carefully constructed lives, including Jay's. But tears threatened to overwhelm her. Leaving wouldn't help *her*. She would leave in the same shape as she'd arrived.

She heard footsteps and she jerked to attention. Maybe it was just Jay.

"Faith?" Bruce called, his voice sending fear through her veins. "Are you all right?" He emerged from the shadows and cautiously walked toward her, his gait slightly unsteady. "What's wrong?"

Faith started back to the hall, brushing past him. Except for the faraway sounds of the music, it was amazing how quiet it was; the crows that nested up in the trees seemed to have vanished.

No dogs barked.

No crickets chirped.

Just the distant hum of party noise.

She was freezing cold. She pushed away the fear, the tingling in the back of her neck, and just concentrated on ignoring Bruce, the way she would a stray dog. She heard Bruce's footsteps behind her. She hadn't really gone that far from the hall, but it felt as if it would take an eternity to get back to it.

She yelped when Bruce caught her arm.

"Don't touch me!" Faith jerked her arm, but Bruce seemed to have been expecting it because his grip was tight. She tried to move sideways, along the railing of the corral, but her dress was snagged on something.

Bruce pinned her to the railing.

"Faith, don't run away," he pleaded.

No. This wasn't happening. It couldn't be.

JAY HURRIED OUTSIDE, Gil close behind.

"Where do you think she went?" Jay asked. Why did he feel so clueless? Why wouldn't she tell him what was bothering her?

Gil shook his head. "You go check the track and the bleachers, I'll go back toward the parking lot."

Jay nodded in agreement. "You'll shout if you find her?"

Gil raised his hand, already moving away. Jay headed in the direction of the small dirt track where motor cross races were run during the summer months. They were a perfect place to sit if one wanted to get away and think. Jay was sure he'd find Faith sitting on the top bleacher, staring into the night sky.

"Be there, Faith," Jay whispered, a sick feeling resting like a rock in his stomach. "And after I find you and finish shaking you, I'm going to make you tell me what's wrong."

He broke into a trot and shouted, "Faith!"

FAITH LOOKED UP. She thought she'd heard Jay calling her.

"Let me go, Bruce," Faith said, twisting against his grip. "You're hurting me."

"Not until you tell me what's wrong," Bruce insisted. "You've been avoiding me ever since you got back in town. Every time I try to talk to you, you—"

"You know exactly what's wrong." She turned her head to listen for Jay. Had she imagined it?

"No. I don't."

"Bruce, I'm not going to let you do it again."

"Do what?" Bruce looked genuinely hurt. "Faith, what we shared was beautiful."

"You raped me."

Bruce shook his head in denial. "You wanted it," he insisted, his usually mild voice replaced by anger. "I remember. I would never rape a woman, least of all you."

Faith looked at him in disbelief, tears crowding the backs of her eyes. "What do you mean 'least of all me'?"

"I love you, Faith. I've loved you since you were fourteen."

Faith shook her head. "You were Patty's boyfriend. I was a little kid."

Bruce swallowed hard. "You were always more beautiful than Patty. You were always nicer to me."

"But you *married* her."

"Because it was the only way I could know what was happening to you once you left. If you'd ever shown any interest in me, I would have divorced—"

"You *raped* me, Bruce. There was no way I'd ever consider any kind of relationship with you. I knew I needed to leave when they took your word over mine." Faith tried to laugh but it turned into a sob. "You took advantage of that. You took advantage of the fact that my mother and Patty thought you were the golden boy."

He shook his head. "I know Patty married me for my money. I know she never really loved me. But you were different. You *liked* me."

Faith nodded as tears spilled over. "You're right. I did like you. I liked you a whole lot better than Patty did sometimes. But I never loved you. Not like I loved Jay."

"You turned him down."

"Because I didn't want to get married. Not because I was in love with you."

"You undressed for me."

"I said stop." Again, Faith tried to wrest herself from his grasp.

"But you kissed me. You *touched* me."

Faith nodded and swallowed hard. "Yes. I did. And I take full responsibility for that. But I don't take responsibility for the fact that when I said stop, you didn't. You didn't even stop when I screamed."

"No." Bruce tightened his grip, and Faith winced in pain.

"So, Bruce," Faith asked quickly, still blinking back her tears. "If you didn't rape me, how come you're holding on to me so tightly? How come we have to have this conversation with you trying to break my arm?"

Bruce let go of her so fast she stumbled over the uneven ground and landed on her butt. She didn't notice the jolt of pain screaming up her spine, only the piercing denial in his eyes. She shook her head, tears streaming down her face. When had it become so hard to breathe?

She crawled backward like a crab, before turning onto her hands and knees and trying to stand up.

"Don't run away, Faith," Bruce said from right behind her.

Faith felt something jab into her knee. What was it? A rock. Adrenaline surged through her. With her back to Bruce, she felt for the rock. It wasn't a round smooth rock, but a jagged piece of granite about the size of a small orange. She frantically dug with her fingers in an attempt to dislodge it from the ground.

She could hear Bruce behind her.

"Faith? Are you okay?"

He was awfully close so she dug harder.

The rock gave just a bit.

Her nails hurt, but with one last jerk, the rock was free.

With a sob of relief, she clambered to her feet and backed away slowly, putting more distance between them.

"Stop right there," Faith warned, liking the weight of the rock.

Bruce stopped and looked at her as if she'd lost her mind.

Maybe she had.

But she had a rock. And it was in her hand.

CHAPTER THIRTEEN

BRUCE STARED AT HER, his brown eyes uncomprehending. "What's wrong, Faith?" He moved closer.

"Leave me alone," Faith said, calm returning to her body. "I'm armed. I've got a rock."

Bruce was clearly alarmed. "What do you plan to do with it?"

"If you don't stop where you are, I'll throw it at you." Faith couldn't help the hysterical laugh that started in her throat. Part of her realized she sounded like an eight-year-old.

Bruce took a cautious step forward. "You don't want to do that."

"Stop!" Faith hefted the rock. "I don't want to hurt you, but I will if you don't leave me alone."

Bruce ignored her and continued to approach.

"I mean it. I'll throw this."

"Faith, you don't have anything to be frightened of. Put the rock down."

"Bruce, stop. Now."

Bruce shook his head. "Put the rock down."

"See, Bruce?" Faith said sadly, tears sliding down her cheek. "I *did* ask you to stop and you didn't. You did exactly what you're doing now."

That stopped Bruce. He licked his lips and looked

away, taking off his glasses. Faith could see him clench and unclench his fists, then suddenly his eyes opened wide in horror.

"Oh, God," he whispered, the prayer dragged out of him, as he stared at her as if seeing her for the first time.

"God, Faith." Bruce just shook his head, his face wilting in remorse. "I didn't stop. You're right." The words were hoarse.

A long silence, and Faith felt more tears course down her cheeks. She let the rock fall to the ground.

"Faith…" Bruce opened his palms to her. His eyes were inexplicably sad.

But Faith just wanted to get away. She wasted no time and turned—right into a solid body, which didn't yield at all. She looked up and found her upper arms caught in a firm grip. Faith moved back quickly, her heart pounding.

"Don't touch me!" she hissed as she struggled to free herself.

"Whoa, Faith. It's me, Jay."

He was sweaty, out of breath. He looked like he'd been running.

Faith stopped, her body trembling. With a wail of relief, she hurled herself at him and sobbed.

"What happened?" he asked urgently, his arms going around her.

She shook her head.

Jay pulled away, and Faith felt deserted.

"No, Faith," Jay said, his voice flat. He tilted her face up to his. She could see the emotion glittering in his eyes. "You're not going to do this to me. Tell me what happened."

Faith just buried her face into his shirt. She didn't want to think about it anymore. She didn't want to think about Bruce or the rape. All she wanted to do was go home.

"Tell me, Faith," Jay whispered in her ear, unsteadiness in his voice. "Trust me."

FAITH'S DISTRESS WAS PAINFUL to see, and Jay's frustration mounted when Faith remained absolutely quiet, but he couldn't force her to talk. Finally, she pulled away, standing on her own a little unsteadily. He held her elbow.

"Let's go back to the party," she said, her voice very tired.

She looked like hell. Her hair was a mess, her face was streaked with dirt and mascara, and her pink dress was stained at the knees and ripped along one side. Jay felt impatience clog his throat. He'd accepted her reluctance to talk before—she was entitled to her secrets—but it had gone on long enough. The secrets were harming her.

He gently took Faith's hand, studying the torn fingernails.

"Faith, what happened?" he asked again as compassionately as he could, but she avoided his eyes and started to walk away. Jay turned to Bruce, who appeared deathly pale. "Bruce?"

That inquiry stopped Faith in her tracks. She whirled around, shaking her head at Bruce, pulling on Jay's arm. "Jay. Let's go back. I'm ready to go."

"I'm not," Jay said angrily. "I leave you two to dance and somehow you both end up in the middle of nowhere. Faith looks like she's been attacked. Bruce, you look like you've seen a ghost. I need someone to explain this to me."

Faith exhaled sharply. "It's a long story, Jay. It's too much for me right now."

"Bruce, is it too much for you?" Jay asked, then watched Faith and Bruce communicate with their eyes.

"Bruce, tell me what you know," Jay insisted. He could feel a vein throb in his temple.

Bruce swallowed hard. After a moment, he said, his voice unsteady, "It's not my place to tell."

"For God's sake, Faith." Jay couldn't contain his frustration. "What the hell is going on?"

Faith remained silent, slowly shaking her head.

The noise of a crowd gathering behind them startled them all.

Gil spoke. "I'm glad you found her. I was about to call in the police." His father's sharp eyes locked on Faith.

"Yes, I found her," Jay said briefly. "She's had a long night, I think I'll just take her home."

"Bess has her purse."

"Thanks." Jay put his arm around Faith's waist and guided her through the crowd.

"Faith!" Dearie Weaver was suddenly in front of them.

Jay sensed Faith stiffen next to him.

"Mom."

"Are you okay?" Dearie's concern seemed a little

airy, but she grasped Faith's arm, helping her. "You'll feel better once you fix your hair."

"She's fine, Mrs. Weaver," Jay said quietly as he and Faith continued on to the hall. "She's just a little tired."

With the music playing in the background, Jay waited for Faith while she and Dearie disappeared into the ladies' room.

Patty strode toward him with purpose, her arm ready to push open the door. "Where is she?"

Jay held up a hand to prevent her from entering. "Don't, Patty."

"I don't believe this! She can't even attend a party without an excess of melodrama. *Damn it.* I worked hard to make this night perfect and now it's ruined."

Jay turned a thoughtful eye toward the dance floor. People were dancing. Conversations continued. "It doesn't seem to me that the party is ruined."

Patty inhaled sharply as she surveyed the room.

Jay knew he was right. There might be a few people who continued to speculate about what happened, but for the most part, any rumors would circulate and die within a few days and probably within twenty-four hours, even though whatever had created the chasm between the sisters had lasted nearly eighteen years.

"Have you seen your husband?"

"Bruce?" Patty's back went rigid. "What does Bruce have to do with this?"

Jay shook his head. "I don't know, but I think a lot. You might want to find him."

Patty looked at the door to the ladies' room, but Jay blocked her way. "Go find your husband, Patty."

FAITH PRESSED HER FOREHEAD against the bathroom mirror, fighting the urge to cry now that she was safe. Dearie fussed over her, but Faith was in no state to appreciate her motherly concern.

Bruce had finally admitted the truth.

One tear leaked out. Did it matter? Did it change anything? She didn't know.

"I don't know how you managed to tear this beautiful dress," Dearie fretted as she tried to patch the rip with a safety pin she took from the strap of her slip. "What were you doing out there anyway?" Dearie's tone felt like a light slap.

"Just getting some air." Her voice felt faint. *She* felt faint.

"I hope you weren't trying to rekindle something with Bruce…"

Faith's throat closed as she stared at her reflection in the mirror. She looked like hell and her mother thought—

"No," Faith said succinctly. "In fact, I learned he wants to rekindle something with me."

"Well, of course he does." Dearie straightened. "Men always want what they can't have. Bruce is no exception. That's why we needed to make sure that he married Patty."

Faith stopped still. She could feel the thudding of her pulse in both temples. "What are you talking about?"

Dearie dabbed a wet paper towel at the smudges on Faith's face. "Pity about the dress."

"Mom. What do you mean that you needed to make sure Bruce married Patty?"

Her mother threw the paper towel away and wet another one. Finally, they faced each other, Dearie's eyes bright and defensive. With a practical shake of her head, she said, "You know how much money we spent on Patty, not to mention the time and effort. Surely, it had to pay off somewhere."

"You knew he raped me?"

Dearie turned and didn't respond.

"But you said you believed him." Faith bit her lip. "You believed him over me."

The words hung in the air.

Dearie broke the silence, her voice clipped. "We *had* to, Faith. There was no other choice."

"Did Patty believe me?"

"We never talked about it."

"But if you knew—"

"That's water under the bridge. What matters is that you're home and things are all right. You've grown into a beautiful woman without my help. Things are all right."

But Faith wasn't all right. She had waited eighteen years for her mother to tell her she believed her. And when Dearie finally did, it wasn't healing at all. All Faith felt was a hollow in her heart where family should have been. For so long, Faith had thought her parents, her *mother* didn't believe her. Now she realized that her mother had known the truth all along and had chosen to ignore it just to ensure a good marriage for Patty.

JAY PARKED IN FRONT of the cottage and got out of the car. Without waiting for him, Faith struggled to open up the large door, at the same time fumbling in her purse for her keys. Before she could get to her feet, Jay was there, taking the keys from her and helping her out of the car, his touch firm on her hand. When Faith entered the cottage, a feeling of comfort engulfed her. She was safe. She put her purse on the small coffee table, the same table where she, Andy and Sam had played Memory.

Then she realized that Jay was still standing in the doorway.

"Do you want to come in?" Faith asked uncertainly.

He took a long time to answer. "Do you want me to come in?"

Faith nodded and took a deep breath. "Yes. I do."

Carefully, he entered and closed the door behind him. She slipped off his jacket and carefully laid it over the back of the couch. Then she went to the bathroom and threw up.

After a while, she slowly pulled herself up and rinsed her mouth. Then she washed until the tips of her fingers stung from the soap.

When she wearily emerged from the bathroom, Jay was in the kitchen, putting on the kettle. He'd gotten out two cups with saucers, and a package of herbal tea lay on the counter.

"Chamomile," he said briefly, his eyes skimming her from head to toe. "It might make your stomach feel better."

She flushed, embarrassed that Jay must have heard every wretched heave. "I understand if you need to go."

Jay's blue eyes were impossible to read. "Do I look like I'm going anywhere?"

She shook her head. He'd taken off the bow tie and cummerbund, and unbuttoned the collar of his white shirt, now stained with her tears and dirt.

"Why don't you change into something more comfortable? A shower might make you feel better," Jay suggested. "The tea will wait."

Faith could only agree. Twenty minutes later, she sat on the couch, her legs curled underneath her. Her bulky sweats wrapped her in warm comfort as she sipped on a steaming cup of tea. A shower had made her feel almost normal, but she still couldn't shake the fog she was in. Bruce had admitted he'd raped her. And her mother had known all along.

Once the first tear fell, the rest came out in a thunderstorm. She cried for the eighteen-year-old who didn't get away and for the thirty-six-year-old who did. She cried for her mother who believed she needed to sacrifice one daughter for another. She could feel Jay sitting next to her, taking the cup from her hand and pulling her as close to him as he could get her. She could feel the comforting thud of his heart against her face. This was love.

They sat that way for a long time. After a while, Faith's sobs receded to just an occasional hiccup. Then she pulled herself away from him, taking the tissues that he stuffed into her hand.

"Wow," Faith said, pushing her still-damp hair out of her face.

Jay smiled as she blew her nose. "Yeah."

They were silent, and Faith fiddled with the tissues now balled in her hand.

"So do you want to tell me what happened?" he asked casually.

She looked away, and Jay felt a stab in his heart. Even now, Faith wasn't prepared to talk, wasn't prepared to trust him with her secrets.

"It's a long story."

"I have time," Jay said honestly. He did have time. He had all evening.

She swallowed and blew her nose again. He handed her the box of tissues and she took it, studying the floral pattern.

He waited some more.

"Bruce raped me on prom night," she finally said.

Jay sat perfectly still, trying to ignore the roar in his ears. "What?"

She glanced at him nervously and nodded. "You heard me."

"And the reason you never told me this was..." He could feel rage pulsing through him, an emotion so intense it scared him. For the first time in his life, he understood the need to kill. "You should have told me," he said quietly, his fist clenched to control the fury that threatened to overwhelm him.

Faith gave a half laugh, half sob. "And what would I have told you?"

"That you'd been raped."

Faith looked away, and more tears fell. "You wouldn't have believed me."

The tone of her voice cut right through Jay, and he

said more angrily than he intended, "You never gave me the chance to believe you."

"You were so upset that I didn't want to get married."

"At the time—"

"You *left* me!" It was a heartbreaking cry. "You left me on the side of the road. I waited for you to come back."

"I did go back," Jay pointed out. "I went to get you about twenty minutes later but you were already gone. I went past your place, and your mother said you'd gone out with some friends."

"Bruce came b-by right after you left—" She hiccuped and tried again. "Bruce came by and asked if I needed a ride. I didn't think y-you were coming back. You were so mad."

Jay tried to juggle all the pieces, while grappling with a gut-burning truth. Faith had been raped. It explained everything that had happened eighteen years ago, her argument with her sister and her parents, her abrupt departure. It explained everything that was going on now. Why she was a walking contradiction— so affectionate, so close to his boys, but so distant from him, even though she'd admitted she loved him.

Bruce had raped her.

Jay swallowed hard. And it was all his fault. He had been so consumed by her rejection that he'd left her on the side of the road. If he hadn't left her, she wouldn't have had the chance to get into a vehicle with someone she thought she could trust.

"I was upset." Faith kept talking, almost rambling at this point. "Everyone was mad at me. My parents were mad because I'd told them I wasn't going to college. You were mad because I didn't want to get married. Bruce was the only person who seemed to understand, who understood why I wanted to be free.''

''So you went with him.''

Faith looked at Jay helplessly. ''He was Patty's boyfriend. He was at the house all the time. And he'd always paid attention to me. Mom was so busy with Patty and her beauty queen circuit. Dad was working to pay for it. When Patty started dating Bruce, I found someone who listened to me, who didn't mind me tagging along.'' She paused. ''I lied to you earlier.''

''When?''

''When I first came out to look at the cottage—and you asked it I'd cared for Bruce. I said I never had. But I did. I actually had a small crush on him, but I never wanted, or at least, I didn't think that I wanted...'' Faith's brow furrowed in concentration. She shook her head helplessly and Jay reached out to take her hand.

''He had a six-pack of beer stashed in the back of the pickup. He took me to a phone, so I could call my parents, and then we went up to the reservoir. I never thought—'' She choked on her words.

Jay handed her her cup of tea, and she took it gratefully, taking a long swallow.

''Why didn't you tell me? Later, when I asked?''

''I'd already told Patty and my parents. They didn't believe me.''

''How could they not believe you?'' Jay asked, puzzled.

Jay watched Faith's face become still. Finally, Faith

said, "It was a difficult time. Everyone was angry. They knew I'd willingly gotten in his car. Besides, I'd lied to them about going to the reservoir. And they'd probably suspected I had a crush on him. I guess they thought I wanted to sleep with—"

"He was your sister's boyfriend," Jay stated flatly, not able to stop the small tickle of betrayal. "And you were my girlfriend. We never even—"

Faith swallowed and snatched up three more tissues to use on her eyes. "I know, Jay, I know. You have no idea how much I've regretted what I did. I've thought about how a series of stupid mistakes basically changed my life. But I didn't want to be raped." She shook her head emphatically.

"So what happened?" Jay found himself sickeningly interested. It was like a car wreck he couldn't stop staring at.

"We were at the reservoir, and I let him undress me. I helped him undress. But then I knew that I didn't want to lose my virginity in the back of his truck. I didn't want to sleep with him." She shrugged, but her chin still trembled. "I said stop and he wouldn't. I screamed but he just kept— Later, it was so hard to explain. When the family discussed it, all they knew was that I went with him, that I'd been drinking, that I'd undressed. Therefore, I got what I deserved."

Jay couldn't say anything, anger and remorse choking him.

Faith took a deep breath. "It was a different time. Date rape wasn't even a concept. Rape to my mother and father, to Patty, meant a hooded stranger jumping out from the bushes on a dark street. That wasn't my sister's boyfriend. Not Bruce Young. They believed something had happened, but they chose to think I wanted it.'' Her eyes were bright red. And she talked fast as if to justify her family's bad behavior. ''And for the longest time, I thought I got what I deserved.''

Jay shook his head, and said quietly as he took her hand, ''No, Faith. No one deserves it.''

She gave him a watery smile. ''I realized that after I saw the movie *Accused.* I cried for three days. And then I went into therapy. But it doesn't matter how many times people told me I wasn't responsible—I needed my family to see that. I needed Bruce to admit the truth.''

''And did he?''

She nodded. ''Yes. Tonight, he did.''

FAITH WATCHED JAY'S FACE. He sat with his body angled away from her, his eyes staring into the distance. She waited nervously. Finally, he cleared his throat and said, his voice low, ''That explains then. What about now? Why couldn't you trust me to believe you now?''

Faith wrung her hands. ''You're a different person. You're not the same boy I was in love with. I wanted to tell you, but I just couldn't.''

''Why not?'' The words seem to be wrung from him. ''Faith, it must have been terrible for you.''

''I wanted to, Jay, I really did, but honestly, I didn't know if I could trust you.'' The words came out before she could stop them.

Jay stiffened. His face paled. ''What do you mean?''

''Because of what you said to Andy.''

''Andy?'' Jay was clearly confused. ''What did I say to Andy?''

''Weeks ago, at Patty's. You told him you thought he couldn't remember the conversations he had with his mother.''

Jay furrowed his forehead. ''I remember. I still don't think he can. He was way too young.''

Faith shook her head. ''That's exactly what I'm talking about.''

''Faith, you've lost me.''

Faith gave a strangled laugh. ''If you can't believe your own son, why in the world would you believe me? Before tonight, I couldn't prove Bruce had raped me, any more than Andy can prove he had conversations with Becky. Your disbelief is powerful. Do you know what it did to Andy? It made him so insecure that he felt he had to do anything to find proof. He even tried digging up the floor in your old bedroom, looking for a secret compartment that he swears Becky told him about.''

Jay shook his head. ''Those are completely unrelated incidents.''

''Are they?'' Faith took a deep breath. ''I don't think so. I think they're exactly the same thing. You're a man who needs evidence, Jay. You need petitions, tax forms, receipts. I couldn't tell you because I didn't have evidence. Besides, it wasn't important if I was just going to leave.''

''So does this mean that you're thinking about staying?''

The words were spoken in such a low tone that she could hardly hear him.

Faith looked away. "Jay, you don't understand."

"Tell me what I don't understand."

"As long as I am here, you would never have any peace. Patty would make sure of that. I care for you, Andy and Sam far too much to..." Faith paused and then said, "To ruin your lives, the way I've ruined mine."

JAY COULDN'T STAND IT. Faith looked completely defeated. Even when she sat up, swallowed hard and said matter-of-factly, "I've started over so many times I'm used to it. It'll be easy for me. It won't be easy for you. And I won't ask that of you."

Jay felt as if his heart was slowly being removed from his body, valve by valve.

"What about us?" He could hear the strain in his voice. He had just found her and now she was gone.

"There can't be an 'us.'" The words came out haltingly. Faith stared down at her fingernails, careful not to pick at them. He looked down, too. Her small hands looked sore, but that must not even compare to the pain inside her. Why else would she be so desperate to protect herself in silence? It also explained why she never stayed with one family for long. That way they couldn't get too close.

Faith continued, "I don't know if I can stay. I don't know if Patty would let me stay. And you can't leave. You've invested too much of your time and heart into this community."

"I don't think you're giving this community a fair chance."

"To do what?"

"To support you. Patty is not the be all and end all for this town. No one person is. Certainly, I'm not. It's the community that survives. And believe me, Faith, the community has bigger problems than whether or not you stay with us."

She continued to avoid his eyes.

Jay gave a short, bitter laugh. "I can't believe it."

"What?" Faith gave him a startled look.

"After all of this, you still won't trust me."

FAITH TRIED TO DENY his words, but if she did, she'd be lying.

"You don't trust that I can love you for the long term, for forever," he said. "So you're going to leave. You're going to go back to searching for a place to rest, a place to find peace, even though you have family right here."

Her back stiffened and her cheeks flushed, the implication of her mother's full knowledge scalding her. She said shortly, "I don't have family here. My sister can barely stand me. My parents can't see beyond Patty. I don't have family."

Jay was silent for a long time, then asked, "You really think you don't have any family?"

She shook her head. "I don't."

Her answer hurt him—she could tell.

"I had thought—" he spoke clearly, his posture tightly coiled, almost defensive "—you had us."

Jay's simple words sent goose bumps radiating from

the base of her skull to her shoulders, making her chest feel that much tighter, as if she couldn't breathe.

"You know what I think?" Jay asked, sounding very much like he was planning to tell her regardless of whether she wanted to know.

Faith wasn't sure she could stand any more.

"I think you believe you don't deserve to be part of a family. That's why you move from house to house."

All Faith could do was stare at the floor.

"And I think you're scared that you're not enough just the way you are."

Faith couldn't control a new wave of tears. Jay didn't know how right he was. Neither daughter was good enough for Dearie.

"Give us a chance," Jay pleaded softly. "We'll show you how important you are to our family. Hell, my father's practically adopted you. You'll probably be holding Phoebe's hand in the delivery room."

Faith shook her head. "I can't."

"Try."

"No." She gazed unsteadily into his blue, blue eyes. "I won't. I won't do that to you and the boys."

Jay rested his head in his hands, and when he looked up, Faith was moved by the tears in his eyes. "Faith, you say it's about us. At least be honest. It's about you. You can't trust anyone. I've lost one love already. The boys have lost their mother. We don't want to, but we'll survive if we have to lose you, too. But I think you need us just as much as we need you."

She shook her head. "It's for the best."

With a long exhale, Jay finally nodded and stood

up to leave. "You take care, Faith." Before walking toward the door, he leaned over and dropped a sweet, soft, tender kiss on her lips, a kiss that spoke of longing and need, of loneliness, of trust.

FAITH SLEPT FOR HOURS. The phone seemed to ring constantly, and through the fog of sleep, she heard myriad voices leaving messages on her answering machine. Jay checking in on her. Patty. Bess. Phoebe. Her mother. Jay again. And again. And again. Each time Jay called he encouraged her to pick up the phone, but she just rolled over and continued to sleep, her dreams a montage of scenes, happy ones, sad ones.

The only constant in her dreams was Jay, walking with her on the beach, touching her, kissing her, loving her. *Trust me. Trust me.* In her dreams he never left her. In fact, it was just the opposite. He was like the air she breathed or the water she drank and bathed in. He surrounded her internally and externally. If she went away, she'd be leaving the very essence of herself behind, the fluid that made up her body, the oxygen that sustained it.

How could she leave, her dreams asked her, when everything she ever wanted was right here?

When she finally woke, it was late afternoon. She tried to sit up and groaned. Her knees hurt, her fingers hurt, her back hurt. After she went to the bathroom, she crawled back into the bed.

If only the phone would stop ringing.

"Faith, pick up the phone." Jay sounded haggard. "Faith, please."

The next time she woke it was pitch dark.

Then it was light again.

She peered at the clock.

The phone rang again. She waited to hear who it was.

"Faith, it's Gil—"

This time she answered it, staggering out of bed.

"Hello?" Her voice was cracked and froggy. Her jaw ached from lack of use.

"Hey, Faith." His voice was blessedly matter-of-fact, cheerful even.

Faith breathed a sigh of relief. "Gil," she croaked.

"How are you doing?"

Faith felt warmed by the concern in his voice.

"I don't know," she said faintly. "I just woke up."

"I was just wondering if you'll be able to pick up the boys today after school."

The boys. She stood tall, squinting against a headache. She'd forgotten about the boys. "What day is it?"

"Monday."

"Monday." She shook her head. "I guess I lost a day."

"Can't blame you. When are you going to put my son and my grandkids out of their misery?"

Faith blinked, everything coming back to her in a rush. *Under no circumstances am I going to let you blow into town, shake it up and then when nothing can ever be the same, blow out again.* Patty's accusing voice rang in Faith's ear.

"What do you mean?" she finally asked Gil.

"Well, Jay's been telling Andy and Sam that you've got to leave next weekend. Surely you're not leaving, are you? We've just fixed up the cottage. By the way, Phoebe's sorry she missed the party, but didn't think she should chance it.''

Faith perked up. ''Did she have the baby?''

''Any day now.'' Gil's voice was conversational. ''Bess has got the rooms all set up for the twins, so when it happens, they'll stay with us for a couple of nights, until Phoebe gets home from the hospital. Then Bess is going to go to stay with them for a couple weeks, to help out. Actually, Bess was wondering, if you didn't mind, if you could pick up the twins for one or two afternoons a week during that time, just to give Phoebe some rest.''

Faith swallowed hard. ''Well, if I'm around, certainly, I'd be happy to help.''

''I know how much Phoebe enjoys your company. It's kind of lonely out on the dairy by herself. She hasn't had much chance to develop any girlfriends. Now, about those children.''

''Which ones?''

''Can you pick up Andy and Sam today?''

''Yes, of course.''

''You sure, now? It's no bother for me at all. You know how much I enjoy my grandsons' company. This is Jay's busiest week, so don't be shy about telling me if you're not up to it. Jay said you'd probably want to pack because you're leaving....'' Gil's voice trailed off.

Exactly how did one leave behind air?

''I'm not going any time soon. I still haven't hired a nanny. And I can't leave before Phoebe has the baby, can I?'' she said reasonably, realizing that Jay had been absolutely right. Life did go on in their small town.

"We hope not. Well, good then." Gil sounded pleased with himself. "I know the boys are anxious to see you. Andy keeps muttering and smiling about a promise you made him. I know someone else who wants to see you as well."

Faith felt tears fill her eyes. "I know."

"Faith, he's not the best at expressing his feelings."

A small laugh escaped her. "He seems to do well enough."

Faith put down the phone. *We'll survive if we have to lose you, too. But I think you need us just as much as we need you.* She closed her eyes. He was absolutely right. She did need them. She needed to go with Sam on his field trip to the Hershey's chocolate factory. She needed to help Andy with his homework. She needed to answer Jay's phone and organize his messages. She needed to help Bess with the twins, so Phoebe could have time with her new baby. She needed to be part of that family.

A knock on the front door startled her. She peered out the bedroom window and saw Patty's car. Her heart dove to her stomach. In all this time, Patty'd never once come to visit. There was another knock. Faith pulled on a robe and went to open the door.

CHAPTER FOURTEEN

"HI," PATTY SAID BRISKLY, her voice business-as-usual.

"Want to come in?" Faith opened the door wider.

Patty didn't look like she wanted to come in. She looked like she wanted to talk right on the front porch. But she entered, her high heels clicking on the hardwood floor.

"This is nice," Patty said, her eyes sweeping professionally over the interior. "I didn't think it would be so cute."

Faith shrugged. "I like it."

Patty perched on the edge of a straight-back chair, the least comfortable chair in the room.

"You never did intend to leave, did you?" It wasn't a question but a statement.

Faith looked compassionately at her sister. "I did plan to leave."

"I don't believe it." Patty swept an elegant hand around the room. "You wouldn't have done this work if you planned to leave. You wouldn't have gone to the party with Jay if you planned to leave. I saw how you watched him."

There was nothing Faith could say to that so she asked wearily, "What can I do for you?"

''I need a favor from you.'' The words seemed forced from Patty's mouth.

''Yes?''

''Don't formalize any charges against Bruce.'' Patty lifted her chin, her blue gaze challenging.

Faith refused to meet that challenge. ''Would you like some tea?''

''No. Did you hear me?''

Faith ran the water in the kettle and put it carefully on the stove. Then she rummaged through the small cupboard for some herbal tea. Chamomile, Saturday night. Peppermint, Monday morning. She found herself a mug and watched the water, looking for signs of boiling.

''Did you hear me?'' Patty asked again.

Faith nodded. ''I heard you,'' she replied mildly. ''I wasn't even thinking about pressing charges. It happened eighteen years ago. I don't have any driving need for legal justice. I don't want Bruce spending any time in jail. I just needed him to say it out loud.'' Faith concentrated on the kettle. No steam yet. What was it about watched pots? She tried to make her breathing even and steady.

Patty gave a sigh of audible relief. ''Then there's no reason for anyone else to—''

''I told Jay,'' Faith said.

Patty nodded as if she'd expected that.

''I didn't think Bruce would tell you,'' Faith said quietly.

Patty's cheeks were bright. ''I didn't want him to. In fact, I told him not to. I told him the past was the past. But he insisted. I—I didn't want to believe it.''

"Why not?" Faith met her sister's eyes.

Patty's face flushed, but she didn't answer.

"Because you'd rather have a husband than a sister." Faith's voice was low as she poured the now-boiled water over the tea bag. "So I stopped being your sister when you took his word over mine. I stopped being a daughter when Mom decided it was easier to let me go than to find you another husband."

Patty sat motionless.

"And neither of us deserved that." Faith couldn't hide her hurt.

Patty opened her mouth and then closed it. Finally, she said stiffly, "You're right. But I needed Bruce." Patty's voice was raw. "Mom needed Bruce. Our family needed Bruce. So much money went into those pageants and I still wasn't popular or accepted. I wasn't like you. People never liked me the way they liked you. Or the way they liked Bruce. When you told me what happened, I couldn't stand it. Even my boyfriend liked you more. I always knew you'd find someone to love you. I just had Bruce."

It was the most honest thing Patty had ever said to Faith.

Faith looked at her sister in wonder. "You are one of the most beautiful women I know. Why would you think you'd never find anyone besides Bruce? Why would Mom think that?"

"Because we knew I was never going to leave." Patty's voice was defeated. "Rich, eligible men don't settle in Los Banos every day."

Poor Patty. Sadly, she made sense. "Are you sure

you don't want some tea?'' Faith held up the kettle as a peace offering.

Patty hesitated, and then shook her head and stood. ''No. I've got to get back to work. I have two houses to show later this morning.'' She strode to the door, then paused. ''There's a meeting for the Literacy Alive! program next Tuesday night. A couple of the ladies who met you through Sam's class thought you'd be interested in helping out.''

''I'll think about it.'' And she would, too.

''Good enough,'' Patty said, her eyes staring into the distance. ''They also heard you can throw a mean frozen game hen.'' She gave Faith a small smile before closing the door behind her.

Faith sat down, stunned.

Jay had been right. All she'd had to do was trust him.

She bit her lip, and her heart, which had felt like it was wrapped tightly with broken bits of string, began to wriggle out of its bounds.

FAITH WAITED FOR SAM at the entrance of the elementary school. He was talking to a small group of his friends, but when he saw her, he came running, his backpack flopping against his legs. When he reached her, he flung himself at her, almost knocking her over, but she didn't care.

''I told Andy you'd come today. I told Andy you were going to stay.'' Sam was so excited he was jumping up and down.

''Well, we'll just have to see.''

''*No!*''

''What's wrong?'' Faith asked in concern.

"'We'll see' always means no." Tears began to form in his eyes.

Faith hugged him fiercely. "Not always, Sammy."

"So you're staying?"

"I need to talk to your dad."

"Do you love him?"

Faith took a long time to answer. Finally, she nodded. "Yes, I do."

"Then don't forget your promise."

"What did I promise?"

"You promised Andy that if you loved Dad you'd stay with us."

"We'll see."

Sam didn't look too happy with her answer, but he let it go to change the subject. "You're going with us on the field trip tomorrow, right?" Sam looked at her anxiously.

"Yes, of course. I promised your teacher I would. Now, what do you want to do for a half hour before we have to pick up Andy?"

"Let's go see Dad." Sam pointed in the direction of Jay's office.

"I don't know, Sam. He's pretty busy. Taxes are due at the end of the week."

"He's got candy on his desk. Root beer kind."

"I don't think so."

"Grandpa takes me, and Dad doesn't get mad."

"I don't think he'll get mad. I just haven't ever interrupted him at work before."

Taking her hesitation as an affirmative sign, Sam pulled on her hand. "I know where it is. It's really close. We can walk."

They walked until they reached the small office space, conveniently located across the tree-lined street from Los Banos City Hall. Sam confidently pushed open the door.

"Hiya, Mrs. Masters," Sam said, greeting the woman behind the desk. Faith hung back.

"Hey, kiddo. Here to see your dad?"

Sam nodded. "Is he with a climate?"

"Climate?"

"I think he meant client," Faith supplied.

"Are you Faith?" the woman asked.

Faith nodded warily.

The woman broke into a welcoming smile and extended her hand. "I'm Debbie. We've talked on the phone."

Faith took the woman's hand, surprised at the genuine friendliness in her face. "You're the one who keeps Jay sane," Faith replied.

"I try." Debbie just smiled and leaned over to Sam. "Your father doesn't have any clients right now, so go on in."

She straightened and addressed Faith as Sam pounded down the hall. "I hear you've done wonders with the boys."

Faith reddened.

"It was great of you to fill in for the crunch."

"I just wanted to help out."

"Well, I for one wanted to tell you how much his employees appreciate it. When he's happy, we're happy," Debbie said as she lifted up the files she held in her hand. "Got to make copies. Pretty soon, I'll have a 1040 form permanently tattooed to my hand."

"Then they'll change the form."

Debbie chuckled.

With a profound sense of well-being and anticipation, Faith waited for Sam, studying Jay's simple reception area. On the tasteful wood paneling, Jay had hung his certificates, handsomely framed. *Under and by virtue of the provisions of an Act of the Legislature of the State of California creating a State Board of Accountancy. This Certificate is granted to* Jason Miller Whitfield *to practice as a Certified Public Accountant.*

Miller. She'd forgotten his middle name. So much she didn't know about him, so much she could learn if she spent a lifetime with him. All she had to do was stay.

"SHE SAID WHAT?" Jay peered over his glasses at Sam, who was ricocheting off the walls of his office. He shouldn't have let him take the second root beer candy.

"She made us a promise."

"A promise?"

"Uh-huh." Sam nodded and sucked hard on the candy with a loud slurping noise as he squatted to examine a large pile of paper.

"Don't touch that, okay, Sam? It took Debbie and Dad a long time to get those exactly in that order."

"I won't touch." He hovered over them. "See? I'm not touching."

"So what promise did Faith make you?" His head was full of numbers, but this intrigued him so much more.

"Can I have another candy?"

"You already have one in your mouth."

"When I finish the one in my mouth, can I have another one?"

"Yes," Jay said impatiently. "So what did Faith promise you?"

"She promised Andy that if she loved you, she'd stay."

This was definitely more intriguing. "When'd she say that?"

"When we had our sleepover at Grandpa's."

Jay's face fell. "Well, Sam, that was a long time ago. I don't think you should set your heart on Faith staying. She has other children to look after."

"Children she likes better'n us?" Sam shook his head. "Uh-uh. She said she loved us."

"But sometimes it takes a little more than love."

"Why don't you ask her if she's staying? She's out there."

Jay didn't want to ask her, but it certainly couldn't hurt to see her. Or maybe it could. It still stung that she couldn't trust him, even if he understood why. It had taken her eighteen years to develop the shield that protected her heart. He didn't think she'd lower it in just a few weeks. Maybe if she wandered around for a few more months, she'd realize that she missed them and come back. Unlike Becky, Faith could come back. That thought had sustained him these last thirty-six hours. He took off his glasses and followed Sam down the hall, his palms turning sweaty at the sight of her.

"Hi," he said nervously.

Startled, she looked up from the certificate she was reading.

"Hi." She gave him a half smile, then said hurriedly, "I hope we're not bothering you."

He shook his head. "No, I needed a break, anyway."

"Deadline time, huh?"

He indicated the copiers, which seemed to be running constantly. "If those don't blow up, we'll actually make it to Friday."

"Ask her, Dad," Sam directed.

Faith gave him a puzzled look.

"Later."

Sam's face fell and he kicked at the floor with one foot. "'Later' means no, too."

Jay studied Faith, who averted her eyes.

"I'm glad you could pick up Sam and Andy. We weren't sure. I guess Dad called you?" When had conversation with Faith gotten so hard?

She put her hands behind her back. "Well, Sam's got his field trip tomorrow and I wanted to be sure to make that. I promised. I also haven't hired the nanny yet."

"An' she doesn't break her promises," Sam put in meaningfully, sucking on another candy.

They stood awkwardly for a moment.

"We should go and get Andy. Let you get back to work."

Jay nodded absently, his eyes tracing the lovely lines of her face. He would miss her when she was gone. "See you tonight?"

She nodded back. "Tonight."

JAY WEARILY WALKED UP his driveway at one in the morning. The past four days had been hell, but the crunch was over. The tax returns or extensions were filed and he was exhausted. His office was officially closed for the next four days and all he wanted to do was sleep for two of them. He felt rather like a college student who'd just finished his last exam before summer break.

He was grateful that Faith had decided to postpone leaving, because even though he really wanted to talk to her, business took every ounce of his concentration. It seemed as if all he could do was grunt at her. Faith being Faith took no offense at his rudeness. She filled in the best she could, taking messages about his council work, relaying the important business, tactfully rerouting the less urgent. However, business all but went out of his mind when he ran into Bruce at the office supply store. They'd held a wary exchange ending with a tacit understanding about Faith. Jay wanted Bruce to know that Faith was *his*. Bruce acknowledged that with quiet dignity.

Now Jay pushed open the door and listened for sounds of life. Except for the hum of the television, the house was quiet. He found Faith in the family room reading a book on antiques, several pages marked with sticky notes.

''You're free!'' she remarked with a shy smile.

It was so nice to see her curled up on the couch under a throw quilt. He could almost make himself believe that Faith would always look the way she did tonight, that when he walked home from work, she would always be waiting for him. Always. He swallowed hard.

"I am," he said as he sat down next to her, deliberately close, his body enjoying the physical contact with hers.

She didn't move away, didn't even shift.

His heartbeat accelerated.

"Guess what I found?" Faith said quietly.

Jay shook his head. He felt as if time and Faith were slipping through his fingers. Instead of telling him, she searched through her backpack and pulled out a scruffy steno tablet secured with a rubber band. She handed it to him.

"What's this?"

"I think it's Becky's journal."

Jay stared at the book, his throat constricting. "It's *what?*" His voice was hoarse.

"I think it's her journal. I didn't read it," Faith assured him. "I know it's private."

"Where did you find it?"

Faith indicated the book in her lap. "I've been studying about the kind of antiques Becky collected. Dressers like the one in your bedroom often had false panels and secret doors. Andy thought the secret door was in the floor. It was actually in the dresser. See, Whitfield? This is proof. Children do remember the conversations they had with their mothers."

With a trembling hand, Jay took the notebook. He carefully pulled off the rubber band, which disintegrated in his hand. His eyes clouded when he saw Becky's familiar writing. He read a few words. His chest tightened, but it didn't hurt. It wasn't the intense pain that he felt he had to dull with work. That was because of Faith.

"Thank you."

Faith smiled. "You're welcome. Enjoy it."

"So, I guess you'll be leaving soon," he commented casually.

Faith fiddled with the pages of her book, her heart pounding. Jay'd been so busy these past few days, it'd given her plenty of time to think about what she wanted. She had attended Patty's Literacy Alive! program meeting, and while her sister wasn't warm, she wasn't hostile, either. Bruce had entered the house as the meeting was breaking up, apparently stopping by to pack a few of his things. Faith had found herself giving him a sad smile. Yes, it would take time to get used to seeing him. And it would also take time for him and Patty to sort out their marriage. Dearie had opposed their separation, but this time Patty ignored her mother's protests. Since the party, Faith had come to realize that healing took time—something she had a limitless supply of. She didn't need to budget it; she wasn't going anywhere.

"I guess so," she said slowly, in reply to Jay's question.

"I saw Patty today," Jay mentioned.

"Oh?"

"She said that you'd volunteered for the community reading project."

Faith was silent.

"I didn't think you'd volunteer for anything if you were leaving," he ventured.

Faith didn't know how to say it.

"I guess that's it, then," he said with a sigh, pushing off the couch to stand up. "I'm beat. I think I'm going to bed."

Faith watched him get up, his body moving slowly, his fingers raking through his hair.

"Yes!" Faith blurted.

"Yes?" Jay's eyes were guarded. And she didn't blame him. She'd put him through a lot.

"Yes, I thought I might stay for a little while." She could feel words spewing out of her. "After all, the nannies I've interviewed haven't really been very impressive."

JAY FELT A SMALL PRICK of hope. Suddenly, he wasn't tired at all. He took a deep breath and said bluntly, "Sam said you made Andy a promise."

Faith's face became very still, as if she were waiting for something.

"And what would that be?" she asked, her voice uncertain. "I promised Andy I'd help him with his homework."

"You also promised him that if you loved me, you'd stay." There, it was out. She could accept it or reject it. If she rejected it, they'd live. Nevertheless, Jay waited, his breath held.

"I guess I did." Faith's voice was very faint.

Jay's heart thudded, reminding him that it needed oxygen. He exhaled sharply. "You said you loved me."

She nodded and bit her lip. Her brown eyes met his.

"Do you break your promises?"

She didn't speak, but he could see her answer in her eyes.

She loved him.

She was going to stay.

"Do I need a new nanny?" he asked.

A small smile played on her lips, and she replied, "I don't know, Whitfield, do you?"

They stared at each other for a long time and Faith took a step closer to him.

"Instead of a nanny..." Jay whispered in a voice that didn't sound like his. He gently rubbed his knuckles over the soft curve of her cheek. "I'd rather have a wife brave enough to take on an overworked council member and two lousy kids."

EMOTION CLOGGED FAITH'S THROAT. "I'd rather be a wife," she said softly.

"You need to be able to trust me."

Faith could barely stand the brightness of his eyes. "I can do that. I'm learning how. You were right about Patty and about me needing to give the community a chance. You were right when you said I needed you as much as you need me—and that I had a family all along."

They stood still for what seemed like eternity. Close, so close, that she could hear Jay's shallow breathing.

"Weaver, will you marry me?" Jay asked gruffly.

"I'm nothing but trouble, Whitfield," she said, straightening her shoulders and tossing back her hair, the beads brushing against his arm. He tugged lightly on one.

"I need a little trouble. It keeps me on my toes."
Jay's voice was raspy.

"I'd want to put Becky's antiques in this house."

"Done." Jay pulled her to him, wrapping his arms
tightly around her shoulders.

"The boys would have to have regular bedtimes."

"Of course."

"You'll have to be patient if I don't learn this trust
thing right away."

"You're a quick study."

She nodded, her heart untangling as the pieces of
string unknotted. "Okay."

"Okay, what?"

"I'll marry you, Whitfield."

The phone rang, causing them to jump apart. Both
of them laughed, as if they'd been caught doing something they shouldn't.

"Hello!" Jay said cheerfully, his hand reaching for
Faith's.

"Jay," Gil said with no preamble. "Has Faith gone
back to the cottage?"

"No, she's right here with me." Jay cinched an arm
around her waist and pulled her in close to him.

Faith laughed softly, as he indicated that she should
listen as well.

"Good. Mitch and Phoebe are in transit to the hospital. Bess is with the twins, who are still asleep, but
Phoebe really wants Bess to be with her."

"I'll be right over to sit with the twins," Faith said
into the receiver. "That way, Bess can go to Phoebe."

Gil breathed a sigh of relief.

"What are you doing, Dad?" Jay asked.

"Just thinking that we're going to need more places for Sunday dinner. I'm going to the hospital, too. Stink will do the 4:00 a.m. milking. Thanks, Faith. You're a lifesaver."

"No," Jay said once he hung up. He held her in a tight hug. "No, not a lifesaver, just part of the family."

Part of the family. Faith closed her eyes, feeling Jay's strength, his love, and finally, finally—peace.

Silhouette
bestselling authors

KASEY
MICHAELS

RUTH
LANGAN

CAROLYN
ZANE

*welcome you to a world
of family, privilege and power
with three brand-new love
stories about America's
most beloved dynasty,
the Coltons*

*Brides
of
Privilege*

Available May 2001

Where love comes alive™

INDULGE IN A QUIET MOMENT
WITH HARLEQUIN

Get a FREE
Quiet Moments Bath Spa

with just two proofs of purchase from
any of our four special collector's editions in Ma

Harlequin® is sure to make your time special this Mother's Day
with four special collector's editions featuring a short story
PLUS a complete novel packaged together in one volume!

Collection #1 Intrigue abounds in a collection featuring *New York Times*
bestselling author Barbara Delinsky and Kelsey Roberts.

Collection #2 Relationships? Weddings? Children? = *New York Times*
bestselling author Debbie Macomber and Tara Taylor Quin
at their best!

Collection #3 Escape to the past with *New York Times* bestselling author
Heather Graham and Gayle Wilson.

Collection #4 Go West! With *New York Times* bestselling author
Joan Johnston and Vicki Lewis Thompson!

Plus Special Consumer Campaign!
Each of these four collector's editions will feature a
"FREE QUIET MOMENTS BATH SPA" offer.
See inside book in May for details.

Only from

HARLEQUIN®
Makes any time special ®

Don't miss out! Look for this exciting promotion on sale in May 2001
at your favorite retail outlet.

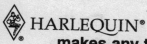

*Harlequin truly does make any time special. . . .
This year we are celebrating weddings in style!*

A Walk Down the Aisle
WEDDING CELEBRATION

To help us celebrate, we want you to tell us how wearing the Harlequin wedding gown will make your wedding day special. As the grand prize, Harlequin will offer one lucky bride the chance to "Walk Down the Aisle" in the Harlequin wedding gown!

There's more...

For her honeymoon, she and her groom will spend five nights at the **Hyatt Regency Maui.** As part of this five-night honeymoon at the hotel renowned for its romantic attractions, the couple will enjoy a candlelit dinner for two in Swan Court, a sunset sail on the hotel's catamaran, and sweet spa treatments.

Maui • Molokai • Lanai

To enter, please write, in, 250 words or less, how wearing the Harlequin wedding gown will make your wedding day special. The entry will be judged based on its emotionally compelling nature, its originality and creativity, and its sincerity. This contest is open to Canadian and U.S. residents only and to those who are 18 years of age and older. There is no purchase necessary to enter. Void where prohibited. See further contest rules attached. Please send your entry to:

Walk Down the Aisle Contest

In Canada
P.O. Box 637
Fort Erie, Ontario
L2A 5X3

In U.S.A:
P.O. Box 9076
3010 Walden Ave.
Buffalo, NY 14269-9076

You can also enter by visiting www.eHarlequin.com
Win the Harlequin wedding gown and the vacation of a lifetime!
The deadline for entries is October 1, 2001.

HARLEQUIN®
Makes any time special ®

PHWDACONT1

HARLEQUIN WALK DOWN THE AISLE TO MAUI CONTEST 1197
OFFICIAL RULES
NO PURCHASE NECESSARY TO ENTER

1. To enter, follow directions published in the offer to which you are responding. Contest begins April 2, 2001, and ends on October 1, 2001. Method of entry may vary. Mailed entries must be postmarked by October 1, 2001, and received by October 8, 2001.

2. Contest entry may be, at times, presented via the Internet, but will be restricted solely to residents of certain geographic areas that are disclosed on the Web site. To enter via the Internet, if permissible, access the Harlequin Web site (www.eHarlequin.com) and follow the directions displayed online. Online entries must be received by 11:59 p.m. E.S.T. on October 1, 2001.

   In lieu of submitting an entry online, enter by mail by hand-printing (or typing) on an 8½" x 11" plain piece of paper, your name, address (including zip code), Contest number/name and in 250 words or fewer, why winning a Harlequin wedding would make your wedding day special. Mail via first-class mail to: Harlequin Walk Down the Aisle Contest 1197, (in the U P.O. Box 9076, 3010 Walden Avenue, Buffalo, NY 14269-9076, (in Canada) P.O. Box 637, Fort Erie, Ontario L2A 5X3, Ca Limit one entry per person, household address and e-mail address. Online and/or mailed entries received from persons residing in geographic areas in which Internet entry is not permissible will be disqualified.

3. Contests will be judged by a panel of members of the Harlequin editorial, marketing and public relations staff based on th following criteria:

   - Originality and Creativity—50%
   - Emotionally Compelling—25%
   - Sincerity—25%

   In the event of a tie, duplicate prizes will be awarded. Decisions of the judges are final.

4. All entries become the property of Torstar Corp. and will not be returned. No responsibility is assumed for lost, late, illega incomplete, inaccurate, nondelivered or misdirected mail or misdirected e-mail, for technical, hardware or software failure any kind, lost or unavailable network connections, or failed, incomplete, garbled or delayed computer transmission or an human error which may occur in the receipt or processing of the entries in this Contest.

5. Contest open only to residents of the U.S. (except Puerto Rico) and Canada, who are 18 years of age or older, and is voi wherever prohibited by law; all applicable laws and regulations apply. Any litigation within the Province of Quebec respect the conduct or organization of a publicity contest must be submitted to the Régie des alcools, des courses et des jeux for ruling. Any litigation respecting the awarding of a prize may be submitted to the Régie des alcools, des courses et des je for the purpose of helping the parties reach a settlement. Employees and immediate family members of Torstar Corp. and D. L. Blair, Inc., their affiliates, subsidiaries and all other agencies, entities and persons connected with the use, marketin conduct of this Contest are not eligible to enter. Taxes on prizes are the sole responsibility of winners. Acceptance of any offered constitutes permission to use winner's name, photograph or other likeness for the purposes of advertising, trade promotion on behalf of Torstar Corp., its affiliates and subsidiaries without further compensation to the winner, unless prohibited by law.

6. Winners will be determined no later than November 15, 2001, and will be notified by mail. Winners will be required to si return an Affidavit of Eligibility form within 15 days after winner notification. Noncompliance within that time period may in disqualification and an alternative winner may be selected. Winners of trip must execute a Release of Liability prior to and must possess required travel documents (e.g. passport, photo ID) where applicable. Trip must be completed by Nov 2002. No substitution of prize permitted by winner. Torstar Corp. and D. L. Blair, Inc., their parents, affiliates, and subsid are not responsible for errors in printing or electronic presentation of Contest, entries and/or game pieces. In the event o printing or other errors which may result in unintended prize values or duplication of prizes, all affected game pieces or e shall be null and void. If for any reason the Internet portion of the Contest is not capable of running as planned, includin infection by computer virus, bugs, tampering, unauthorized intervention, fraud, technical failures, or any other causes be the control of Torstar Corp. which corrupt or affect the administration, secrecy, fairness, integrity or proper conduct of th Contest, Torstar Corp. reserves the right, at its sole discretion, to disqualify any individual who tampers with the entry p and to cancel, terminate, modify or suspend the Contest or the Internet portion thereof. In the event of a dispute regardin online entry, the entry will be deemed submitted by the authorized holder of the e-mail account submitted at the time of Authorized account holder is defined as the natural person who is assigned to an e-mail address by an Internet access p online service provider or other organization that is responsible for arranging e-mail address for the domain associated submitted e-mail address. **Purchase or acceptance of a product offer does not improve your chances of wi**

7. Prizes: (1) Grand Prize—A Harlequin wedding dress (approximate retail value: $3,500) and a 5-night/6-day honeymoo Maui, HI, including round-trip air transportation provided by Maui Visitors Bureau from Los Angeles International Airp (winner is responsible for transportation to and from Los Angeles International Airport) and a Harlequin Romance Pack including hotel accomodations (double occupancy) at the Hyatt Regency Maui Resort and Spa, dinner for (2) two at Sw Court, a sunset sail on Kiele V and a spa treatment for the winner (approximate retail value: $4,000); (5) Five runner-u of a $1000 gift certificate to selected retail outlets to be determined by Sponsor (retail value $1000 ea.). Prizes consist those items listed as part of the prize. Limit one prize per person. All prizes are valued in U.S. currency.

8. For a list of winners (available after December 17, 2001) send a self-addressed, stamped envelope to: Harlequin Walk Aisle Contest 1197 Winners, P.O. Box 4200 Blair, NE 68009-4200 or you may access the www.eHarlequin.com Web si through January 15, 2002.

Contest sponsored by Torstar Corp., P.O. Box 9042, Buffalo, NY 14269-9042, U.S.A.

PHWDACON